WHERE MAN

Inspector James Given
Book Four

Charlie Garratt

SAPERE
BOOKS

WHERE EVERY MAN
MAN

Published by Sapere Books.

20 Windermere Drive, Leeds, England, LS17 7UZ,
United Kingdom

saperebooks.com

ISBN: 978-1-80055-081-0

I hold the world but as the world, Gratiano,
A stage where every man must play a part,
And mine a sad one.
The Merchant of Venice

ONE

A blue and cream bus emptied its cargo of country people at the stop, hummed on the roadside for less than a minute, and rattled on its journey to the next village. Travellers fanned along the three rows of market stalls to gather vegetables, fish, meat, cheese, and a dozen other essential supplies to take them through the week. Ten chimes from the tower of Sainte Cécile's echoed above our heads and, as if part of the mechanism, a side door in the church swung open on the last one. A thin man, with a shock of black hair and striking, film star looks, stepped into the weak early March sunshine. He looked both ways, spoke for a moment to an elderly woman carrying two baguettes, then ambled over to my stall.

'What do you recommend?' The man ran a finger round his dog-collar and, with a frown, surveyed the vegetables. 'Louise, my housekeeper, she cooks for me, but she's away at her sister's so I'm fending for myself tonight. I can stretch to frying chicken and need something to go with it.'

It may have only been my first season looking after the stall, so I was no expert on vegetables, but I'd never experienced the luxury of a housekeeper and knew well enough how to prepare a meal. I suggested potatoes and carrots might be simple and bagged some for him. I even offered him tips on how to cook them.

'You're not from these parts, are you?' the stranger asked. 'English?'

'I came to France with my wife in December. We're living on Malo Legrand's farm. You know it?'

He stuck out his hand. 'I do; I've known Malo a long time. I'm Francis Guen.' He jerked a thumb over his shoulder. 'Parish priest in there.'

It didn't need much in the way of detective skills to work this out from the clothes he wore.

'James Given.'

'It's a strange time to come here, isn't it?'

'We thought we'd be as safe from the war here as in England.'

In Brittany we were as far away from the German border as at home, and if the Nazis overran France, the Channel would prove no major barrier.

'Where in England are you from? I have friends in Birmingham.'

'I lived and worked in Kenilworth, in Warwickshire.'

The priest looked blank. 'Warwickshire?'

'In the English Midlands. Kenilworth would be about twenty miles … sorry, thirty kilometres. I grew up in the city, and Rachel, my wife, lived in Birmingham before we married. My family is still there.'

The smile he'd worn since we met widened. 'Excellent. Perhaps you've come across my friends?'

I opened my mouth to tell him it was an enormous place, so I'd be unlikely to have met his friends, when two customers behind Father Guen shook their heads and glared at me. I took the hint.

'Will there be anything else?' I nodded towards the women and he turned, tipped his hat then lifted his bag.

'I'm sorry, Monsieur Given, I mustn't keep you from your work. Perhaps we could meet, and you might give me some news?'

'That would be nice.'

'Next Wednesday, say eleven o'clock, after early Mass finishes?' He pointed across the square. 'Over in the Café de Léon?'

I agreed, and the priest wandered away. As he did, my next customer, a small, gnarled woman of some age, dressed in black with a white lace bonnet, thrust a handful of apples forward and, without waiting for me to weigh them, dropped the fruit in her bag. She scrabbled in her purse, found a few centimes and held out her hand. I took her offering, thanked her and wished her well. She beetled off to grace another stallholder with her sparkling conversation, and a small, slim woman now stood in front of me wearing an impish smile. That smile brought something to her features to make her attractive, even though she didn't carry traditional good looks. Her nose was a little too flat, her cheeks a little too rounded. She spoke in English.

'Don't mind Madame Villét, she means no harm. Mind you, she's not always so engagingly chatty.'

I laughed. 'Your English is good.'

She raised an eyebrow. 'A little better than your French, I think.' She clapped her hands in front of her lips. 'I'm so sorry, that sounded very rude. I like to practise my English whenever I can, and it came out wrong.' Even in her apology she had playfulness in her voice.

'That's no problem, madame. You are right; it still needs a little work.'

'Have you been here long?'

'Only about three months. My wife and I arrived in December.'

'Ah, that explains it. Then you're doing very well for such a short time. It can't be easy trying to earn a living in a new country with a different language.'

'Thank you. I learnt some French at school then travelled all around the world for a few years, picking up bits of a dozen languages along the way. My wife says I need to concentrate more on remembering the less common words, but I get by. Where did you learn English so well?'

'I lived in London for the final two years of the last war, so my English became good.'

'What work did you do?'

'Nothing important. I was only a typist in the army. A little different from what I do now.' She pointed across the market, and I turned to see a single-storey stone building attached to the side of the Mairie, the mayor's offices. 'I work in the library over there.'

'I haven't been yet, though I keep promising myself I will because my wife says you have a good collection. My sister has been sending books over from England, but I don't know how long she can continue with an invasion on the horizon.'

'Well, if it happens, we can't be sure the library will remain open either. Perhaps you should come in before it is too late. I'm sure we could find something suitable for you. I'm there most days but if I'm not, ask for me, Lisette Perron, and they'll tell you when I'll be back.'

'That's very kind of you, Madame Perron. I'll call in.'

'And if you have any difficulties with words or phrases you don't understand, I'd be happy to help.'

Whilst she selected fruit and vegetables, the librarian gave me advice on places in the area I should visit if I got the chance. When she walked away, I could see life in France was getting better all the time. Some friends in England thought the French aloof and uncommunicative, but this was far from my experience. I'd found going the extra mile to learn their culture and language went a long way.

As soon as Madame Perron went out of view, Father Guen appeared by my side again.

'I see you have met our librarian. She could tell an interesting tale or two if you get to know her.'

'How so?'

He tapped his nose and glanced in both directions, as if checking the coast was clear. 'It is said she was Deuxième Bureau — military intelligence.'

Before he could say anything further, a soldier, barely in his twenties, arrived and lifted a cabbage from the pile on the stall, peeled back the outer leaves and sniffed. 'These fresh?'

The priest turned away. 'You're busy. I'll tell you more when we meet.' Francis scurried back towards his church and I attended to my customer.

'Picked yesterday, not one kilometre from here. Best you'll get this time of year.'

He weighed the cabbage in his hand, stuck his nose in it again, then placed it in his bag and asked for some potatoes. The soldier paid me then went on his way, whistling. I wondered how long it would be before they'd send him to the Belgian border, where troops on both sides were squaring up for battle.

After I'd returned from the market, Malo Legrand, our landlord, ambled the twenty yards from the back door of his farmhouse to the barn where I was unloading boxes from the cart. I'd never enquired why his house and the one we rented from him were so close together but assumed, as is often the case in the countryside, an eldest son married at some time in the distant past and wanted somewhere to live apart from the parents. The two homes, ours much smaller than his, backed onto a yard surrounded by two barns, a cowshed, and our garden.

In contrast to his family name, Malo wasn't a big man. In his sixties, with a thin but muscled frame, he wore brown corduroy trousers, patched and turned up because they were too long. Like many farmers, he hid his affluence under a facade of poverty, wearing shabby, sometimes second-hand clothes and refusing to spend money on even the most basic of house repairs.

'How did we do today, James?' he asked.

'We did well. The sun brought people out. There are potatoes and apples left, but they will keep. Other than those, the rest will see you through the week or can go to the pigs.'

'You make sure you take some for that pretty wife of yours, never mind the pigs. They'll find what they need easily enough.'

Malo was thrifty, but he wasn't mean. His weekly donation of vegetables and fruit from the farm had helped stretch our savings whilst we were finding our feet in Vieux-Croix. I thanked him and filled a small box with produce after he left. I finished the unloading and walked over to our house, where a tortured violin grated through the open window. My wife, Rachel, was enduring one of her pupils.

When we'd moved into the house, we decided to live in the kitchen, which was more than big enough for two of us. This allowed us to use the old living room for Rachel's lessons. It had worked well so far, despite the woeful musicianship of some of her charges. I often took to the fields when an aspiring violinist came round, but this one had caught me by surprise.

The squawking continued whilst I removed my boots and washed the dust of the day from my hands. I checked my reflection in the mirror over the sink and smiled. The outdoor life and healthy diet agreed with me. I'd shed a good few pounds and my skin had swapped its office pallor for a farm-labourer's tan. The downsides were a few deeper lines and clothes stitched up the back to make them fit. These were a small price to pay.

I put on the kettle to boil, then knocked at the music room door. Rachel popped out her head.

'Oh, didn't hear you come in. Good day?'

'Good enough. Met some nice people. Would you and your student like tea?'

'That would be lovely. We'll be finished in a minute.' She pushed me away and closed the door when I mouthed 'Good'. Rachel was building a nice little group of paying customers, but I was glad I spent most of my days out in the fields or away at the local markets. A woman had taught music at the school until a year earlier, but she'd married and moved away. Listening to the performances taking place in our little home, I suspected music hadn't been her main subject. Thankfully, this one stopped before I'd finished laying out the cups.

Rachel came out, followed by a girl of seventeen or eighteen, carrying a well-worn violin case. My wife swung an upturned hand in my direction. 'Marie-Clair, this is my husband, James.'

The frown the girl had been wearing disappeared, and smiling eyes shone through her horn-rimmed spectacles. She pushed back a lock of wavy, brown hair. 'Very pleased to meet you, Mr Given.' Her Breton accent had a sing-song quality, different to the Parisian French drilled into me at school, the accent I'd become used to in my dealings with our new neighbours. 'Your wife tells me you are a policeman, yes?'

I shook my head. 'Not now. I left that behind in England. Now I'm just a simple farm worker.'

Marie-Clair's face dropped. 'Oh dear, that is a shame.'

'A shame?'

'I hope to join the police soon and thought you might be able to give me some advice.'

'Well,' I began and looked across at Rachel. 'When you're here again, we can talk. Write some questions before you come; it will help put your thoughts in order. Then I'll answer them if I can.'

Rachel came to my rescue, a playful smirk on her lips. 'Tea?' She turned to the young woman. 'Tell my husband how the lesson went, Marie-Clair.'

'It was very good, Monsieur Given. Madame is a very good teacher. I think I am improving all the time.'

It took all of my self-control to avoid laughing. Immersed in her lesson, poor Marie-Clair obviously hadn't heard what emanated from the house. We finished our drinks, then Rachel took her payment and accompanied the aspiring violinist outside. When she returned, I wagged a finger.

'You're very naughty, Mrs Given. That girl hasn't a note in her head, and you're relieving her of her mother's money.'

Rachel's brows knitted. 'Why do you imply Marie-Clair has no father? I didn't think you'd met her before.'

Now it was my turn to smirk. 'Elementary, my dear Rachel. She had a wide, gold wedding-ring on a chain around her neck. Unlikely to be hers, so possibly her mother's, but it's obviously too big or she'd be wearing it. So a man's. It might be her brother's, but if an older, married brother died, the ring would have gone to his wife. Yes? Much more likely to be her father's, in which case he must have passed away. Am I right?'

'I thought you said you weren't a policeman any longer.'

'You know what you always say about old habits.'

My wife plonked herself down onto a dining chair and laughed until the tears ran from her eyes. I stood, hands on hips, waiting for her laughter to subside.

'So what's so funny?'

'Well, you're completely wrong, Sherlock. Her father is a very successful businessman, and the ring is her grandfather's. It is a sad story, though. He set up as a blacksmith when he was young and built a good living from the forge, enough to send the boy to college and give him cash to get started on his own. When the old man retired, he kept his hand in by shoeing friends' horses; then one reared up and kicked him in the head. Killed him outright. Marie-Clair loved him; that's why she wears the ring.' She began to giggle again, and this time I joined her.

'Well, at least mine was a plausible explanation. I can't get it right all the time.'

'Marie-Clair's a nice girl — can't play the fiddle for toffee and I'm not sure she ever will, so perhaps I should stop taking her money anyway. She's desperate to become a detective, though. Are you going to help her?'

'I will if I can, though I'm not sure of the system here.'

'Surely the skills are the same the world over?'

'Probably, I've just never thought about it. How was your day?'

'Nice enough, though I missed you. It will be nice to have you to myself for the rest of the weekend.'

She pecked my cheek, put away the cups and teapot, then went into the garden, where she'd begun to establish a vegetable plot and a couple of flower beds. I looked out of the front window, across the road to the simple war memorial and Malo's small orchard beyond, with buds just forming, and thought of where the harvests might take us this year.

The plan we'd made before leaving England was to rent a house in Brittany, then follow the soft fruits and grapes south, returning in the autumn to pick apples and pears. As we'd become more settled in Vieux-Croix, me with the work on Malo's farm, and Rachel with her music lessons, our dream was softening at the edges. We'd agreed to wait awhile before heading away, see how the weather was in this part of France in the spring and if we still needed to be somewhere else to feel the warm air on our faces. My new life gave me the freedom of the outdoors I'd craved in my years in the police in Kenilworth, so my desire for the fruit fields of my early twenties was fading. We both felt this to be a good place with friendly people and enough work to get by.

A shadow passed the window, followed by a tap on the front door a few seconds later. Henri, the postman, touched his hat's peak and handed me two letters: one with an English stamp and postmark, the other with neither. I asked about his family, and we exchanged thoughts on the weather before he strolled on his way.

I closed the door and opened the one from England, knowing by the handwriting it was from my father. Rachel came through the back door before I'd read the first paragraph.

'Was that Henri?'

'It was. A letter from Papa and one for both of us which looks official. Give me a minute.' I skim-read my father's then re-read it more slowly. 'He says he's had word from Uncle Gideon. The family is here in Brittany. Papa wants me to visit him. Says he's looked on a map and it's only thirty miles from here.'

Gideon was my father's brother who, having escaped the Nazis in Germany, had made his way across the Continent seeking safety. When war was declared, my father demanded I travelled over to look for him and his family, but I narrowly missed him in Paris. I knew he'd moved to Brittany, but I'd not realised he was still here and so close to our new home.

'You'll go?'

'I suppose I'll have to. No excuse if he's so near, and Papa won't let up until I do. I'll need to check with the boss when I can take some time off. I imagine I'll need a couple of days at least.'

'What's the other letter?'

I opened the envelope and extracted good quality paper bearing the address of the town hall. 'It's from the mayor's office. We have to go to see him.'

In the afternoon, I wrote two letters of my own. The first was a brief reply to the mayor, Alain Sitell, confirming that the date and time he'd suggested was convenient. It coincided with when I'd agreed to meet with Francis Guen, but the mayor was a powerful man, and not one to cross in a small French commune. My second note was to the priest, apologising that I needed to change our arrangement, and suggesting we meet an hour later than planned. I hoped he'd still be available and I wouldn't miss out on our chat. I'd have much rather have been in a pleasant café with my new friend than dealing with some mindless bureaucracy.

The sun dipped below the horizon when Rachel and I left home to walk to the Mairie to drop off the letter. Within minutes our lane was in darkness with only a faint glimmer from the moon, and I was thankful for a torch despite treading this way several times a week in daylight. It was less than a quarter of a mile, but the temperature had fallen like a stone and left us shivering.

'Why do you think he's asked to see us, James?' asked Rachel.

'I've not a clue; there was nothing in his message to say. I expect it's because we're strangers, and he wants to be sure we're respectable enough to be in his town. You know how these petty officials are. We'll tell him what he needs, and no more, then he'll leave us in peace.'

We walked across the now deserted market square and found the priest's house behind Sainte Cécile's. I poked my apology through his letterbox, not wishing to disturb him, and we continued on our way. As we turned the corner, the wind almost lifted my hat and the temperature fell a couple of degrees further. I pulled Rachel to my side and she snuggled even closer. There was not another soul on the streets, just us in our own world. This was, without doubt, the best part of the day.

TWO

The following Wednesday, Mayor Sitell greeted us at the door of his office fifteen minutes after his secretary buzzed through to tell him we'd arrived. She'd asked us to sit, offered us a pleasant smile, then returned to her typing.

The mayor's office faced the entrance, across a wide hall of grey stone with a marble mosaic floor, light oak panelling, and anonymous doors. The only three marked were the one we sat outside, the library, which also boasted a sign declaring it was for staff only, and the police office.

No-one left the room before the mayor came out, so I assumed he'd wanted to show us how important he was by keeping us waiting, a technique I'd witnessed more than once in my career. The man was almost exactly as I'd expected him to be. Shorter than me, and even rounder than I was before Rachel took me under her wing. His neatly shaven moustache and slicked-down hair gave the impression of an older, fatter Clark Gable, who we'd seen at the cinema as our last night out before leaving England. What I hadn't expected from this bastion of officialdom was the broad smile and firm handshake as he guided us to two leather chairs on one side of his enormous desk. On the wall behind him were potent symbols of his position, the tricolour and the framed photograph of President Lebrun.

'Take a seat, Monsieur and Madame Given, please. May I offer you coffee? Or perhaps tea?'

We shook our heads in unison. I, for one, wanted to be out of there as quickly as possible.

'I apologise for dragging you in; you will understand when I explain, I hope.'

My palms were sweating, and I understood how innocent people would have felt when I'd called them into the police station for interview.

'How we can we help?'

'It is simple, though I wish it was unnecessary.' Sitell cleared his throat, not as though he had a cough or cold but more as if he were nervous. 'This war brings with it lots of threats, lots of fears —' another throat clearing — 'and as a result, lots more paperwork. I am told I need to produce a file on all foreigners living in the commune.'

'And is this a big task, Monsieur Sitell?'

The mayor laughed and slapped the desk. 'Not at all. Why, there are no more than four or five of you locally — and two of you live in the same house.'

'So what do you need to know?' Rachel asked.

'First, tell me a little about yourselves. Ages? Where are you from? What work you did before you came and what you are doing now. That kind of thing.'

We gave him the basics. I kicked Rachel under the desk when she knocked three years off her age, but otherwise we told him the truth, keeping to the minimum we could get away with.

'So, Monsieur Given, you were a policeman?'

'I was.'

'For how long?'

'About ten years. Before that I was at sea.'

'And you gave up being a detective — why?'

I gave him the answer I'd offered everyone since I left my job. 'Because I became fed up with the evil I had to deal with every day —' I took my wife's hand — 'and because I married this lovely lady, who made me want to start a new life with her.'

'That I can understand.' He paused for a few seconds. 'May I ask about your politics?'

I leaned back in my chair. 'Politics? How do you mean?'

'Were either of you, for instance, members of a political party in England?'

Rachel and I shrugged, both shaking our heads. He consulted his typed set of questions then scribbled for a moment on his pad. I leant forward, trying to see, but he shielded the words with his left hand.

'What are you writing, monsieur?'

'Only your responses, nothing to worry about. This question of politics is important in these times, do you not think? We need to be sure they would not lead you to be sympathetic to our enemy.'

If he'd known a little more of the truth about us, he wouldn't have needed to ask about our political persuasion, but I wasn't about to reveal that nugget for his scrutiny.

'And you, Monsieur Given, you would have been too young to be active in the last war?'

'I was fifteen when it ended. Listen, where is this going? We're just a newly married couple, hoping for new lives in your beautiful country.'

'Please don't become difficult, Monsieur Given. I have to ask these questions of everyone. I have a friend, a mayor in a nearby commune, and he told me last week he had three German families living there. Now, what do you think he should do? They tell him they are opposed to the Nazis, but he has to check, doesn't he? That is all I am doing, just seeking anything which may give cause for concern.'

'Well, you'll find nothing with us. What the Germans are doing is abhorrent.'

'If that is the case, then why are you not in your country's forces fighting them?'

I closed my eyes and rubbed my thigh, and Rachel squeezed my hand. 'Because I was injured in the last case I worked on. Stabbed. In the leg. The army decided that even if I could walk, I was not fit enough to be shot at. I have the paperwork at home if you need to see it.'

'Ah, I understand. Your reaction to my questions is therefore quite understandable. Especially as our countries are allies.' The mayor looked up from his notes and coughed again, a habit which was starting to grate. 'It would be helpful if you could bring the papers to my secretary to add to your file. Now, I have one last question if you don't mind.'

I clenched a fist at my side. 'If you must.'

'May I ask your religion?'

I felt the air sucked from the room and I froze for what seemed an age, though his lack of reaction showed it must have been much less than a second.

'Roman Catholic,' I heard Rachel say, 'though we don't attend church regularly.'

'Easter, Christmas,' I said, following her quick thinking, 'weddings, christenings and funerals. Those kinds of things.'

Sitell lay down his pen. 'I have to admit I am the same, but you must go more often.'

'Sorry?'

He smiled. 'It is a good way to meet people in a small community. They will welcome you as strangers, and you'll soon find you have lots of friends here.' The mayor stood, said he had all of the information he needed and led us to the door. He cleared his throat one more time. 'A final issue, Monsieur and Madame Given. If you leave the area for more than a day or two, please let me know where you are going, and why. It will be important that I communicate this to the relevant authorities.'

I didn't forewarn him I'd be leaving for a few days to visit my uncle. There'd be time enough to let his office know when I'd put my travel arrangements in place.

When we stepped outside, having confirmed with the mayor's secretary when I would take in the required documents, I kissed Rachel and waved her off then made my way to the Café de Léon.

Sainte Cécile's and the Mairie dominated the square, edifices of the church and state in balance, but the space between belonged to commerce. Once a week the market emerged to complement the patisserie, grocer's and two bars lining the third side. The café where I planned to meet the priest stood on the corner, and in the summer there would be tables and chairs on the pavement, but these were now stacked in an open-fronted lean-to beside the building. Through the large front window, I could see Father Guen tucking into coffee and a confection of chocolate and pastry, something I preferred to resist. A bell rattled when I pushed inside, and the priest raised a hand in greeting then waved me over to join him. We were the only customers and the remaining tables were laid for lunch, the two-hour respite from the working day. White tablecloths, wine and glasses, menus and sparkling cutlery waited for diners to trickle in soon after midday.

'Are you well, Monsieur Given?'

I told him he should call me James.

'Then you will call me Francis.' I glanced at his dog-collar and he hooked his index finger behind it. 'Ah, don't worry about this thing. It is part of my working clothes, and we are friends, yes?'

'I hope we will be.'

We talked of the weather until a waitress in a white blouse and black skirt brought me a drink, then he asked me about his friends in Birmingham, French names I'd have remembered if I'd ever come across them.

'I'm sorry, Francis, I don't recognise any of them. It's a large city. Only half the size of Paris but still big, and I've not lived there for many years. I could ask my father if you wish.'

I was fairly certain Papa did not know the priest's friends either. He had a wide circle of acquaintances and customers, but they were largely Jewish, not Catholic.

'There is no need to make enquiries of your father; it was only idle curiosity on my part. One loses touch, you know, and England, whilst so close, sometimes feels so far away.'

I looked round this little café and thought of the farms, the market and our new life here. It wasn't hard to agree with his sentiment. I told him it would be no inconvenience to ask my father as I'd be writing soon anyway, so an extra line or two in my letter would make no difference. 'Speaking of living in England, Francis, tell me about the librarian. What you said on Saturday made her sound very mysterious.'

'Ah yes, Madame Perron. An interesting lady.'

'In what way?'

'Lisette Perron was a trainee shorthand-typist when the war started, and like so many of our generation she volunteered to join the army. Her intelligence and a bent for languages brought her to the attention of her superiors, and she was posted to London. It is rumoured she worked with your military intelligence service, translating messages into French and then into code ready for transmission.' There was a gleam in Francis' eye as he recounted this story. 'Who knows what else she got up to, eh? Perhaps even a spy?'

If she had been a spy, then we had something in common. In some of my cases I'd worked with a man called Mitchell, no first name other than Mister, who was connected with MI5. Due to wartime restrictions, he'd arranged transport for us to France and provided fake identity papers for our safety in the event of a German advance. Unsurprisingly, he'd asked for something in exchange. If I heard anything on the grapevine he might find useful then I was to pass it on. There'd been nothing worth mentioning so far, but this tidbit about a potentially useful contact might be a small repayment for his help. I made a mental note to ask him about her.

We ordered more coffee and I told Francis about our meeting with the mayor.

'So you will take his advice and attend Mass?'

'If I tell you something, Francis, even outside the confession box, would you promise to keep it to yourself?'

'You'll have seen I like to gossip, James, but only about unimportant things. Things half the population of the town and surrounding countryside would already know. When it comes to the confessional and to my friends, I am like a clam.' He squeezed his lips tight against his teeth, breaking into a gentle smile when it was clear I'd got the message. 'What do you want to tell me?'

I checked the café owner and waitress were out of earshot. 'There is a small problem with Rachel and I attending your church.'

'Oh?'

'We're Jewish.'

The priest leaned back and rubbed his chin. 'Ah, I can see how that might be a problem. Even more so with our German friends knocking at our door. What will you do if we can't keep them out?'

'Hopefully we'll have enough warning before they get this far to head for the hills. Perhaps even back home.'

'Still, Alain Sitell is right, you should try to blend in. You know, there is no synagogue within fifty kilometres of here, and we both worship the same God in our own way. Why not use my church to keep in touch with Him?'

I said we'd think about it. He asked me what had prompted us to move to France.

'Years ago, I spent a long time at sea and got a taste for the open air. When I left that life, I picked fruit for a short while, then something terrible happened which caused me to join the police. A little over a year ago my reason for joining disappeared, and I realised how constricted I felt being a murder detective. My last two cases were particularly bad and I lost a partner so, when Rachel came along, I decided to pack it in. We've kept a place in England in case we ever need to go back, but, for now, we want to spend time together with as little worry as possible. Does that sound so bad?'

'Not at all, James. It sounds perfect. Though I suspect ploughing, sowing and selling vegetables on the market won't be enough to keep you amused for too long.'

'Well, until it becomes boring, that's all I intend to do.'

We both laughed and talked for another ten minutes, mainly him telling funny stories of the antics of the locals, until the church bell chimed and he checked the clock.

'Heavens, is that the time, James? I must be going. I have enjoyed our talk. Same time next week?'

Without hesitation I agreed, and we walked to the door.

As he set off across the square, he turned. 'And will I see you on Sunday?'

I grinned. 'Perhaps.'

I needed a stamp if I was to write to Mitchell, so I called into the post office before I went home. As I entered, a tall man, broad with tousled blond hair, blocked my path. He apologised and side-stepped, but I went the same way; more apologies then we repeated this a couple more times until I stopped and gestured him past.

Monsieur Peston, the postmaster, pushed his glasses up the bridge of his nose and grinned when I reached the counter.

'Happens all the time, our customers dancing in the doorway for our entertainment.'

'I'm glad we are able to keep you amused.'

'Mind you, your dancing partner wasn't strictly a customer, he was just looking for information. People see the post office and think we'll know everyone in the area.'

'So what did he want?'

'Said he has a friend in the army and thinks he was posted near here. He was asking where the military camps are.'

'And did you help him?'

His grin expanded to a loud laugh, and he tapped his tell-tale drinker's nose. 'No chance. We are at war, you know. I'd never seen the man before in my life, so I wasn't about to tell him anything. I was tempted to send him on false trail, but he was a big man and I wouldn't fancy my chances if he came back. I just told him of the two out towards Rennes, which anyone can see from the road, then said the army handles its own postal services but if I could think of anything I'd get in touch.'

'So you don't know who he was?'

'I didn't say that, did I?' The postmaster turned, lifted a sheet of paper from the shelf behind him, and waved it at arm's length. 'He left me his details, just in case. His name is Ménière, David Ménière, and he is living on the road to Dinan.'

Another morsel to feed to Mitchell. I paid for my stamp and wandered home thinking about the letter I'd pen when I had time.

THREE

On the Sunday after I'd met with Francis, Rachel and I attended his church, partly to get to know more local people, as suggested by the mayor, and partly to paint a rosy picture of us being Roman Catholics. The news from the eastern border wasn't good. There was little actual fighting, but it was becoming clear Germany would soon invade Norway, then Holland and Belgium. If they were successful, then France would surely follow. At home we'd heard reports from my father's friends of how Jews were being treated in Germany and the countries it had occupied. Treatment my own uncle had fled from, and which was certain to be repeated everywhere they went. We had the false papers, courtesy of Mitchell, but I'd no idea how good they were. We needed to be in a position where our neighbours could vouch for our religion.

The belltower of Sainte Cécile's, built of local granite, cast a shadow over the market square and the smartly dressed families making their way into the vestibule. A bottle neck had formed where parishioners stopped to dab water on their foreheads, and as we moved closer I could see they were making the shape of a cross. Inside, the church was full, though quiet and still, and the grey walls and stunning marble floor served to accentuate the beauty of the stained-glass windows down each side and over the altar. The silence was broken only by shuffling of feet as people found their seats, and by the gurgling of a baby on the front row.

We took places near the back, and when the crowd was settled, Francis, wearing robes as white as the ground beneath him, emerged from a side room and took his position facing his congregation. Like an orchestra conductor, his right hand described a cross in the air, and he spoke in a language I took to be Latin. All in the church, other than Rachel and me, mumbled a response. Their priest climbed several steps on one side and stood behind an ornate wooden lectern. In French, he then welcomed the congregation and explained they would be baptising a child when the Mass was completed. I assumed this explained how many were in attendance.

From our seats we took the cues from our neighbours, kneeling, standing and miming prayers as convincingly as we could, when Francis returned to the Latin service. All religions have rituals, so although the building and artefacts were unfamiliar the experience wasn't, and I knew it was something we could participate in with a little practice.

Francis was at the church door when we were leaving, and he shook my hand. 'I'm so glad you could make it, James.' He winked. 'Not too stressful, I hope?'

'Not too much, no. You haven't met my wife? This is Rachel.'

'It is nice to meet you, Madame Given, and I hope to see you here with your husband often.'

He introduced us to some of his parishioners, making sure we were noticed by the mayor, almost last to leave the church from his privileged seat at the front. Alain Sitell tipped his hat and smiled, though he didn't pause to speak before ambling over to join a gaggle of men. Shortly afterwards, Rachel tugged at my elbow and we made our way through the arched door to the outside. Malo Legrand stood by his car, talking to the librarian I'd met in the market the previous week.

Rachel leaned in and kissed the farmer on both cheeks. 'I hardly recognised you, Malo. So very smart.'

My employer had certainly cleaned up well for church, his frayed overalls replaced by a nicely pressed suit, his battered boots by polished black brogues. He blushed very slightly and ran a hand through his grey hair. 'Lovely to see you, Madame Given. Have you met Madame Perron? She is our librarian.'

'Ah, now I recognise her. My apologies, madame, I was trying to place you. You know how it is when you see someone in a different setting.'

Lisette Perron smiled thinly then turned her attention back to the farmer. 'I must go, Malo, I have lunch to prepare. I will see you again soon, I hope.'

With a bow in our direction, she wandered away from the church and across the square. Why had she been so curt, the opposite to when we'd last talked? My stupid male vanity made me wonder if it was because Rachel was at my side. I mentioned the difference to Malo.

'Poor Lisette. She is the nicest of women but sometimes gets a bee in her bonnet. I'm sure she meant nothing by it, but I must say she did seem a little distracted this morning. I saw her talking to her boss, the mayor, before Mass and they appeared to be disagreeing. Perhaps her mind was still on something at work.'

'Maybe so. A little village politics.'

Malo grabbed his car door handle and moved to lift his hat to Rachel.

'Before you go, Malo, could I ask a favour?'

'Of course, what is it, James?'

'You know how we've been ploughing the bottom field, and the other two are already done?'

'Yes?'

'Well, when it's finished tomorrow there will be nothing more to do for a week, is that correct?'

'Not until we're putting in the seed. Why?'

'I need to take a short trip and hoped I may be able to have a little time off. Just Tuesday to Friday. I'll be back in time for market.'

He rubbed his chin. 'I don't see why not. There's nothing urgent to be done. Nothing I can't manage myself anyway.'

This was a big concession from him. He'd only taken me on because he'd pulled a shoulder in the autumn and it had taken a good while to heal. I'd been asking round all the local farms if there was any short-term work, and Malo knew he'd have trouble handling the horses in the early part of the season. He'd offered to pay me a decent rate with the house thrown in for as long as we needed it, so I jumped at the chance. So far he'd treated me very well, even though he knew I might be moving on later in the year.

'Thank you, Malo, it means a lot to me.'

'One thing, though. Will you be going on your own?'

'I will. Why?'

The farmer threw back his head and laughed. 'Don't make a habit of it. If you leave your lovely wife alone too often, I might convince her to run away with me.'

He pulled open the car door, climbed inside, and, still laughing, he drove off with a wave.

Monday, though hard work, was easier than the week before, when we'd harrowed four fields ready for sowing and ploughed two left fallow the previous year. I'd taken the horses out at first light to be sure we'd finish by the end of the day, though, in the event, there'd been no snags and the work was done by mid-afternoon. So, thanks to Malo's generosity, I could get on with preparations for the visit to my uncle.

I'd hardly a minute to spare since talking to the postmaster and Francis, and had no idea if the information I'd collected about Lisette Perron and David Ménière would be of any interest to Mitchell, but he'd asked me to keep my ear to the ground so that's what I was doing. I'd met Mitchell when we were both investigating the same person for different reasons; I'd had him down as a respectable witness to a murder, while Mitchell had had him as an enemy agent. I wouldn't have suspected the man of being involved in espionage, but he was. At the time, I'd considered myself good at unearthing evidence on murderers, robbers and run-of-the-mill thugs, but Mitchell's was a different world where I was a stranger. One of secrets, bluff and counterbluff. If what I'd found in the last few days was of use, he'd add it to the dozens of tips he received every day and draw a clearer picture of our enemy's activities and intentions.

At the top of my letter I included the fictitious return address Mitchell had provided in case it was intercepted, then addressed the envelope, in the French style, to a stamp collecting supplies company in Paris. My MI5 contact had said it would find its way to him in a few days. He'd joked that any reply would follow the same route back so I should think about taking up philately.

The contents of the letter were straightforward: a stranger had been asking questions about army bases, and I'd become aware of a local woman who'd worked with MI5 during the last war so might be persuaded to work with them again. There were no codebooks to consult, nor invisible ink involved, so Mitchell must have thought either my intelligence would always be low importance, or his delivery precautions would be enough to keep it secret.

Though I considered it unlikely the French postal system had yet been infiltrated by German spies, I went along with the rest of Mitchell's planned smokescreen and posted the letter. Whilst in the town, I called into the library to consult a travel guide for hotels and the route I'd take to where my Uncle Gideon was living. The room had a quiet stillness, and sunlight from the one large window caught Lisette Perron's face at the desk. In contrast to our meeting outside church, she smiled when she looked up from her work.

'Ah, monsieur, you've found us. It is Monsieur Given, yes? I think this is how Father Guen addressed your wife.'

'That's right. James Given. It's nice to see you again.'

'So how may I help you today?'

I told her what I was looking for. She led me to a corner of the library, then scanned the shelves with the tip of her finger, finally removing a well-worn copy of Baedeker's guide to Northern France.

'This is old, I'm afraid, but it is all that we have.' She pointed to a wooden desk and a chair with a rush seat. 'Sit there and you can go through it. If you need any help, please ask. I'll bring you the bus and train timetables in a moment.'

I thumbed the guide until she returned with the timetables. I checked my route first. It would be a long journey, though under thirty miles, requiring a bus to Dinan, then a train to Dol-de-Bretagne, with the inevitable wait in between. It was clear I'd probably not have time to reach my destination and find my uncle in one day, so I returned to the Baedeker to look for accommodation. When I'd finished, I asked the librarian if she would just check that I'd translated correctly. She quickly read the entries on which I'd made notes and confirmed I'd got them right.

'Some of the places may have closed or changed name since this was written, monsieur, but I don't believe you will have a problem. In France it is not unusual to just turn up and request a room. Where you are going is a reasonably-sized town with a railway station, so there will be plenty available.'

I thanked Madame Perron for her help, and we chatted for a few minutes about my trip, then I left her to her work. I was still tempted to telephone a hotel from outside the post office but decided I'd take the librarian's advice and leave it to chance. If I found my uncle quickly, then I'd stay with him and would not need to pay for accommodation.

FOUR

As I'd expected, the journey from Vieux-Croix to Dol-de-Bretagne a week later took hours. There'd been a flurry of snow overnight, so the bus was half an hour late then trundled from village to village on treacherous roads. As a result, I missed the train I was aiming for and had to spend an extra hour and a half in Dinan station. Even the fantastic mosaics in the rebuilt ticket hall didn't amuse me for too long so I shivered for most of the time on the platform, which made the most of the easterly gale blowing down the tracks.

Dol, as the locals call it, was bathed in afternoon sunshine by the time I arrived. The wind had subsided a little and the town's streets were damp from the showers which arrived after the snow. I was still pleased to take shelter from the cold in the Hotel de la Gare, only minutes from the station, where the owner, a trim little man in cravat and waistcoat, confirmed he had a room available.

The hotel was as neat as my host. There were three floors with freshly painted shutters on the upper windows, a highly polished reception desk on one side of the entrance and a smart dining room on the other. He showed me to my bedroom at the back of the second floor, seeming almost offended when I insisted on carrying my small case. The room was compact but adequate, with a single bed and a view of the railway station from the window. As I unpacked my few clothes into the wardrobe, a goods train rattled past and I prayed the service wouldn't continue through the night.

I was starving, having not eaten since leaving home hours earlier. It was far too late to begin an extensive search for

Uncle Gideon and his family, so I ensconced myself in the hotel dining room and asked to order a late lunch. A waitress apologised because the chef had now finished until dinner, but she said she would ask the manager if it was possible to prepare something. A short while later, I tucked into a chicken escalope in a delightful cream sauce, accompanied by potatoes and vegetables, followed by a slice of the finest apple tart I'd eaten in a long time. When I'd finished, the manager came through and enquired if everything was satisfactory.

'It was excellent, and the room is very comfortable.'

'Will you be staying long, Monsieur Given?'

'Possibly only one night. I'm looking for my uncle, and when I find him I'll stay with him afterwards. Would there be a problem?'

'We are not busy at this time of year, so a flexible arrangement is perfectly acceptable. If you need your room for longer, it will not be a problem either. Your uncle, does he live locally?'

I explained Gideon had written to my father, saying he'd arrived in Dol from Paris. I showed the manager the address and asked if he knew it.

'It is only ten minutes' walk from here, by the cathedral. If you finish your coffee, you will be there before it is dark. Do you wish to pack and cancel your room?'

'No, no, that would be too rude. I will stay the one night at least. My uncle may not have space for me anyway; I've no idea how big a house he has. I will go to look and then move tomorrow if it is convenient for him.'

We talked for another few minutes until the reception bell rang and he made his apologies, so I drained the last of my coffee and went upstairs to collect my coat. A clap of thunder gave me reason to take my umbrella as well.

With my uncle's address in hand, along with scribbled directions from the hotel owner, I strolled for ten minutes along a straight, tree-lined road which took me to the main street, with shops on both sides. A couple of turns later I found my way to, and under, the ancient stone and timber arch he'd described. Thunder rumbled again and as a deluge began I hurried into a small courtyard with four houses on each side and piles of rubbish on the ground, a magnet for the rats scurrying away when I came into view. The whole place stank of decay and old stone. The building I wanted was at the far end, with less rubbish than its neighbours. It was narrow, rising to three floors, with paint peeling from the door, shutters and window-frames. I knocked. A woman in her mid-sixties, dressed in black, answered. She cocked her head and peered through wire-rimmed glasses.

'Yes? Do I know you?' She spoke in halting French, so I replied in English, which I knew she understood.

'It's me, Aunt Miriam, James … Jacob Geffen … your nephew.'

The creases in her cheeks disappeared as her chin dropped. 'Jacob, Dov's boy. You visited us in Bremen. Yes?'

'I did.'

Years earlier, when I was at sea, I'd jumped ship in a north German port and sought out my uncle's home in nearby Bremen. The family was welcoming and had been settled in the city for a long time, though, even then, Gideon knew there was trouble on the horizon. He told me a man named Adolf Hitler had been released from prison and was building a following, blaming the Jews for the economic problems in Germany. I'd only stayed with my uncle for two nights and hadn't seen him or his wife since, even though, at my father's insistence, I'd spent large chunks of the last year trying to find them.

My aunt ushered me inside and climbed the stairs to the first floor, telling me that an elderly, bedridden lady lived below them, which was why she had to answer the door. In a leather armchair by the fire sat a man older than my father, but still his image. He recognised me straight away, rose and shook my hand.

'Jacob, Jacob, welcome. What are you doing here? Is everything all right? Dov isn't ill? Your mother?'

'It's nothing like that; everyone is well, Uncle. Papa was worried that you were in danger and asked me to come to see you.'

'But so far?'

'It's not so far — I'm living in France now.'

'In France? Where?'

'A small place called Vieux-Croix, about thirty miles from here. I'd have come to visit sooner, but I had no address for you until Papa wrote last week. He's been so worried about you since your letters stopped.'

'I know, I know. It has been such a difficult time the last few months, not knowing how long we could settle in one place. We were in Paris for a while.'

'I was there looking for you, but you'd gone.'

'Is that so? You are a good person, Jacob.'

He continued with his story, which was a long and frightening one. I'd heard some of it before, but not in such detail. The family had fled Germany in late 1938 when Hitler's thugs were terrorising the streets and it was clear Jews would no longer be safe in the country. The family went south first, heading for Switzerland, but the further they went the more abuse they received. Instead, they swung west at Essen, skirting through Holland and settled briefly in Belgium, where they thought they'd be safe because the country was neutral. It soon became clear that they wouldn't be, because Germany had other plans. Once again they'd packed up their lives and crossed the border into France, slowly making their way to Paris. My uncle said they'd made for Brittany because it was far from Germany and there was nothing to say England would be safer. This was how they'd ended up in Dol-de-Bretagne. They'd been devastated that my cousin, Lev, had left some months earlier and gone home to Bremen to work against Hitler, saying he could do more good that way than he would running away to France.

'Have you heard from him?' I asked.

'We had a letter a week ago telling us he's now moved to a Dutch border town; he didn't say where. He thinks the Germans will attack that front next so is preparing for the fight.'

'He's a brave man; you must be proud.'

'I think the boy has courage. And stupidity. I'd give anything for him to be here with us.'

I asked about their daughter, Anna.

'She is well. A seamstress and well-regarded. She works for a tailor, just down the street.' My uncle glanced at his wife and she nodded. 'Anna married a man in Belgium, but he turned out to be no good. A drinker and womaniser. Thankfully, he decided not to come with us. She'll be home soon.'

Outside it had become as dark as my uncle's news whilst we'd drunk coffee and chatted, though his face lit up when he heard footsteps on the stairs.

'This will be Anna; she'll be so pleased to see you.'

A woman around forty years of age pushed open the door and came inside. Rain dripped from her coat onto the wooden floor. She looked at me then her father, suspicion etched on her tired face.

'This is Jacob, Anna. You remember him? He visited when we were still in Bremen.'

Recognition came slowly as she pushed her fingers through damp hair. 'Ah, yes. You'd run away from sea. I remember you now.' She laughed. 'Such a long time ago — where did all those years disappear to?'

I joined in with her laughter and stood to shake her hand. Instead, she pulled me to her and gave me a hug.

'It is good to see you again, Jacob. You are staying for the night … or longer?'

'My hotel is booked for tonight. I thought it unfair to just drop in on you and expect you to put me up.'

'Then you're staying for dinner at least?' Anna looked towards her mother.

'Of course, Jacob must eat. What would he think of his uncle and aunt if we didn't feed him? And he must stay here for a night or two if he has time.'

The hotel was expecting me and I'd already had a good feed in the afternoon so I'd leave them in peace to their meal, but I would be happy to accept their offer the next night.

With promises to talk with my uncle the next afternoon, and to eat with them that evening, I left to walk back in the rain past the dark shops to my hotel. One or two bars were still open, with men drinking against the counter, but I wasn't tempted to join them. Not tonight. I was in too good a mood, despite the weather.

It had rained all night, though without the thunder, and, thankfully, the railway line had stayed quiet after I got back so I'd slept well. I'd risen late, then eaten a simple breakfast of coffee and croissants, the latter delicious. I preferred tea in the mornings, though I'd not had good experience of it in France other than at home, so I stuck with coffee. Then I'd spent an hour with a newspaper, reading endless articles on how the war was progressing. For the moment, it was quiet except at sea, where there'd been casualties on both sides. The conflict between Finland and the Soviet Union had ended and Herman Goering, the German leader's deputy, had asked his people to collect metal objects and donate them as a present to Adolf Hitler for his birthday. I threw the paper down after I'd read this last article and decided to take a walk.

The streets close to the hotel were deserted. They always are around a market, wherever I am, except when I reach it. Then there are people everywhere. I never understand how it happens. Do they all leave home a short while before me and stay longer than it takes for me to buy my few items? I've tried varying when I walk down, and my route, but the same phenomenon always occurs. Empty streets, bustling market. An English friend of mine maintains that all French towns and villages are like this, so it is a great illusion, the French not really existing outside of the shops and bars. Whilst an amusing notion, I know it isn't true. Since we'd moved to our home in Vieux-Croix in December we'd met several locals in their homes, so I know they do exist beyond the market.

When I arrived on the main street, stalls lined it on both sides, leaving only the narrowest of paths between them and the shops. This market was much bigger than the one where I sold Malo Legrand's vegetables, and I spent a good hour pottering round tables which offered everything from lace to ironmongery, honey to live chickens, and boots to cheese. I was paying for some chocolates to take home to Rachel when large spots of rain began to spatter, causing the merchants to gather their goods under cover. I abandoned my wandering and dived into a café hoping for lunch, even though it was barely twelve o'clock.

My usual approach in a strange town would be to seek the busiest place, on the basis that if the locals think it's good then it must be worth a visit, but the shower forced me to find the nearest café to avoid being drenched. One small table remained near the window so I could continue to take in the sounds and sights of the street. The waiter took my order for the plat du jour and a glass of water, and I settled to watch the water bouncing off the cobbles while I waited.

The food arrived as the rain stopped and I ate slowly, observing the soaking stallholders pack away their wares, drying them as best they could. Some would have a long journey home and they'd all have work to do, trying to save what they could from rot and water damage. It might be a lean week for those who'd lost a couple of hours' trade and not made enough sales before the rain came down.

Not long after I'd finished my veal and vegetables, I saw my Uncle Gideon passing so I knocked on the window and waved for him to join me. Over our coffee he filled me in on some of the lighter stories of his travels, having told me most of the bad ones the night before.

I asked him about what was happening to Jews in Germany when he left, and he surveyed the scene outside the window for a long minute before shaking his head.

'You see out there, Jacob? Ordinary people going about their ordinary business. No politics, no cruelty, just getting on with their lives. That's how it used to be in Bremen. We were accepted. Seen as a little different in the way we worshipped but allowed to go about our business every day and with no animosity. Until Adolf Hitler and his like came along: a small minority saying we Jews were the cause of all of the problems in Germany. Not the French, the Americans or the British who'd defeated the country, but the Jews, who wanted nothing more than to feed their families and live in peace.'

'And it changed?'

'Those we thought were our friends began to avoid us. The fascists had become stronger and stronger, increasing their control of the press and employment, so people either believed what the papers told them or were in fear of losing their jobs so acted the way Hitler wanted them to. Bad things were said to us in the street. Bricks were thrown at our people's businesses. Soon it became unbearable.

'We thought our lives were in danger, and we had to get away. But that is all behind us now. We are here in this lovely country and safe.' His voice cracked on these last few words, but he gathered himself and smiled. 'And we are making proper contact with our family again. Will you join us this evening for Shabbat? I know Anna would love to see you again before you go back home to your wife.'

I agreed I'd be with them in time for dinner, and we parted on the street. I made my way back to my hotel, pleased I could soon put my father's mind at rest that his brother was safe and well.

I arrived back at my uncle's half an hour before dark and the house was already prepared for Shabbat, the rooms cleaned, table laid and candles waiting to be lit around six o'clock, when the sun would be deemed to be set. The smell of warm food in the oven was scrumptious, full of memories of my parents' house on Friday evening.

Whilst Aunt Miriam and her daughter fussed over the final preparations, my uncle asked what I'd been doing before coming to France. The last time I'd seen him, other than the previous day, was before I'd returned to England, so there was a lot to tell about my remaining years at sea and my time with the police when I got home. He listened to it all then asked the question everyone seemed to have. Why had I left it behind?

'In the end, day after day, being surrounded by violence and evil became too much. I knew for my sanity I needed to get away and work again in the open air. I only joined the police with one purpose: to bring the men behind a friend's death to justice. When that possibility disappeared, I was free to do what I wanted.'

'But surely you were providing a public service? Doing good? That was important, wasn't it?'

'It was, or at least I thought so for a long time. Then I saw nothing was changing. I'd put one villain behind bars, and another would pop up to take his place. One thing I've become sure of is that no matter how many rats we dispose of, there's plenty more in the sewers waiting to crawl out. I can do as much service to the public now growing vegetables and picking fruit.'

My uncle shook his head, then leaned forward and put his hand on my knee. 'I'm not so sure, Jacob. The world can be a wicked place, and we need men like you to protect us.'

I'd been told this before and believed it, only to find more deaths followed which I couldn't prevent. Before I could protest, he held up his hands, palms outward.

'You must do what you think is best. If God has chosen this path for you, then he knows what he's doing. If he hasn't, he'll show you soon enough.'

Anna called to us. 'Come to the table, come. Everything is ready — and I'm starving.'

After dinner my uncle led us in the traditional giving of thanks for the food we'd taken then asked me to join him, his wife and Anna in a corner. He explained there was no synagogue close enough for them to travel to, so they reserved this small space to make their devotions.

'It is only right, Jacob, on this Shabbat, that we offer our prayers to show our gratitude for God leading you to us.'

I suspected his first offering was one the family had repeated every day in their flight across Europe. *Blessed are You, Lord our God, Who has kept us alive, and sustained us, and enabled us to reach this moment.*

It occurred to me that these words would just as easily be spoken by Francis in his church, acknowledgement of the mystery of how we make it through every day in a world where we can't predict what's coming round the corner. Some put it down to the intervention of a loving God, others to luck. I couldn't decide, so for now I went through the motions, as I did in Sainte Cécile's, to keep up appearances.

When the thanks and calls for intercession were completed we sat by the fire and talked more of our lives, his in Russia as a child, me of my wanderings round the ports of Europe, Africa and America. I asked Anna about her marriage.

'I was foolish. Tomas was charming, swept me off my feet you might say. Hardly together three months when I discovered he was stealing my savings to spend on other women. Mother and Father had already decided to move on, and I thought I'd be staying with my new husband until I found what a snake he was. I left him where I found him and came with them.'

'So do you plan to stay here?'

'I have a nice little job, but I'd like to set up on my own one day, perhaps a small workshop somewhere.'

'That would be nice.' I turned to her father. 'And you, Uncle Gideon, will you stay here or go to England? Papa would put you up until you found somewhere.'

'There is no need, Jacob. We are happy here for the time being.'

'But what if France is overrun?'

'Then so be it. This will be God's will. To take this country, Germany will need to conquer Holland and Belgium on the way, and if he succeeds then what is to stop him crossing the water to take England as well?'

I had to admit this fear was real and shared by me and many at home. 'You're a good distance from the border here, Uncle, and close to the sea, so if they do break through you'll still have a chance to escape.'

'But the first thing they'll do is secure the ports. We'd never get across.'

'Then get to know some fishermen. They'll have sturdy boats and, I'm sure, for a fee will carry you over. If you've not got the money then contact Papa; he'll send enough.'

I pushed and pushed but my uncle was insistent he'd be staying put. In the end I had to settle for a promise he'd keep in regular touch with my father and be truthful in his reports of how the family were getting on. Months earlier Papa threatened he'd travel to France to find his brother, and I knew the only way to avoid this was for him to be sure Gideon was safe.

On the doorstep, before I left, my aunt, uncle and cousin hugged me and told me to make sure to visit again soon. I'd only taken a few steps across the quiet courtyard when I heard footsteps behind me. I tensed in the darkness until I looked back to see Anna.

'Don't worry, Jacob ... James, I'll make sure he writes regularly. He can be stubborn, but if the Germans come I'll get him to England somehow.'

I thanked her and said a final goodnight, then set off down dark streets for my hotel and bed. My conversations with Uncle Gideon and Anna had set me wondering if my decision to come to France had been entirely sensible.

FIVE

Next morning, after throwing questions around throughout a sleep-starved night, I rose early, ate a light breakfast and caught the train to Dinan with nothing resolved. I was lucky this time to have only ten minutes to wait between train and bus, but when I climbed on board my bad thigh was throbbing with all the walking and travel of the past few days.

My wife was shivering at the stop when I climbed off.

'Why on earth are you out on an afternoon like this, Rachel? Has something happened?'

'No, nothing's happened. I just wanted you home.'

We'd walked a few steps and she stopped.

'You're limping. Is the leg bad?'

'Just a bit sore. I think I might have been doing a bit too much. Funny really, out in the fields it doesn't bother me, but as soon as I'm on the streets I start to feel it. Anyway, enough about me, are you sure everything is all right?'

She paused for a moment. 'Actually, something has happened, but that's not what brought me out.'

I gave her a hug and we cuddled as we walked, staying close to buildings to avoid the worst of the east wind, which whistled with a vengeance. On the other side of the lane trees whipped back and forth, dirty grey clouds skimming the sky above them.

'So what is it?'

'The librarian, you met her?'

'I did, Lisette Perron.'

'The poor woman's been found dead.'

'What? How? I only spoke to her a few days ago.'

'They're saying it must've been an accident because she was discovered yesterday evening in the river with her bicycle. Georges Moreau went down to fish for his dinner and found her near the bridge. He ran to fetch the policeman, Pascal Jaubert, who arranged for her body to be taken away.'

'And they're sure it was an accident?'

'One or two of the more nervous old ladies have double-locked their front doors, convinced there is a cold-bloodied killer on the loose, but what else could it be other than an accident?'

Most murders aren't really in cold blood. They might be planned, and they might be brutal, but the killer almost always has a reason, albeit distorted, for her or his actions. Jealousy, revenge, envy, lust. Something has made their blood boil and tells them the only way forward is to destroy the person who generated the emotion. Even in cases where the perceived wrong has occurred years before, something has happened to unlock the anger and caused the river to burst its banks.

I was pleased to push open our front door into a warm living room. Rachel had stoked the fire well before she left and soon had the kettle singing.

On the table lay a letter bearing a Paris postmark and return address of the stamp seller in the first arrondissement, the same address I'd used for the one to Mitchell.

In his reply, Mitchell thanked me for the information and requested that I find more on David Ménière. He also wrote that he'd done a little digging and found that the librarian was still on his department's payroll. She'd been on a small retainer since she'd returned to France but had reported nothing for years, though she'd made contact with her link officer only two weeks earlier. Lisette Perron hadn't forwarded any information, only enquired if the path was still open. She'd been told it was.

He wound up his letter with a footnote saying he'd enclosed a couple of stamps 'just to get your collection going'. On the envelope containing one, an 1887 halfpenny vermilion, a stock number was scribbled, which I knew would be a telephone where I could reach Mitchell in an emergency.

Rachel and I sat in opposite armchairs whilst I read, then, with our hands wrapped around our cups, I told her the story of my trip.

'Do you think he'll go to join your parents, James?'

'I don't know. He said he wouldn't, but perhaps Anna will make him see sense.'

'Possibly he's right, though.'

'About what?'

'That it's only a hop and a skip for the Germans to get to England if they make it to here. In fact, from Belgium or northern France it's much closer to Kent than to Brittany.'

'Are you worried? I've been thinking the same thing, but we would have the Channel between us. Do you *want* to go home?'

'Not yet.'

I looked to see if she was telling the truth, but I couldn't tell. She flashed a smile in my direction.

'I love it here. It's peaceful and people are friendly. I have you all to myself.' Rain rattled against the window, and the smile broadened. 'And summer will be here soon.' Rachel left her seat then plonked down onto my knee. She snuggled her head against my shoulder. 'Let's try not to think about it. The world can be frightening enough without us worrying about what might not happen.'

We sat for a very long time by the fire, saying nothing, but my thoughts hovered between German tanks and the dead librarian. It was only when Rachel stirred and said she'd prepare dinner that I went back to our earlier conversation.

'How well did you know her? Madame Perron?'

She shook her head. 'Hardly at all. She'd stamped my books in the library and we'd said hello at church last week when you were with me.'

'I'd only spoken to her myself a couple of times, but there was something about her. Feisty. I thought you might have become friends.'

'Well, she was quite distant when we spoke with Malo. And now she's dead.' She turned from chopping potatoes. 'Are you planning to take a look at what happened?'

I snorted. 'No. Why would I? I've told you, all that's behind me now. Besides, you've said it was an accident.'

Rachel came behind my chair and planted a kiss on the top of my head. 'Good. I don't want you in harm's way anymore. What would I do without you?'

The words had barely fallen from her lips when there was a tap on the door. Rachel opened it.

'Marie-Clair? What are you doing here? Our lesson is tomorrow.'

'I know, madame, but I heard your husband has returned. My mother saw you waiting at the bus stop. May I speak to him?'

'Of course, come in.'

I stood and offered the girl a seat. Rachel excused herself and went back to preparing our meal.

'What is it, Marie-Clair? Do you have a problem?'

'Me? Oh no. Can I ask you a question?'

'Go ahead.'

I now switched between English and French without thinking, and imagined that, before long, Rachel and I might speak our adopted language all the time, even when at home. Marie-Clair drew a deep breath.

'Why did you join the police, Monsieur Given?'

'It's a long story.'

'So tell me.'

'A woman I loved very much, someone I thought I might marry, was murdered.' Marie-Clair glanced at Rachel. 'It was a long time ago, many years before I met my wife. I thought if I joined the police I could catch her killers. Why do you ask?'

'Because I've been thinking and thinking about something since I heard of Madame Perron's death.'

'Thinking of what?'

'I've been wondering if wanting to be a police officer is a vocation, like being a nun. Is that how you felt?'

I laughed. 'Never. As I said, it was a means to an end. More than just a job but not something I'd wanted to do my whole life. When those men got what they deserved, I stopped.'

'So you were on a mission.'

'I suppose you could say that.'

'Perhaps that's what it is, then. This feeling. I need to know what happened to Madame Perron.'

'Then, first of all, you should talk to the policeman. See what he has to say. If you're still not happy she had an accident, come back to see me and we'll talk about what you might do next.'

Marie-Clair leapt to her feet and bashed the side of her head with the heel of her hand. 'Of course. Why didn't I think of doing that? The policeman, Pascal, is my cousin. It will be no problem getting him to tell me what he thinks.'

I walked her to the door, and she shouted a goodbye to Rachel, then walked off into the evening. I stayed on the step watching her go, shaking my head and thinking how fine it would be to be young and enthusiastic again.

The following Sunday the church was full again, though there had been no baptism, and we'd discovered this was because it was a special day in the Christian calendar, Palm Sunday, the day their Jesus rode into Jerusalem, only a week before his crucifixion. The service made me feel uneasy, with its message that he'd been betrayed by the Jews.

Afterwards, Rachel and I were amongst the first to leave the church, being handy for the door from our pews near the back. Father Francis shook my hand, then pulled me by the elbow to one side.

'James, may I have a word?'

I glanced at the queue of expectant parishioners giving me filthy looks for laying claim to their shepherd. 'Now?'

'No, after they've all left. It will only be five minutes. Come to my house and I'll make us a drink. I have English tea, or something stronger?'

'Tea will be fine, Father.' He raised an eyebrow. 'Sorry … Francis. We'll wait outside until you're ready.'

One by one, the congregation filed past him, some pausing for a brief conversation, most simply bowing their heads and shaking hands. Some nodded to us as they went by, others looked away, probably not happy with the extra attention the newcomers had received.

When the crowd had dispersed, the priest joined us and led us to a large house beside the church. He took us through an ornate hall to a high-ceilinged room at the front of his home. It seemed to me that the whole of our small cottage would fit into this one space. I didn't hide my envy too well.

'I know, James, it is disgraceful for a single man to live in such a large house, but it isn't my choice. The parishioners who built the church obviously thought they needed to demonstrate the importance of their priest by building him an impressive home. Do you know, it has six bedrooms. Six! I can only imagine my predecessors had many servants or many visitors.'

A woman pushed open the door. She carried a tray which she put on the table in front of my wife, and Francis introduced her as his housekeeper. Rachel and the woman shared a few words, then she left.

'You know Louise, Madame Given?'

'Only in passing. We've met in the shops once or twice. She seems very nice.'

'She's a saint. I don't know what I'd do without her.' He poured the tea and offered cake, which we both refused.

'Was there something you wanted, Francis?'

'Yes, yes, of course. I mustn't keep you. There were actually two things.' He walked to a bureau in the corner and brought out a sheet of paper. 'This came through my letterbox two days ago. I hear others have had them too.'

It was a printed handbill, about six inches by four. Cheap. In short sentences it spelt out the threat to "ordinary, decent, people" of Jewish ownership of businesses. Just the kind of material I'd seen in Germany years earlier. I showed it to Rachel then handed it back.

'There will always be things like this, Francis. It means nothing. I even saw them in England. What do you want us to do?'

'Nothing, James. I just wanted you to be aware of it. Someone in our small community is spreading hatred, and I will do my best to find out who it is. In the meantime, you need to be careful.'

'But no-one here knows we're Jewish.' I leant back in my chair and looked at Rachel then at the priest. 'Do they?'

His cheeks flushed. 'You surely don't think I'd have told anyone? You confided in me, and I don't betray my friends.'

'No, no, Francis. I'm sorry. It's just that we haven't told anyone other than you, and I thought for a minute you might have let it slip. If you're saying you haven't, then that's good enough for me. We'll be careful, as you suggest. You said there were two things?'

The priest poured more tea. 'You heard my homily this morning on the death of poor Lisette Perron?'

'I did. I met her a couple of times and she seemed pleasant. Why?'

'Lisette was very active in the church. She had … how should I say it … an interesting love life, and I think her good works were a way of atoning for it. She came to see me on Thursday, the day before she died.'

'And?'

'I'm uneasy about saying. It wasn't in confession, but I feel she was confiding in me. I've struggled over the past few days as to whether I should say anything.'

I gave him the stock policeman's answer, perhaps less than he deserved. 'If you think it has a bearing on her death, then you should tell the police.'

Francis looked at Rachel, then back to me, and pressed his intertwined fists against his bottom lip. 'She told me she was struggling with a dilemma. Said she couldn't explain more. I asked if it was about a relationship and she said it wasn't, not directly, but it was something she'd discovered. I couldn't get any more out of her.'

'And you believe this relates to her death? How?'

'I don't know, James, perhaps she just needed someone to listen and it's nothing to do with what happened to her. Even if it didn't, I wish I'd pressed harder.'

'You can't blame yourself, Francis. It isn't your fault she didn't open up, but I don't think you have any choice. You must tell the police. It may not be connected, but they at least need to know.'

'Pascal Jaubert already has Lisette's death recorded as an accident. He'll not change his mind.'

'He might if you give him fresh information.'

'I doubt it; he'd just think I was being dramatic. Couldn't you take a look?'

'Me? How could I? I've no power to do so. I'm no longer a policeman.'

'But you were one, James, and I suspect a good one. You know about these things. That's why I'm telling you.'

I shook my head and looked to Rachel to come to my rescue, which she did.

'I'm sorry, Father Guen, but my husband left all that behind in England.' She laid a hand on mine. 'He had a very bad time there at the end, even being badly wounded, and we don't want him going through that again. Please don't ask him to.'

Francis sighed. 'I apologise, James, I shouldn't have burdened you with this. As you have said, it is probably nothing, but I've hardly slept since poor Lisette's death thinking about her words. I'll do as you suggest and tell Pascal what I know then leave him to act as he sees fit.'

He poured more tea and turned our conversation to the weather and tittle-tattle about his flock until we stood to leave.

'Remember what I said, you two keep your heads down. There are people who will happily blame Jews, and foreigners, for any misfortune they are facing. There are others who will stoke the flames for their own ends. Both need to be watched.'

Rachel and I held hands as we walked from his door and stayed silent all the way home.

SIX

I'd told Francis the truth when I'd said I was no longer a policeman, but all I'd done was leave the force. Years of investigating, picking away at details to unravel mysteries, is a hard habit to break. I've never been sure if I had a particular turn of mind or if it was a skill I developed, but now I would always look for alternative perspectives on any problem placed before me. Someone once accused me of picking at scabs until they bled, and this was how it felt with the two questions raised in the last week. Was David Ménière, the man I'd briefly met in the post office, a spy, or was he really looking for a friend in the forces? Did Lisette Perron have an accident, as concluded by our local policeman, or was there something more sinister about her death? These, inevitably, led to a third question. Were the two connected?

So, if I followed up on Ménière's activities, then wasn't I just acting as an amateur detective with no valid reason to refuse Francis' request to look into the librarian's death? Except murder investigations had taken me to some very bad places. Places I didn't want to go to again.

Rachel and I had discussed this from every angle when we'd returned from church, with me defending my inclination to do Mitchell's bidding to the point where she went off to practise her cello for hours. She was still cool as the March night when we went to bed.

But I couldn't help myself: I needed to pay back our debt to Mitchell. I convinced myself I'd ask a few questions then leave it to the boys in military intelligence to do the heavy lifting.

Late on Monday morning, after I'd finished my jobs around the farm, I was outside David Ménière's house. I'd extracted the exact location from the postmaster, and it hadn't been difficult, his need for gossip seriously outweighing any sense of confidentiality. It was in the middle of a short terrace a couple of hundred yards from the marketplace. I'd have liked to have taken a spot across the road but there was no cover, so I'd have stuck out like a sore thumb. Instead, I walked past several times, seemingly consulting a slip of paper, as though looking for a specific address. The upper windows of the five stone houses were shuttered, and the doors all needed a coat of paint. I turned a corner at the end of the row and peeked over the wall. The gardens I could see were neat and planted with vegetables. These gardens were divided by hedges, some made up of free-growing shrubs, others neatly clipped, Ménière's looking like it hadn't been tended for some time.

A path ran along the back of the houses, with a gate between each, so I watched for a few minutes to make sure the coast was clear then pressed the latch of the first gate. As I did so, an elderly face appeared in the window of the end property, a lady who fixed me with rheumy eyes. My smile and lifted hand only solicited a deeper frown, so I retreated to the main road. I needed to dive back round the corner to avoid being spotted by Ménière, who had just stepped from his front door. He headed away from me in the direction of the market square, so I counted to ten then followed at a decent distance, just another shopper ambling into town. His height and straw-blond hair ensured he'd not be difficult to keep in view. The man went into the tobacconists, so I took a spot outside Francis' church, leaning against a wall, consulting my watch every minute or two and shaking my head. Someone waiting for a friend, nothing more. Ménière progressed from shop to shop before turning into the Bar du Marché. I took my chance and followed, taking an empty table next to Ménière and nodding to him as I sat down.

'Cold out there.'

He glanced out of the window then back at me. 'I expect it is. What can we expect at this time of the year, eh?' The postmaster had said Ménière didn't have a local accent, and the difference was noticeable straight away.

'Had any luck?' I asked.

'Luck? In what way?'

'Your search. We bumped into each other a few days ago. Monsieur Peston, the postmaster, said you were looking for your friend.' I rose and offered my hand. 'I apologise, sir, you must think me very rude. My name is James Given. The postmaster only mentioned it because he knew I have a half-brother in the army and had also been hoping to find him stationed nearby.'

My lie seemed to satisfy Ménière, and he turned to face me more directly. Bernard, the owner, came to take our orders, a glass of beer for him and mint cordial with lemonade for me, a Diabolo Menthe.

'I've not found him so far, Monsieur Given; they move about so much at present. This is why I've been trying to locate all of the camps. Perhaps we might compare notes some time. I'll tell you the ones I've visited, and you can do the same for me. That way, we can share the load and may have some success.'

'I think that might be very helpful, Monsieur…?'

'David Ménière.'

'Ah, thank you. Do you live in Vieux-Croix?'

'I do, just a short walk from here. Do you?'

'On a farm, just outside the town. If you give me your address, I'll drop round a list when I've had time to think about it.'

He told me and I wrote it down, even though I already knew where he lived. Ménière said he was a salesman and only in Vieux-Croix for a few weeks, probably moving on soon. I steered the conversation round to the dead librarian to see his reaction. There was none, other than a dispassionate "so sad".

'Did you know her?'

'I don't believe we'd met. I heard of the lady's death when I returned from a trip the day after she was found.'

'A holiday?'

'No, not really. I had some business to attend to in Paris. I managed a little sightseeing but mostly work, I'm afraid.'

I asked where he'd stayed in Paris. He tilted his head to the side.

'Why?'

I laughed. 'I'm sorry, my French still isn't perfect and sometimes comes out wrongly. My wife and I are planning a trip later in the year, and any recommendations would be helpful. It's fine if you'd rather not say.'

'No, it is not a problem. It was a small commercial place, the Hotel de la Paix, in a back street close to the Eiffel Tower. Comfortable and not expensive. When are you going?'

'Not for a while. It will be our wedding anniversary, and we thought it might be nice to spend it in the capital.'

'Ah yes, you British always seem to think of Paris as romantic.' He drained the last of his beer and stood. 'I'm afraid I must be going, Monsieur Given. It was nice to talk to you. Don't forget to let me have a list of the camps you have visited.'

The minute he closed the door I scribbled as detailed a description as I could, in preparation for my next letter to Mitchell.

Later that day I had two more letters addressed and ready to post.

The first was to Mitchell, via the Paris stamp dealer. There wasn't much to add to what I'd already sent to him, except that I'd made contact and had a better description of David Ménière to offer. As I wrote, I wondered again if I should have waited a few days to try to take a photograph. Since he'd left me in the bar it had been preying on my mind, but I couldn't work out how to take one without raising his suspicions. I had to hope my powers of description were good enough for Mitchell to identify the man. In addition to painting the most accurate pen-portrait I could of the possible spy, I told Mitchell I'd found where he was living and gave a full account of my chat with him. I didn't give an opinion on whether I thought he was telling the truth, mainly because I couldn't decide. What he'd said sounded plausible enough but, with practice, any lie can be disguised.

The second envelope bore the address of the hotel in Paris where Ménière said he'd stayed, his visit neatly slipped into our conversation, perhaps a rehearsed story to give him an alibi. It made sense to check it, though I was far from sure why he'd need an alibi anyway. The story I'd concocted was that a friend had recently returned from travelling and had provided their hotel as one of the places he'd be staying when he got back. I wrote that I hadn't seen him for two years so was hoping to catch him there, and it would be most helpful if they could let me know if and when he'd arrived. There was always the chance they'd tell Ménière, but this seemed unlikely unless he visited regularly. I'd need to keep my fingers crossed.

Both of the letters were in the box to catch the midday collection.

Having lost a good part of the morning in my checks on Ménière, I needed to catch up on the work Malo was paying me for. Rachel had thawed overnight, then turned icy again when she'd heard my plans at breakfast. Nonetheless, she made me a good lunch, even though we ate it in silence. Soon after we'd cleared away our dishes, Marie-Clair arrived for her violin lesson. I reached for my overcoat a moment too late. The girl put down her case and stood, arms folded, in front of me.

'Before you go out, Monsieur Given, could I tell you something?'

I sighed. 'Please don't ask me again to investigate Madame Perron's death, Marie-Clair. I've told you I'm not a policeman anymore.'

'No, I know. I just want to tell you what I've found and ask some advice.'

I sat in my armchair and gestured for her to take the other. 'Go ahead then, if you must.'

'As you suggested, I spoke to my cousin, Pascal. He's not very bright, you know. Not bright enough to be a decent policeman at least. It's his view that Madame Perron had an accident, that's all. He says she must have been cycling too fast down the hill and skidded down the bank, bashing her head on a rock in the river.'

'This is what I'd heard. Isn't that the most likely explanation?'

'It's *one* explanation, but surely you've had cases where things weren't as they seemed at first glance.'

She didn't know how right she was. In all of my recent cases, the obvious had turned out not to be true, or, at least, there had been more to the situation than was first thought. Left to some people, they would have been wrapped up and filed away without a second thought for the victim or their loved ones. There are always, everywhere, sloppy or corrupt police officers who take what's in front of them at face value, refusing to dig any deeper than is convenient. Nine times out of ten the answer is what it seems, but we still need to consider alternatives. Otherwise the cruel and calculating get away with murder. Literally.

'What makes you think there's another possibility, Marie-Clair?'

She shifted in her seat and fixed her eyes on the floor. 'Nothing really. It's just that it would be so much more exciting if the librarian had been murdered. Don't you think?'

I laughed. 'So now we have it. You just want some amusement at the expense of poor Madame Perron.'

Marie-Clair looked up, a hint of red in her cheeks. 'Not exactly. I'm interested in how it would be investigated, that's all.' She stood and snatched up her violin case. 'If you're going to make fun of me, monsieur, I'll have my lesson and leave you to it.'

The girl was keen, and not afraid to challenge authority, I gave her that. What harm could it do if I took her through a few basic steps in crime detection? If anything emerged, I could leave it to her and our policeman to see it through.

'I'm sorry, Marie-Clair, I didn't intend to upset you. What if I told you I've heard a story which makes me wonder if there isn't more to this than meets the eye?'

'You have?'

'Possibly. I need to do some more checking before making a decision. Would you like to come with me when you're finished to ask some questions?'

I didn't need to wait for an answer. Her face said it all.

For the hour of Marie-Clair's lesson I escaped from the house, chopped some logs for Malo and hoed weeds from a couple of beds of broad beans. The month had been chilly, but pods were starting to form, and we'd have the beginnings of a harvest within a few weeks unless a late frost knocked them back. Clouds were low on the horizon, moving quickly as a front in our direction, so it looked like we'd have milder weather for the next few days. I checked my watch, and even though I'd told Marie-Clair I'd be finished when she was, I needed to make sure Malo and I could do the work we planned. I went to the second barn, behind the farmer's house, where the machinery was kept. We always cleaned after we finished, but it did no harm to brush away the dried mud and to grease the moving parts. The buckles and harnesses needed no attention, so it took me no more than thirty minutes to get everything ready. Even so, when I returned into the house, Marie-Clair was waiting, on the edge of her seat.

'You're ready? Come on then, grab your coat.'

'Certainly, I'm ready. Where are we going, Monsieur Given?'

'There's a man I need to find out more about. Question his neighbours, that kind of thing. The thing is, he knows me, so I'll perhaps need to melt away and let you do the talking. Are you prepared for that?'

She gulped. 'I … I expect so.'

'Good. Also, we need to keep this secret, so don't tell anyone what you've seen or heard.'

'Of course, monsieur.'

I changed out of my work-coat and boots into more respectable ones, dug out a notebook and pencil from the kitchen cupboard, and we went out into the windy afternoon. On our way through the town, I told Marie-Clair to knock on Ménière's door first when we got there. If he answered, she was to ask about a fictitious previous tenant, a friend who owed her money. When he denied any knowledge, which he was bound to do, she would then tell him she'd ask the neighbours in case any knew of her friend's new address. I ducked around the corner to keep out of sight until Marie-Clair came to find me.

She hadn't needed the story because Ménière wasn't home, so we knocked on the door of each neighbour in turn, now with me in the lead role. One was out and the old lady who'd spotted me last time peered round her curtain and shooed us away. A young man answered the next door.

'Good afternoon, monsieur. My colleague and I were looking for the gentleman who lives along the street here, a Monsieur Ménière. Do you know him?'

'A little, though not well.'

'Would you know when he'll be home?'

The man rubbed his chin. 'Afraid not. He hasn't lived here long.'

'Is that right?'

'Only a few weeks. Seems a decent enough bloke, though could be a bit quieter and tidy his garden up. Listen, what's this about?'

'I'm sorry, monsieur, I can't go into much detail.' I glanced at Marie-Clair and we both shook our heads. 'No, it wouldn't be right. All I can say is that we've been asked by a debt-collector in Paris if we could have a word with him.' I was sure with this approach none of the neighbours would mention our visit to Ménière.

The young man tutted. 'I can't help you there. We've only ever said hello or nodded in the street. Doesn't look the type to spend a lot of money. Funny, you never can tell.'

At the last house, a balding man in his sixties confirmed Ménière had only been in the house about a month. 'He knocked a day or so after he arrived. Said hello and asked if I knew of any army camps locally. Said he was looking for a friend based in one.'

'And did you?'

'I thought it sounded a bit suspicious with a war on and all, so I told him I didn't.'

'Very wise.'

'Well, you don't know, do you? I was glad I kept quiet. The next time I saw him he was in the library, bothering that woman who died. He became quite irate with her when she wouldn't deal with him right away. Wanted largescale maps of Brittany, and she told him to wait until she'd finished dealing with another customer.'

When we walked away, I asked Marie-Clair if she'd learnt anything.

'I could see how you didn't dive in straight away with the questions, and how you gave them a reason to talk to you.'

'Good. In my experience, people are always willing to gossip, you just have to get them started. If you start to question them straight away, unless you've got them in a cell of course, then they'll automatically be suspicious. Give them the impression you're clarifying what they've said, and they'll continue to open up, not realising how deep your questioning is going. Got it?'

'I think so. Did *you* learn anything?'

'I did, two things.'

'Tell me.'

'One isn't important to you, only to a friend of mine. The other was that Monsieur Ménière told me a lie. It might mean nothing, but I think perhaps we need to look just a little further into this after all.'

Marie-Clair's face lit up. 'So what do we do now?'

'You go home and change into some boots then meet me at my house in half an hour. We'll take a look at where Madame Perron died.'

SEVEN

Marie-Clair dashed half a step in front of me through the orchard opposite my house, then across the field almost all the way down to the road leading to the river. Twice I'd had to ask her to slow down and let me keep up. Twice she'd laughed and told me I was like an old man.

The young never seem to give leeway to those who are not as fit and lively, unless they are obviously elderly. Although my leg injury hadn't resulted in a visible limp, I was no longer able to run or walk long distances without pain. To preserve my dignity, I said a good detective moved at a speed where they'd see what was around them. She laughed again.

'But Madame Perron didn't die anywhere near here; what would there be to see? You're just making excuses because you're a slow-coach.'

I stopped. 'May I ask you something, Marie-Clair?'

She strolled back and put her hands on her hips. 'Yes?'

'Do you believe the librarian was murdered?'

'Well, it's a possibility, isn't it?'

'It is. So, do you know which way our killer, if there is one, left the scene?'

'No, of course not. How could I?'

'Then he, or she, could have come through this field. Agreed?'

Marie-Clair made a silent 'Oh' and returned up the path, darting this way and that until I called her back.

'Could we have missed something, Monsieur Given? I'm so stupid, rushing along, I never thought.'

Now I laughed. 'I doubt we've missed anything. In fact, I can't see any reason why they'd bother coming this way. There's nothing but Malo's farmhouse and fields for miles beyond my place.'

'So why did you say it?'

'Well, I had to slow you down somehow, didn't I?'

The girl clenched her teeth. I was reminded of how wet behind the ears my police partner, John Sawyer, had been when we'd first worked together. And I owed my life to him.

I walked on and waved for her to join me. 'Come on then. Let's get down there. See what we can see. But take it easy.'

It took us five more minutes to reach the road, which sloped gently from the village until it dropped steeply a hundred yards from the bridge over the River Fourion. It was a beautiful spot to die. The open fields on our left, with grazing cattle, dropped in green banks beyond the road down to gurgling water, shaded by woodland on the other side.

I asked Marie-Clair to go to the bottom and work her way up. 'I'll come down the hill towards you. Check for anything unusual, particularly any signs of a skid; the librarian would have braked hard if she ran out of control. We'll cross in the middle so we both cover the same ground.'

The exercise took us a quarter of an hour, but we found nothing. Marie-Clair raised the obvious question.

'So why no skid marks?'

'There are a few reasons why we might not see the traces. She could have veered off the road further up, hoping the grass would slow her down. Or her brakes could have failed.'

'Perhaps someone made them fail, or maybe she didn't crash her bicycle at all.'

'Let's not get ahead of ourselves.'

At points like this, the first time on a potential crime scene, I always feel my skin becoming more sensitive and my pulse quickening. Even my ears pick out sounds they'd missed earlier: the wind moving through the trees, the rattle of machinery in the distance, birdsong. This heightened alertness comes on the edge of discovery, when the air tells you things are different to what you thought they were. I walked to the grass bank and beckoned Marie-Clair to follow.

'We'll do the same again, closer to the edge this time. Let's look for where she came off the road. Try to stay on the hard surface as far as you can so we don't disturb anything.'

Before I'd trekked up to my starting point, Marie-Clair shouted me. 'There's something here.' She was only yards from the bottom of the hill, where there was the track of a car tyre, parallel with the road. The grass was flattened and muddy between there and the river.

'Well spotted, but I don't think it's relevant. This is where they lifted her out. We'll find nothing here, even if it's where she went in. Your cousin, Pascal, has made a real mess.'

We restarted our check of the bank but found no evidence of where Lisette Perron left the road. This could have meant nothing.

'We've had snow, wind and rain over the last few days, so the narrow track of a bicycle tyre could easily be obliterated. It might even have been where those fools churned up the ground. It would have been much better if Pascal had looked for it when the body was discovered rather than letting half the village clomp all over the place. I can't imagine he'd have allowed them to do it if he'd found bicycle tracks.'

Marie-Clair's face dropped. 'So there's nothing more we can do?'

'We can keep looking. Firstly along the bridge, then on the other side. If there's the slightest chance of foul play, we examine the entire area, not just where the ground would have been affected had it been an accident.'

There was nothing to see on the stone bridge, though I didn't expect there to be. Traffic and the weather would have hidden anything relevant within a week. Below, the water flowed but, pretty as it was, the term 'river' seemed something of an exaggeration. It was no more than twenty feet wide and even at this point in the year was no deeper than two feet. Several large boulders broke its surface, and the bed was covered with smaller ones. If the librarian had, in fact, crashed into the water, it was easy to see how she'd have cracked open her skull. On the far side the road veered sharply left to follow the river as it tumbled down the valley to meet the Rance five or six miles away.

The other bank was bordered by a rough path and was leveller than the one we'd looked at so, again, we worked from one end each. A minute after I began, a branch cracked in the woods behind, and I had the feeling someone was watching me. When I swung round, there was no-one and no further sound to suggest anyone moving away.

At the point where it would have been easiest to climb the riverbank, I spotted a deep impression in the grass. Twelve inches behind it was another. I called Marie-Clair.

'See, here.'

We squatted and I moved the top layer aside with a pencil. In the mud were footprints.

Marie-Clair glanced at me. 'There was someone here?'

'Looks like it. What else do you see?'

She pushed her glasses to the bridge of her nose and peered close to the ground, examining the print from every angle. The girl shook her head. 'Sorry, I can see it's a footprint, but there's no tread to identify who it might belong to. I can't see anything else.'

I stood and took a few paces to the left, then planted my boot in a similar position. 'Come here.' She did. 'Now can you see any difference?'

She repeated her examination. 'The other one is deeper.'

'Exactly. Someone trod here carrying something heavy. Let's look for where they came out.'

Marie-Clair discovered another set only a short distance from the first. She grinned from ear to ear when she reported they were shallower. 'Think I'm getting the hang of this. So they dumped whatever they had in the river. Suspicious, eh?'

'Perhaps. Keep searching.'

Up and down the road. Nothing by the edge. Then a yard in, backwards and forwards. At one point I shouted to Marie-Clair to slow down.

'Keep it methodical. Check every inch.'

There was nothing.

Marie-Clair smiled when we'd finished, then noticed I didn't. 'You're not happy?'

'Why are there only two sets of footprints?'

'How do you mean? Only needs one down and one back.'

'What about the bicycle? If the first trip was with a body, how did the bicycle get in the river?'

Her brow furrowed, then she clicked her fingers. 'He threw it in the river from the bridge!'

'Perhaps. Or maybe these footprints have nothing to do with Lisette Perron's death.'

'Well, how would you explain them? Someone carries a heavy load down to the river then he comes back without it.'

'Easy. Imagine the trips were the opposite way round? He, or she, could have gone to the river empty-handed and taken something out, like a rock. We also don't know when this happened; it might have been before the death, or since the body was removed. You must always keep an open mind, Marie-Clair, and try to think of the alternatives. And don't assume all killers are men. I've covered enough investigations to know that isn't the case.'

'So what do we do?'

'I'm doing nothing. You're the one convinced there's more here than meets the eye. Check the weather in the week before the librarian was discovered, particularly how much rain fell. Next, you must talk to your cousin again. Was anyone on this side of the river when they recovered the body? Was it his car parked where we found the tyre mark? Did he see any sign of the bicycle leaving the road, either skidding or tracks in the grass? If he did, you might ask him why he tramped all over them rather than preserving the evidence.'

All the way up the road back to town, I glimpsed her looking at me and shaking her head. Even though I'd tried to convince the girl I wanted nothing more to do with it, I was as desperate as she was to hear the answers to those questions.

EIGHT

Malo and I had spent the morning laying hedges and moving his few sheep to graze on the remaining turnip tops. We'd planned to work two fields in the afternoon but, just before we started, the heavens opened and an easterly wind started to blow. He'd told me put away the horses and the harrows, then to call it a day.

I'd only been back indoors for five minutes and looking forward to a restful afternoon when Marie-Clair returned. The previous afternoon she'd left with a spring in her step and a promise to talk to her cousin again, asking the questions I'd suggested.

She greeted Rachel and threw herself into an armchair, frowning. 'That idiot Pascal should be shot. He's pathetic.'

I tried to hide my smile. 'And what's he done to deserve this?'

'I went to tell him what we'd found, and he laughed at me. Told me I was a silly girl imagining things.'

'Perhaps he's right.'

'You think I'm a silly girl?' Her glance told me not to pursue that suggestion.

'No, of course not. But perhaps you've let your imagination travel a little ahead of the facts.' Time for oil on troubled waters. 'On the other hand, Pascal Jaubert may have jumped to a conclusion without looking at the evidence from different angles.'

It was tempting to add she was doing exactly the same, but she'd interpreted what she'd learnt to suit her preference for a juicy murder. The policeman preferred an easier life.

'Could you talk to him, Monsieur Given? He'll listen to your experience.'

'I'm not sure he will. He could see it as interfering where I have no right. Anyway, I've told you, I really don't want to get involved. I'm a farm worker now, not a policeman. I'll happily give you advice, but that's as far as I'll go.'

The girl took a deep breath. 'But I don't know where to go next. If he's ignoring me, there's no point in looking for anything else because he'll ignore that as well. If you can convince Pascal to keep an open mind, then it gives a glimmer of hope when I find something new.'

'I'm still far from certain he'll take any notice of a retired English police officer, but let's be clear. If I do this, I'm doing no more. On that understanding, do you want me to come with you to talk to your cousin?'

I didn't need to ask twice; she was up out of her chair almost before I'd drawn breath. Rachel insisted we ate lunch before heading out, and Marie-Clair gobbled it down as fast as she was able. For fun, I asked for seconds. The girl fidgeted the entire time I chewed, then almost dragged me out of the door into the wet afternoon.

Marie-Clair and I used the public entrance to the police station on the side of the single-storey wing. Vieux-Croix was only big enough to warrant one policeman, and he covered a large area under the direction of the mayor, so we were lucky to find him in. Marie-Clair introduced me to the chubby man with a black moustache and a sour expression behind the front desk who stood and nodded when he shook my hand. He looked in his early twenties but could have been two or three years either way.

'Ah, Monsieur Given, the mayor mentioned you recently. You were a policeman in England, yes?'

'I was. A Detective Inspector.'

Pascal Jaubert raised an eyebrow. 'So how can I help you today?' He threw a glance in Marie-Clair's direction as if he'd already guessed the reason.

'Mademoiselle Levaux here is my wife's music pupil and has an interest in becoming a police officer.'

'This I know.'

'She asked me to show her how I might investigate a crime, so we've been taking a look at the death of the librarian, Madame Perron.'

'But no crime has taken place there, monsieur. She died in an accident.'

'It certainly looks like one.' Marie-Clair made to interject, but I raised a finger to stop her. There was no point in antagonising Pascal Jaubert at this point. 'Would you be so kind as to take me through your reasoning for this conclusion? It would help your cousin, I am sure, to be aware of how complex, or how simple, these things sometimes are.'

The policeman stood. 'If we are to discuss this properly, perhaps we should go into my office.' He locked the door and asked us to follow him. The room reminded me of the one I'd had in Kenilworth, basic and functional. Grey walls, a small Government-issue desk with chairs either side, and two wooden filing cabinets. The features which distinguished it from mine were the French flag on the wall and a photograph of Jaubert, the mayor and President Lebrun looking down.

He offered us seats, settled in his own and glowed with the opportunity to share his deductions with a fellow professional, even one who was no longer active.

'My reasoning is quite simple, monsieur. The road is quite steep near the river, as I'm sure you have observed. It had been raining on and off for two days, and the surface was slippery. Madame Perron would not have been a very good cyclist; none of these women are, are they? She simply skidded on the wet road, bounced across the grass and went over the handlebars, bashing her head on the riverbed. Very sad, but if you think about it logically, she was a librarian — who would have wanted to kill her?'

'Indeed.'

'So I think the young lady might need to reconsider her detective skills, yes?'

'That may be the case, but Marie-Clair and I have been considering some alternative possibilities. Would you humour us and explain a couple of things? Just so she gets the practice.'

The policeman tutted. 'I'm a very busy man, Monsieur Given. I really don't have time to play games.'

He got my best patronising smile. 'I've nothing but admiration for the work you are doing here, Monsieur Jaubert, but I'm sure you remember how enthusiastic you were when you began your career. Marie-Clair now shares that enthusiasm, and it would be really helpful if you could pass on some of your experience.'

It's amazing how many people cave in at the merest hint of flattery. He shrugged and admitted he could possibly spare a few minutes.

'Your cousin has, I believe, told you of the footprints we found on the opposite bank to where you concluded Lisette Perron had entered the water?'

He reiterated that he'd discounted them as irrelevant because it was clearly an accident, and the footprints could have been created at any time.

'But, as you just said, the weather had been very wet in the two days before Madame Perron died. We've checked the reports, and it had been mostly dry for two weeks before this.'

'Perhaps so. What is the point you're making?'

'Only that the depth of those footprints could not have occurred if the ground was hard. So they would not have been there more than two days before the accident. Agreed?'

'Agreed.'

'Good. Could you tell us where the bicycle was in relation to the poor woman's body?'

He frowned and I could tell this question had piqued his interest. 'It was by her side.'

'Closer to the bridge or further away?'

'Closer.'

'And how far would it have been from the bridge?'

'Probably about two metres. Where are you going with this? What's the relevance of how far it was from the bridge?'

'I was just wondering if someone could have thrown a bicycle as far as the body, and it sounds like they could. Was there damage to the bicycle?'

'The front wheel was buckled. Exactly the same as it would be if the bicycle had bounced over the grass and into the river. Are you suggesting this wasn't an accident, Monsieur Given?'

'No, no, I'm not suggesting anything of the sort, just throwing some ideas around. Can I ask if Father Guen came to see you?'

'He did.'

'So you are aware that Madame Perron had told him she had discovered something about a local person, and it was troubling her?'

'The priest reported this, yes. But I can't see the relevance. These women gossip all the time, then get in a flap if what they hear doesn't fit their cosy view of the world.' He grinned across at his cousin. 'Isn't that so, Marie-Clair?'

She tensed then settled back in her chair. 'You're a fool, Pascal. Monsieur Given, who has solved more murders than you've had hot dinners, is trying to help and all you can do is make silly jokes.'

Inwardly I groaned. This interview would now be over. The policeman flipped his notebook shut and stood, knuckles on his desk.

'I'm sorry, monsieur, I suggest you are wasting your time and mine. This young lady has an idea fixed in her head, and the facts won't shift it. You would be well advised not to listen to her. What is more, as we have established, you are not now a detective, so you should not be poking about in business that does not concern you. I'd thank you to leave now and let me get on with my work.'

There was no more to be said but as we left, Marie-Clair turned and stuck out her tongue at Jaubert. I tugged her by the sleeve and chuckled like a fool all the way home.

Rachel was ironing when I arrived back. She was the most efficient of workers, despite her artistic prowess and this always surprised me. Perhaps it shouldn't have, but for some reason I presumed the sensitivity she needed to play a violin concerto would compromise her ability to carry out practical tasks. On one side was a neatly folded pile of clothes, on the other an equally neatly stacked basket of those which had been pressed. Her movements were strong and rhythmic: an item laid on the board, a splash of water from the jug by her left hand, then stroke, fold, stroke, until the piece was finished and laid in the basket, creases straight and sharp. I slipped my arms round my wife's waist from behind and kissed the nape of her neck. She leaned into me.

'That's nice. Good day?'

'Curate's egg.'

'Egg?'

'Good in parts. Your young Marie-Clair was cheery but her cousin, the policeman, was difficult.'

Pascal Jaubert had reminded me of a colleague or two I'd had in England, always preferring to take the easy route. I could never figure out why they'd joined the police if they didn't want the challenge of solving crimes. For me, the discipline of assembling the jigsaw, putting piece after piece in place until the full picture emerged, had been fascinating. The one aspect of the job I'd enjoyed.

'In what way difficult?'

'We discovered a couple of things he'd overlooked down by the river, but he didn't want to know. He's stamped the case file as "accident" now and is not going to be shifted. I daresay he's told his boss, the mayor, it's all sorted out and doesn't want to go back to tell him differently.'

Rachel lay down her iron, then sat at the kitchen table. 'So Marie-Clair was right? There is more to it than first thought?'

'I'm not sure. If I'd been investigating, I'd have wanted to dig a bit more. Without trying too hard we found a person had carried something heavy to the river and came back without it. Also, there were no skid marks to show where Lisette Perron tried to stop herself. The bike could quite easily have been thrown in later from the bridge. Of themselves the details are all circumstantial but linked with what she told Francis they might add up to something.'

'How would Jaubert have missed such things?'

'It's easy when you've an idea in your head. His first thought was the librarian wasn't important enough to have enemies, so it must be an accident. As a result, he simply wouldn't look for anything which might contradict this view. It wasn't wilful, just human nature. Let's face it, he's policing a quiet rural area where violent crimes only occur once in a blue moon, so in many ways his assumption makes sense.'

'So what will you do?'

'That's what Marie-Clair asked me.'

'And?'

'I'll give you the answer I gave her. I'll not do anything. I'm not interested.'

Rachel stood and took both my hands in hers. 'This doesn't sound like you, James. What's going on?'

'Nothing's going on. You know I had a bellyful of death in England, that's why I came here. Even if I wanted to look into it more deeply, I won't have time if we're moving on. It's not going to be long before pickers are needed, then we'll be busy until late autumn.'

This was my safety net. Don't stay in one place long enough to have demands made.

'I've been thinking about this. We don't have to move away too soon, if at all. You've a decent little job, and with my music teaching we've enough to get by. The weather will improve, and we've made friends here; where else are we going to find that's better?'

'But it's what we said we'd do, follow the harvests right down south and back. Enjoy the strawberry beds, the vineyards and the autumn sun in the orchards.'

'That's what we said, but we can change our minds, can't we? Are you sure you're not just running away?'

I dropped her hands and took a step back. 'What happened in those last two cases was more than most coppers would face in a lifetime. Don't you think I've earned the right to run away?'

Rachel's voice became harder than I'd ever heard it. 'No. Frankly I don't think you do. You had a bad time, and no-one knows that more than me, but it doesn't mean you shouldn't do the right thing. If you believe … if even a small part of you believes there's any chance that librarian was murdered, you've got to look into it, even if only to prove she wasn't.'

I walked away and grabbed my coat, then lifted the door-latch.

'You can go out, James, and this might be one of those times you'll dive into the bottle, but the problem will still be here when you get back.' She gently took my elbow. 'And so will I.'

I let go of the latch and slumped in my armchair, coat on the floor beside me. 'I just don't know what I should do, Rachel. I really don't. No-one other than you, Francis and Marie-Clair gives a damn. Even the girl is only interested so she'll have a better chance of getting into the police. Everyone else shakes their heads and accepts "poor Madame Perron" died in a dreadful accident.'

'Perhaps they're too scared to admit it might be more than that. You've already said such terrible things don't happen in towns like this very often. It makes them feel safe if they just accept what the policeman has said.'

'Then why can't we do the same? I hardly knew the librarian and neither did you. It's not my job any longer to try to fix all the evil in the world.'

'I'm not saying you fix all the evil in the world, James. Only in our little part of it.'

A letter dropped onto the mat soon after breakfast. Rachel lifted it, read the envelope, and passed it to me.

'It looks official, James.'

A typed address with no stamp or postmark. I turned the envelope over, but there was nothing to indicate its origin. I tossed it onto the table. Rachel folded her arms and glared.

'Are you going to open it or not?'

Grinning, I peeled the flap and pulled out the contents, slowly unfolding the letter whilst shielding it from her view. My smile disappeared as I read the few lines.

'Well?'

'The mayor wants to see me again.'

'Why would he ask us in a second time? Do you think there's a problem with our papers?'

'Maybe, but he doesn't want to see us both, just me.'

It being Wednesday, I was going into town in any case for my weekly coffee with Francis, so I called in on the mayor's secretary and arranged an appointment with him later in the morning.

The café was busier than the last time we'd been in, but Francis' status guaranteed him his usual table by the window, where we could take in the full beauty of his church across the square. We ordered our drinks and my friend tried his usual trick of tempting me to cake.

'Just the one, James, what harm can it do?'

I prodded my shirt above my waist and shook my head. 'See this? I'm now wearing trousers two sizes smaller than before Christmas, and I'd like to keep it that way.'

He laughed. 'Well, I'm having one.'

I envied his ability to eat what he wanted and still stay as thin as a lath. I loved my food but knew I'd always have to work that little bit harder to keep the pounds off.

When the coffees and his treat arrived, Francis said he'd been to see Pascal Jaubert.

'I know, he told me yesterday. What did he say?'

'Only that he'd make a note and look into it.'

'He'll not, though; he made it pretty clear to me he gave the information no credence, not even coming from you. I took him new evidence and he discounted it without a second thought.'

Francis picked at the edge of his chocolate cake before laying down his fork. 'But how can he do that, James? Surely he has a duty to investigate any new leads which come his way.'

'Not if he's already made up his mind. He and the mayor have agreed her death was an accident, and Jaubert isn't budging.'

'Then you'll need to make him budge, won't you?'

'Me? What's this to do with me?'

'You have the experience, and you know something's not right. I do too, and the more I've thought about what Lisette said the more I've known it. That woman came to me for advice and found me wanting. If I'd asked the right questions, she may have told me what was bothering her, and she may still be alive today.'

'You can't be sure of that, Francis. And if she was killed because of what she'd discovered, and her murderer found out you knew, how long do you think it would be before you were the victim of a strange accident?'

'That's as may be, but it doesn't get us away from the possibility there's a killer loose in our town and you're the one with the skill to catch him or her.' He turned to the window and surveyed the half dozen people passing by. 'Listen, James, I understand you were hurt in England and you want to put it behind you, but this is important. Please reconsider.'

I drained my cup and stood. 'We shouldn't fall out over this, Francis, but I don't think I've any more to say.' I consulted my watch. 'I have another appointment. I'll see you when I see you.' Without waiting for a reply, I headed to the counter to pay then went straight to the door.

Francis called over the heads of the other customers as I pulled it open. 'Take a while to think about it, James. I know you'll make the right decision in the end.'

Five minutes later, I sauntered over to the mayor's office with Francis' parting words spinning in my head. As I dragged open the elegant door of the Mairie, I spotted Pascal Jaubert crossing the hall and disappearing through the inner door to his office. Now I guessed why his boss wanted to see me.

Alain Sitell sat behind the same glorious desk, wearing the same politician's smile, when I was shown in by his secretary. There was a single folder in front of him. I played dumb.

'Is there something wrong with my paperwork, monsieur? I've had no difficulties with it previously.'

'No, not at all. It is all in order.' He paused. 'As far as I can tell.'

'That's good. My wife was worried when we received your letter.'

'Please tell Madame Given I apologise. It was not my intention to cause distress.'

'So, is there something I can help you with?'

Sitell leaned back and interlocked his hands. 'When you came to see me last time, you said you are a retired policeman.'

'I did, and I am.'

'A policeman or retired?'

'I was a policeman but now I'm retired. What is it you want, monsieur?'

He pushed the folder forward and flipped it open so I could read the contents. The top sheet was a typed record of the conversation I'd had with Pascal Jaubert.

'Our police officer has submitted this report,' he said, tapping it with a fingernail, 'as you can see. A report in which he tells me that you have been investigating the death of Madame Perron, that you have been to the spot where she died and have brought to him some alternative findings. Please take a look at the sheet below.'

I did as he asked. It was the official record of the investigation. The first few lines outlined the initial information, including when and where the body was found, and by whom. The middle of the page had space for interviews and other investigations. It was largely blank. The final section was headed "Conclusion and further action".

'And what does it say there at the end?'

'It says Madame Lisette Perron died in an accident.'

'Precisely.'

'But —'

'No buts, please, Monsieur Given. I do not know what it is like in the part of England where you worked, but here we have a quiet little town. One where we have no trouble and want no trouble. Perhaps you are looking to make a name for yourself in Vieux-Croix. To show us French country folk how clever you English are. Is this the case?'

'It isn't, and I'm sorry you might believe that to be how I feel. I have nothing but respect for your country and countrymen, monsieur. My wife and I have been welcomed into your community, and the last thing I'd want to do is cause offence.'

'So why have you been digging for information?'

I explained how I'd only been trying to help Marie-Clair to grasp some of the techniques she may need if she were to join the police force. 'She's young and she's keen. The girl has an enquiring mind and looks like she'd make a good officer. I was simply trying to encourage her. Almost any enquiry, on almost any case, will throw up other possible conclusions to the ones most obvious, but this doesn't mean they are correct. In my experience, a good detective learns to look at the evidence from all angles, fitting the pieces together until the truth emerges. Sometimes this process will lead down the wrong path, but usually it won't, and the diversion will have been worthwhile.'

'And you think Pascal has this wrong?'

'No, I'm sorry, monsieur, that's not what I am saying. What Marie-Clair and I found were just a couple more pieces of the puzzle not considered earlier. We reported them to your policeman, and as far as I'm concerned, that is it. I have no desire to become any further involved than I have been already.'

'That is good to hear, Monsieur Given. Let us consider the case of Lisette Perron closed; certainly Pascal would like you to leave it that way.'

I made one more apology and said no more, because there was no more to say, then left the mayor to the important business of running his little town.

NINE

Marie-Clair lived with her parents in a three-storey house a short walk from behind the church. Five windows on the ground floor, five on the floor above, and three dormers in the attic made an impressive frontage. I took it in for a minute from outside the low garden wall before venturing to the door along a path lined with rose bushes and lavender. The family's maid eyed me suspiciously when I asked to speak to Marie-Clair, then brought her master to the door instead of the girl. I introduced myself and he invited me inside, with the firm handshake of a man successful in commerce.

'You're most welcome, Monsieur Given. Marie-Clair has told us a lot about you. In fact, she's hardly stopped talking about you since you met. Oh, what it is to be young, eh?'

'Your daughter is certainly very eager. In a good way. She'll be a credit to the police when she joins.'

He brushed his fingers across thinning hair and sucked in through his teeth. 'That's nice of you to say, monsieur, but she'll not be joining unless she goes about it the right way. Marie-Clair is bright and must complete her education, then take up the proper training.'

I understood his reservations. Policing is often looked upon by the professional classes as an unsavoury occupation, a vital job someone must do but preferably not their son or daughter. Having seen lots of run-of-the-mill policemen in my time, some poor, many just mediocre, it's not difficult to grasp why they'd have that view.

'You're entirely right, Monsieur Levaux. She must do both of those things.' I glanced at my watch. 'Is Marie-Clair home?'

'Of course. I'll send for her.' He rang a bell, the maid returned, and he asked her to fetch his daughter, then took me into a substantial dining room. 'Please wait here, Monsieur Given, and Marie-Clair will be with you in a moment.'

If I hadn't guessed it from the outside of the house, this room told me the family had money. Oil paintings of what I guessed to be three generations hung on one wall, a fine tapestry on another. On a gilt-mounted corner table stood photographs of the man who'd greeted me, a child of four or five years old, and a striking woman so similar to Marie-Clair it had to be her mother. Before I could take in much else, Marie-Clair bounded through the doorway.

'Have you discovered something more, monsieur?'

'No, I haven't.'

'Then are we going out to investigate something new?'

I laughed. 'No, we're not.'

'So why have you come to my house?'

'I've been to see Monsieur Sitell, the mayor. And so has your cousin.'

'Oh.'

'Indeed, oh. Neither of them are very happy.'

'Then they're idiots.'

I laughed again. 'That may be so, but they're both important men and entitled to their opinion. You'll get nowhere going against them. They're saying the case is closed and you'll just have to accept that.'

'So you're giving up?'

'I'd already given up, Marie-Clair, remember? I handed in my warrant card months ago, before I left England. The reason I came round was to tell you to give it up too. Mayor Sitell and Pascal Jaubert could make life very difficult for me and for you —' I paused as she bristled — 'and for your parents.'

The young woman turned away, shook her head and pulled open the door. 'You'd better go. I don't want to detain you from all the important things going on in your life.'

When I reached the front step, she mumbled a goodbye and there were tears on her cheeks. I held back the door for a moment.

'Listen, Marie-Clair, you'll make a very good detective one day, but don't ruin your chances of a successful career by getting into trouble on this one case. There are times when you just have to accept the decisions of those above you and, for now, both your cousin and the mayor *are* above you. It won't always be that way, so take a deep breath and move on. For my part, I'm a stranger here, dependant on the authorities to let me stay, so please don't think badly of me. It has been a pleasure working alongside you for this short time.'

I released the door and felt sure she closed it more gently than she would have done a few moments earlier. With my head down, I ambled home to tell Rachel what I'd done.

Rachel is mostly good-humoured about, and forgiving of, the thousand thoughtless things I say and do on a daily basis. She's my opposite in that respect. If something annoys me I tend to say so, then it's gone. Rachel keeps quiet, then raises it when the heat has left the moment, a deadly ambush when I least expect it. So when the cold-shoulder appeared after I told her of my conversations with Sitell, Francis and Marie-Clair, I knew I was in trouble.

She'd been waiting for me to return home and stayed quiet as I went through my morning, then made me a cup of tea and went to her music room, where she practised scales on her violin for two hours. At first I thought nothing of it — she often practises for long periods — then she still didn't speak while she prepared our evening meal, other than an occasional affirmative grunt if I asked her a question. She served and we sat. I complimented her on the food and got nothing back. An enquiry about a new student brought a shrug. I was hopeless in the face of this.

'What's wrong, Rachel?'

'Nothing. Why should anything be wrong?'

'Because you've not spoken to me all afternoon.'

'I've been busy. Now eat your dinner before it goes cold.'

I leaned across and took her wrist in my fingers. For a second she pulled away but then relaxed.

'How could you give up so easily, James? It's not like you.'

'Give up? What do you mean give up? I did what you asked me to. I gave your Marie-Clair a few pointers even though I didn't want to, and now the two of you are accusing me of being a coward. Well, I've been stabbed, attacked and near poisoned over the past couple of years. If that doesn't justify me being a bit reluctant to become involved in that kind of mess again, then I can only apologise for not being the man you hoped I was.' I pushed my meal away.

'James, this isn't about us, it's about you. You're the finest, most decent man I ever met, and all I want is for you to be happy. I know not following your instincts and walking away from this will make you unhappy, that's all. I also know you'll find continuing difficult. That's why I've been so quiet. I don't want to push you into anything, but I don't want you miserable either.' She moved my plate back where it should be. 'Now come on, eat your food and then we can talk about this properly.'

I did as she asked. Afterwards I said I thought she was right, I *was* torn. 'But it's not just the past that's bothering me, it's our future.'

'In what way?'

'You must see, Rachel, that we're in a precarious situation here. We're Jewish and the Germans may well overrun France within months, weeks even. We have the papers supplied by Mitchell, but we need friends in high places to accept them. If our local mayor and policeman have reason to question our story, then we may be done for.'

'Do you think they'd cause trouble?'

'Well so far we've been lucky, but if I put their noses out of joint their goodwill won't last.'

'Couldn't you try to keep them on our side?'

'Only if I walk away from this. They've made up their minds Lisette Perron died accidentally and don't want me rocking the boat. I have to say, other than me finding some evidence which might just point in another direction, I can't be certain they're wrong. Nothing positively shows she was murdered, and we've hardly a hint of a suspect.'

'What if you had more evidence about the man you thought might be spying?'

'David Ménière? I'm not convinced it would make a lot of difference, but have you heard something?'

'While you were out, Malo's sister, Enora, came round with some eggs. She was chatting about the librarian again. That's all anyone seems to do these days, small town I suppose.'

'What did she say?'

'The last time she was in the library, she was talking to Madame Perron when they were interrupted by a tall man who Enora didn't know. She said he was very abrupt, demanding to see local maps. The librarian asked him to wait but he insisted he was in a hurry, so she left Enora at the counter until she returned. When she did she seemed flustered and took a moment to write some notes. Enora asked if there was anything wrong but the librarian said she was fine, just needed to remind herself of something she must do when she got home.'

'How do you know it was Ménière?'

'Enora was talking to another library customer afterwards about what happened. He said the man was his neighbour and gave Ménière's name. Does that help?'

'Not really, it only adds a little bit. I already knew he'd lied to me about having met the librarian. I'm not even sure it *was* a lie. He's new to the area and might not have known the woman who died was the one he'd had the tussle with.'

'But what if he saw her writing notes and thought she'd figured out what he was up to? Surely he'd be scared she might report him.'

'It's a possibility, and if I was investigating then I'd follow it up. Sadly, there's not enough of a link between Ménière and Perron to convince anyone. Anyway, unless Pascal Jaubert changes his mind about the cause of death, he's not going to be interested in who might have killed her. Francis already told him she was concerned about something, but Jaubert batted it away.'

'I suppose you're right. I hoped it might help, that's all.'

'And I'm grateful. For this and everything else.'

I pulled my wife over onto my lap and hugged her. She held me close for a long, long time.

Rachel said nothing more about Lisette Perron for the rest of the evening. We both read in front of the fire until I nodded off, only coming round when she shook me.

'Coming to bed?'

I mumbled a groggy confirmation but, once I climbed under the covers and we'd said our goodnights, I couldn't sleep.

Images of the confrontation between the librarian and David Ménière spun around my head, interspersed with the responses I wished I'd made to Alain Sitell, if only I'd thought of them at the time.

By midnight I was still wide-awake. Concerned my restlessness would disturb Rachel, I got up and made a cup of cocoa. I thought I'd get rid of my insomnia by drafting another note to Mitchell, updating him with the information Enora Legrand had supplied. There wasn't enough to bother him with, but at least it would get it out of my head.

After I finished, the cocoa did its work and my eyes began to droop. I went back to bed, only to find I now re-ran my argument with Marie-Clair over and over. This went on until I floated away at around three in the morning.

TEN

The sun blasted through the window as Rachel swished back the curtains.

'You'd best be getting up, sleepyhead. Your little assistant detective is waiting downstairs.'

I groaned. 'What does *she* want? She's kept me awake all night as it is.'

Rachel raised an eyebrow. 'Really?'

'Not like that, you fool. I was thinking about our disagreement.'

'If you say so. I'll make tea and see you down there in a few minutes.' She turned as she got to the door. 'She is quite pretty, though, if you happen to like the younger woman.'

I made to throw a pillow at her, but she skipped out, giggling.

Marie-Clair was sitting at the table with tea and toast when I got down. I wished her good morning and asked why she'd called.

'Are you still annoyed with me, monsieur?'

'No. Actually I was never annoyed, only a little put out you wouldn't accept no for an answer.'

'That's good.' She dipped her knife into a pot of strawberry jam and spread it slowly before she continued with a cheeky smile. 'Because I have some more information for you.'

My second groan of the day and I'd not even eaten breakfast. 'This had better be good, young lady, or I'll be asking your father to keep you under lock and key. Come on, spit it out.'

'After you left yesterday, I went back to Monsieur Ménière's.'

'You did what?'

'Don't worry, I was very careful. No-one saw me.'

'I sincerely hope not.'

'I waited on the corner until he went out, then knocked on the doors on either side. No-one was home. I peered through his front windows, but it was dark inside and I could see nothing, so I went round to the back.'

'Where you'd see no more than I did.'

'I went through the gardens, right to his.'

I clasped my palms over my eyes and shook my head. 'Are you mad? Don't tell me you broke in.'

'Certainly not. What kind of person do you think I am? I just had a look around, that's all.'

'And?'

'First of all, I thought there was nothing. The garden was a mess, full of weeds, and it was still too dark inside to make anything out, but then I noticed the wires.'

'Wires?'

'Four long ones, fanning up from the ground to the roof. At the bottom they were connected to another one which went through the wall. I asked my father, and he said it sounded like a transmitter aerial. He commanded a communications unit when he was in the army, so he should know.'

'So what's our friend up to?'

'You still haven't told me what you *thought* he was up to when you took me out there last time.'

'It was something and nothing. Bits and pieces seeming to point one way but could just as easily point in another entirely innocent direction altogether.'

'So are you going to tell me?'

'I'd purposely bumped into Ménière in town and started a conversation about Lisette Perron's death. He told me he hadn't known her. You'll remember his neighbour told us he'd witnessed them talking in the library. Yesterday, Malo's sister confirmed this because she'd been there at the same time. So he was lying. You'll also remember the neighbour said Ménière had been asking around about military camps where he thought a friend might be based. I'd heard this earlier, and that was why I'd engineered a chat.'

'Wow. Do you think he's a spy?'

'Who knows? Sounds like it when you add the possibility of the transmitter to his questions. What I do know is that you must stay away from him. If he *is* a spy, and if he killed Lisette Perron, then he's a very dangerous man. We don't want you being the next one found in the river.'

Marie-Clair's eyes widened, and the colour drained from her cheeks. It hadn't been my intention to frighten her so much, only to keep her safe. Rachel saw I was out of my depth when I heaped two spoons of sugar into the poor girl's tea and tried to take her mind off it by asking about school and her violin lessons. She answered in monosyllables, her eyes fixed on the front door, and almost leapt from her chair when the fire spit a damp twig onto the hearth.

Rachel, always more resourceful than me, saw the solution. 'Whilst you two are talking about your lessons, Marie-Clair, why don't we go through and practise some scales? I've a spare violin here you can use.'

Marie-Clair nodded, and they went to the spare room. In a couple of minutes, a bow scraped a few notes, slowly at first, then faster as Rachel's student began to concentrate. Though the noise was woeful, I didn't flee the house. Instead, I rewrote my letter to Mitchell, including the latest information provided by Marie-Clair.

She was calmer when she emerged half an hour later and almost back to her confident self by the time she'd walked with me to post the letter. Before I left her in the square, I had a final word.

'I'm sorry for frightening you, Marie-Clair, but we both need to be careful. We don't know how dangerous this man might be. At present he'd have no reason to think we've discovered anything, so there's nothing to worry about and, as long as it stays this way, we'll be safe. Just make sure you keep away from Ménière unless I'm with you.'

Later that week, I sat in the Bar Du Marché playing cards with three men: Phillipe, Eric and Daniel. Phillipe lay down the king of hearts, grinned and lifted the trick to put it face down with the eight others he'd won.

'So, another game to me. A shame we are not playing for cash; I'd be able to retire on what I'd win from you amateurs.' He took a sip of his beer. 'One more?'

Eric and Daniel swore, cursing him for being lucky, then laughed and nodded. Even though he bragged about this one, Phillipe knew the odds evened out over time and next week it would be Eric's turn to rule the roost.

I looked at my watch and stretched. 'Just the one. Rachel will lock the doors if I'm much later.'

Customers packed the Bar du Marché on Thursday nights, the only time it was busy other than Saturday lunchtime after the market was dismantled for another week, and a thick fog of cigarette smoke hung above our heads. Groups of men occupied all the tables, mainly playing cards and talking, as we were, and from time to time laughter would explode when someone came up with a decent joke or played a foolish card.

The four of us now met once a week, sharing a table in the corner of the bar, and playing whichever game took our fancy. Never for money, always for honour, and I won as often as I lost. All three were farm workers and took their goods to market on Saturdays as I did. We'd spoken there a few times, commenting on the weather or how busy we'd been, then Eric asked if I'd like to join them for a drink and cards one evening. I'd said I'd love to but would need to check with my wife which night would be best.

When I'd broached the subject, Rachel had asked if I might have a problem. Drink and gambling. For me, a potent combination.

'I'll be fine. I've not touched a drop for six months and it's just for fun, no stakes involved.'

'Are you sure?'

'Well, a few centimes, but nothing to worry about anyway.' I'd wrapped my arm around her waist and pulled her close. 'You know I don't need those kinds of props when I've got you. All the temptation I could ever handle is standing right next to me.'

My wife wasn't susceptible to flattery, she was far too attractive to be taken in, but she'd pecked my cheek and agreed I should get out and enjoy men's company once in a while. So, with her blessing, my evening with Eric Naud, Phillipe Yacine and Daniel Bisset became a regular fixture in my week. I stuck to soft drinks, much to their amusement, and the stimulus of good company and the cards was enough with the minimum of cash changing hands. Daniel and Eric were a few years older than me and had seen action with British troops in the last war. As a result, they practised their English on me from time to time and, in exchange, offered me help with the finer points of working men's vernacular.

We finished our final hand, with Phillipe winning again, and we chatted whilst draining our drinks. I asked if any of them knew Lisette Perron. They all did.

'I'd know Louis Décast, her husband, more than her,' said Eric.

'She was married?'

'Still is. Well, until she died, obviously. Louis is a car mechanic, has a garage at the Hénon crossroads on the way to Rennes. His wife went back to her maiden name when they split a year or two ago.'

Phillipe threw his two-pennyworth into the gossip. 'They didn't get on for ages, always arguing they were. Even when they parted, they fought whenever they met.'

'He's right,' said Daniel. 'I heard the two of them going hammer and tongs a couple of nights before her accident. I don't know what it was about, but I came upon them behind the library and he was shouting she'd gone too far this time. When they saw me, Lisette stormed off with Louis continuing to yell after her.'

'And you don't know why they were fighting?'

'I expect it was another of her affairs. Always off with men, she was, and it made Louis as mad as hell. Don't know why he married her in the first place, it's not like he didn't know what she was like. A nice bloke, but everyone's got their limits. It came as no surprise to anyone when he threw her out. Even then it looks like she didn't change her ways, but then why should she once she was free?'

'If they're divorced, surely he'd not still be jealous?'

All three laughed. Eric settled first.

'They're not divorced; Lisette was too strong a Catholic. It seemed she was a bit selective about which sins she'd commit. It suited Louis as well, still crackers for her 'til the day she died, I reckon.'

So, a jealous husband. Someone else with reason to think Lisette Perron should be taught a lesson.

A few days later, Rachel and I were on the road to Hénon. The countryside spread in ploughed fields and green pastures as far as the eye could see once we'd left Vieux-Croix, the horizon only obscured by the occasional farmhouse or clump of trees. The morning light sparkled off the green tips of new leaves, ready to burst when the temperature rose another few degrees, and I bowled along smiling in Malo's shiny black Peugeot, with Rachel by my side. She placed a hand on my knee when I started to hum.

'You're in a good mood.'

'And why wouldn't I be? It's spring in France, the sun's shining and I'm out for a drive with my beautiful wife. The only problem I have is what story I'd tell to convince Louis Décast to inspect the car.'

'And?'

'I'll just tell him there's a bit of a knock when Malo takes it over bumps, but he's not sure if it's from the front or back, left or right. That should keep him busy long enough for me to have a chat.'

'You think he might be involved in his wife's death?'

'I'm not sure yet that anyone was involved, except Madame Perron herself. There's still not much to suggest it was more than an accident. The things I took to Pascal Jaubert were only circumstantial, worth another look, admittedly, but not enough to secure a conviction even if we had a clear suspect.'

'So why the ride out here today?'

'Well, Malo offered me the use of his car for the odd jaunt a few weeks ago, and I've not been able to take him up on it. It seemed a good idea to kill two birds with one stone — a trip with you and the chance to have a few words with the librarian's husband to see if anything else comes to light.'

Eric had described the place we were looking for and it stood at the intersection of the main road to Rennes and two country lanes. The back of the building showed it had once been a corrugated iron barn, but a brick frontage had been added in recent years, stepped at the top in the modern style. The words 'Garage Décast' proclaimed function and ownership above wide-open double timber doors. Two tractors, several engines and a pile of tyres decorated the concrete area in front. I pulled into the only space left and climbed out. The dust we'd thrown up settled on the car, my hat and my shoes.

A short man in blue overalls and glasses, who I assumed to be Décast, ambled out, wiping his hands on a filthy rag.

'Monsieur Décast?'

'Morning, monsieur, that's me. Can I help?'

I introduced myself and explained the problem. He scratched his bald pate, wandered round the vehicle, kicked a couple of the tyres and drew a deep breath, which whistled through a gap in his teeth. I found it hard to believe this specimen was ever married to Lisette Perron.

'Any ideas?'

'Could be tricky. Car like this not the same as the trucks and tractors I usually see. Drives quiet, so a little bit of slack anywhere sounds like a wheel's falling off. Problem could be anywhere.'

I smiled at his opening gambit, the same as tradesmen the world over. Make the job sound complicated and prepare the customer for a hefty bill. I played along.

'If you could just take a look, I'd be really grateful. Then it will be up to Malo to decide if he wants to spend the money or not.'

'Well, I'm not too busy this morning. I can just about fit you in. Drive inside over the pit and we'll see if I can find anything.'

He jumped down the concreted hole and ducked his head whilst I manoeuvred the car into position. From beneath he directed Rachel to a stool beside a metal stove.

'Sit there, madame, and keep warm. I'll not be long.'

The place stank of oil, cigarettes and paraffin from the heater. Rachel beckoned me over.

'I can't sit on this seat, James, look at the state of it.'

I wiped the worst of the grime off the top with some newspaper from a pile in the corner, then buffed it with my handkerchief until she was happy there'd be no harm done to her dress. As I stood to take a bow, I glimpsed a photograph of a younger Lisette on a cabinet in Louis' office. It appeared to confirm Eric's assertion that the man still carried a torch for his estranged wife.

Back by the car I crouched, watching and trying to make intelligent suggestions. He only grunted in response and knocked a series of components with a hammer. After ten minutes Décast climbed out and lifted the bonnet, leant inside and shook the engine, then bounced his weight on each wing. He shook his head.

'There's no knocks I can hear. Are you sure old Legrand wasn't imagining it?'

'He's bright as a button usually, but maybe he's so used to the horse and cart that any odd noise on the car makes him think something is wrong. You think there's no problem?'

Another sucked-in breath. 'Wouldn't go as far as to say that. As I told you, it's hard to tell sometimes. Wouldn't want him coming back to me complaining if something happened. All I will say is there's nothing obvious.'

I thanked him for his efforts, and he asked how long I'd worked for Malo. We talked for a minute or two about people I'd met and places I'd visited. Then I asked if he'd known Lisette Perron. He leaned back and peered over the rim of his glasses.

'Why?'

'Oh, nothing, just conversation. Everyone seems to be talking about her death.'

'Hmm. Good riddance.'

'Really? You didn't like her?'

'I was married to her. Are you telling me you didn't know that?'

I held up my hands. 'I'm sorry, I'd no idea. I wouldn't have mentioned it if I had.'

Décast took a step forward then stopped and shrugged. 'No matter, we've been apart for ages, and I haven't seen her for months. She was unfaithful all of the time we were together; it was like a habit with her. Lisette was pretty enough —' he cocked his head in Rachel's direction — 'not as beautiful as your lady, but pretty, and something about her pulled men in like bees round a honeypot. She could have any man she wanted and often did.'

I shuffled my feet and consulted my watch. 'I must be going. Many thanks for looking at the car. I'll tell Malo to be a bit less fussy and to only bring it back when he's sure there's a problem.'

Rachel and I drove off to continue with our trip and to look for somewhere for lunch. She read the map, and I wondered why Décast had lied about when he'd last seen his wife.

ELEVEN

Mitchell's telegram arrived on Saturday morning and Peston, the postmaster, was almost beside himself when he scurried over to my stall.

'This is exciting, isn't it, Monsieur Given? I can't remember the last time we had one from England. Must be important.'

He'd have read it as it came in, so his pretence of ignorant expectation was misplaced, but I knew he'd a passion for mystery so just took it from him without comment. I stuck it in my waistcoat pocket. He waited.

'Will there be a reply, Monsieur Given?'

I shook my head and said I didn't think so.

Peston sighed, hung his head and plodded back to the post office more slowly than he'd arrived. When he was gone, I ripped the telegram from my pocket.

The intelligence officer's reply was short, sweet and cloaked in language to hide its true meaning. Mitchell referred to Ménière, for example, as "our friend" and to the information I'd sent as "your gift". Underneath it all he said Ménière was someone in whom the British Government might have an interest and I should keep him under surveillance. There was no indication what I might be watching out for, nor how long I needed to keep it up. It seemed an impossible task if I didn't know what I should report and what to ignore.

There were other reasons I might want to keep an eye on Ménière, besides the gratitude I thought I owed my country and Mitchell, otherwise I'd have told him where to stick his request.

After I'd read Mitchell's instructions, ripped up the telegram and disposed of the pieces, my stall was busy with everyone shopping for their Easter meals. Most people had arrived early, numbers multiplying when the buses let out half the population of the neighbouring countryside, so by mid-morning we were almost out of vegetables. I was wondering if I should close for an hour to collect more, or just wait until they sold out and then call it a day.

During a brief lull I was still checking stock when Francis hurried over from the church for his housekeeper's order. I lifted it from below the counter and he paid me.

'You never mentioned Lisette Perron was married, Francis,' I said.

'Didn't I? Sorry. Is it relevant?'

'Perhaps not. It's just that I heard she and her husband were arguing a couple of nights before she died. I went to see him yesterday, and he said he'd not seen her for months. Do you know much about him?'

'Only that he's always seemed a decent enough man. Not as regular an attender to Mass as his wife —' Francis raised an eyebrow — 'but then maybe he had less to confess. Perhaps they were arguing about her will.'

An elderly couple walked up and stood beside the priest, picking over the few carrots, potatoes and cabbages I had left.

Francis glanced at the pair then back to me. 'Pop over and see me when you've finished here, and I'll explain.' He nodded to the man and woman, then disappeared across the square, collecting packages as he went.

I served my customers who, thankfully, took most of the produce which was still worth selling and I packed up the empty boxes onto Malo's cart. As I loaded the last few, Francis walked past and pointed over to his house. I held up my hand, fingers spread, to show I'd be five minutes.

His housekeeper let me in when I knocked and showed me through to the parlour where Francis, wearing slippers and no dog-collar, relaxed in an armchair. He reached across to the table to serve the tea and pile of cakes left by Louise. Motes of dust caught the sunlight pouring through his window, and I thought about what a quiet and gentle space he occupied.

'So what's this about a will, Francis?'

'I was talking to Monsieur Gamút, the solicitor. Do you know him?'

I admitted that I didn't.

'Fine fellow. Very generous to the church. He was Madame Perron's solicitor.'

'And?'

'He told me he'd been advising her for a while to change her will, and she'd ignored him until last month. She'd not much of an estate, only a cottage and a small life insurance policy, but she'd left it to her husband in the old will.'

'So she changed it?'

'No, that's the point. Gamút had told her to choose another beneficiary, but she hadn't. Then she went to him recently and told him to prepare a new one in favour of a cousin in Paris. She met her death before she could sign it, but perhaps she told Louis and that's why they fought.'

'Possibly. Would you say he's a violent man?'

Francis shook his head. 'I wouldn't think so, though that's more your domain than mine, James. My job is to forgive the sins, not foresee them being committed.'

I laughed. 'That's a good way of looking at it, Francis, but the flaw in your logic is that I can't predict them either. I simply find out who's committed the sin then bring them in for punishment when I can. Admittedly, I'll leave the forgiveness to you. I've met too many victims to believe saying "sorry" is ever enough.'

'I can see we might need a little work on what it means to be a Roman Catholic, James. It's never as simple as an apology. The sinner needs to be sincerely contrite and promise not to do it again. Isn't that what you'd want from the criminals you've arrested? Spending time in gaol without mending their ways doesn't benefit anyone, does it? Perhaps the victim, the police and wider society feel better when the offender is punished, but it's a pretty hollow victory if he steals or robs again as soon as he's released.'

We carried on like this for another twenty minutes, batting the debate back and forth in a good-natured way until I said I needed to go home. My friend waved me away from his door a short while later and my ride home on the cart was lost in thought, just as the trip with Rachel had been the previous day after I'd spoken to Louis Décast. Had Lisette told him about the will? Was this why they were fighting in the street? Why did he lie to me, and would he kill her for her money? More importantly, was she killed or, as the policeman had decided, was she just an unlucky cyclist?

Until this last question was answered there was no case to investigate, but I was sure neither Rachel nor Marie-Clair would let me rest until it was resolved.

As is the case in late March, a fine day can give way to a cold and blustery evening, and so it was when Rachel and I left our warm house just before dark for the Easter weekend celebration. She'd popped her nose out before she changed and pronounced she could smell snow in the air, so we'd dressed accordingly with scarves, gloves and hats. We were ready for the most arctic of blasts, even though we'd only be outside for the fifteen-minute walk to the Salle des Fêtes, the village hall.

Within seconds of arriving I regretted at least one layer of clothing and I could hardly hear myself think. It seemed like every man, woman and child in Vieux-Croix had turned out and were determined to be heard above their neighbours. The body heat and a large fire, complete with a pig roasting above, made it almost unbearable.

Enora Legrand, Malo's sister, greeted us at the door and guided us to seats at one of the four trestles stretching almost the length of the hall. Opposite were Marie-Clair and her parents. A shorter table, accommodating what I imagined were the great and the good, ran across the head of these rows. Francis waved and Mayor Sitell nodded in our direction. They occupied opposite ends and, other than those, the only one I recognised was Louise, the priest's housekeeper. It surprised me Pascal Jaubert didn't have a place of honour until I spotted him surrounded by men of a similar age in a corner. From the flushed faces and loud laughter, I guessed they had made a start in the drinks department.

Having introduced us to everyone around us, Enora went to play host to more new arrivals, a family I'd seen in church. Rachel settled into easy conversation with our neighbours whilst I tried to avoid Marie-Clair's attempts to catch my attention by talking to her mother. After half an hour, our section of the table was called to collect supper and Marie-Clair almost ran around to fall in behind me, poking me in the ribs when I pretended I hadn't seen her.

'Why are you ignoring me?' she hissed.

I turned and feigned surprise. 'Oh, Marie-Clair, there you are. I wondered where you'd run off to.'

'Don't give me that, Monsieur Given. You knew I was here all the time. So why *are* you ignoring me?'

I told her I wasn't and asked how she was.

'I'm fine, thank you. Have you a minute to spare after we've eaten? There's someone I'd like you to meet.'

Rachel and I avoided the pork, even though it looked delicious, and plumped for lamb and all the trimmings. Everyone seemed to head back for seconds, though when I stood, Rachel caught my arm, tapped my stomach and made me sit. This amused Marie-Clair's father, and he was still laughing when he returned with a plate piled almost as high as his first. I was allowed some freedom to enjoy a small dessert only because my wife wanted a chocolate torte herself. The wine flowed, though not for me, and the conversation flowed almost as freely along and across the tables, rising in volume as the evening wore on.

When the meal finished, and musicians were beginning to clear a space at one end of the hall, Marie-Clair came round the table and tapped me on the shoulder.

'Are you ready to meet my friend now?'

I had no option but to agree, so I followed her to the far corner. She introduced me to a young woman with long blond hair, a good figure and a broad smile.

'This is Jennifer Parmentier. We were at school together, though she was two years above me. She has been away, visiting an aunt, since the day Madame Perron died.'

I said I was pleased to meet her.

'Tell Monsieur Given what you saw by the river, Jennifer.'

'I'm sure it was nothing, monsieur, but Marie-Clair seems to think it is important to you.'

She looked around the room, firstly towards the doors, then as if looking for someone. I suspected she wanted her mother to come to her rescue, so I asked her to continue.

'I saw Madame Perron not long before she died.'

'You did? Where?'

'I was on the bus, travelling to Dinan. I was the only person on it, apart from the driver. We passed over the river bridge and I saw her standing by the rail with her bicycle. I knocked on the window, but she didn't see me. She looked at her watch twice before we took the bend and she disappeared out of view.' The girl clasped her hands to her cheeks. 'And I'll never see her again. She was always so nice when I went into the library.'

'What time was this, Jennifer?'

'In the afternoon, just after four o'clock. The bus only takes a few minutes to get down there, and I caught it at four.'

'You say she was looking at her watch. Could she have been waiting for someone?'

'I think she might. Each time she checked it she peered up the hill.'

'And you didn't see anyone else?'

'No, monsieur, it all happened too quickly. The road from the village is hidden from view as soon as you're halfway over the bridge, and we were travelling quite fast.'

Jennifer was shaking by the time she'd finished, so I thanked her and went back to my seat, leaving Marie-Clair with an arm round her friend's shoulder. Five minutes later she was back behind me.

'So? What now, Monsieur Given? How could Madame Perron have ridden into the river if she was already at the bridge when the bus passed?'

It was a good question but, before I could answer, Enora clapped her hands at the front of the room.

'Now, mesdames and messieurs, we have a most distinguished guest this evening.' The mayor puffed up his chest, and I smiled because Enora's glance at Rachel told me what was coming next. 'We have the exceptionally gifted Madame Given, our newly arrived music teacher, who I'm sure will play for us if we give her a big round of applause.'

Rachel resisted for as long as was respectable then treated us to a short selection of her favourite violin pieces, starting with the Mozart, each followed by the audience's rapturous appreciation. Sadly, my mind was only half there. The other half was trying to find a less obvious explanation for Jennifer's sighting of Lisette Perron safe by the river, beyond where she'd supposedly entered the water.

TWELVE

Some policemen, and I'd hope I'm one of them, consider a situation from all angles and weigh new information as it becomes available. Others take the easy path, arrive at a conclusion and stick with it regardless of what's in front of them. I suspected Pascal Jaubert to be one of these.

There'd been no point in trying to give him Jennifer's report at the meal on Saturday; he'd been too far gone to have taken it seriously, so I'd had to wait until Tuesday, after Easter weekend, to find him in his office. He sat, arms folded, leaning back in his chair, his collar open, his jacket rumpled and the stubble on his cheeks looking at least a day longer than it should have been. I wondered if he'd been enjoying himself with his drinking friends long after the communal meal had finished.

'Monsieur Given, it is nice to see you again. Have you been playing detective once more?'

I ignored the insult and told him Jennifer Parmentier's story.

He laughed. 'This changes nothing, monsieur. Did the girl see Madame Perron ride away?'

'No.'

'So the accident could have happened later. Perhaps she was just resting at the bridge before tackling the hill. Possible, yes?'

'Possible, but not likely, is it? The librarian wouldn't career out of control going uphill, would she?'

'But she may have ridden down again afterwards; you know her body wasn't found until two hours after this. If, as you've suggested, she was waiting for someone, she may have gone home then returned to try again.'

'If she'd done that, then wouldn't whoever she was meeting have realised something was wrong and looked for her? No-one has come forward, I take it, to say they were planning to meet?'

Jaubert examined his fingernails for a few seconds before answering. 'Firstly, we don't know for sure she *was* meeting anyone. Even if she was, there would hardly have been enough time for them to have become alarmed between Jennifer seeing her on the bridge and when she was discovered, especially if she went home first and returned.'

'Accepted, but after she was found, wouldn't they have been in touch with you?'

'Maybe, maybe not. The fact Madame Lisette was meeting this imaginary person by the river suggests they may not be from Vieux-Croix so might not yet have heard of her death. On top of this —' he paused — 'I assume you are aware she had something of a reputation. Perhaps she was meeting a man and, quite naturally, he doesn't wish to become involved.'

I was impressed. To a point. At least the policeman showed the ability to think through various possibilities, even if he then dismissed them in favour of his original conclusion. Sadly, these are almost the worst kind of coppers. Bright enough to do a good job but too lazy to bother. There's many a villain gone free, or worse, many an innocent been jailed, on the back of this kind of sloppy work.

'Both of those are reasonable thoughts, Monsieur Jaubert, but don't you think we now have enough to re-open the case and carry out further investigations?'

He stood and walked to the door, swinging it open. 'You say "we", monsieur, but there is no "we". I am the investigating police officer and you are not. You are no longer a police officer, and I think you forget this. As far as I am concerned, you have brought me nothing to change my mind. Lisette Perron died in an accident. Sad, but true. Now, I am busy, so I wish you good day.'

I stopped in the doorway. 'Before I go, may I ask a favour?'

He sighed the sigh of the weary. 'If you must.'

'Might I bring Jennifer to talk to you?'

'To what purpose?'

'So you can hear her evidence directly. You can note it in your records and then show you've considered what she saw. It wouldn't do if rumours started that you'd not been thorough, would it?'

Jaubert scratched his chin. 'I'll give you fifteen minutes. Bring her here at ten o'clock tomorrow morning and I'll take her statement.'

As I walked from the building, my stubborn streak surfaced. There was more than enough new information to warrant further investigation, and if the policeman wouldn't do it then I'd have to. Much as I hated the idea, I'd never rest if Lisette Perron's death didn't receive the attention it deserved. On top of this, Rachel, Francis and Marie-Clair wouldn't let me forget it.

I'd only had occasion to visit Doctor Hodin once since we'd arrived, with a cold which wouldn't go away. He'd done the usual tests of asking me to stick out my tongue and listening to my chest, then told me to take aspirin and eat an orange or two. He'd spent longer asking me about England than he had on the diagnosis, and I imagined his easy manner and sense of humour would serve him well with his patients.

This time there was only one person in front of me when I arrived in his waiting room after leaving the police station, a heavily pregnant young woman who nodded and smiled as I sat down. I was about to ask her when the baby was due when the doctor called her into the surgery and I was left alone.

The windowless room hadn't been painted for many a year, and the beige paint, wooden chairs and dark-lacquered floor gave it a grim feel. If you didn't feel ill on arrival, you would after a few minutes in this place. Thankfully my predecessor left, and it was only a few moments before the doctor shouted my name.

His surgery was barely brighter than the room I'd just left, though it did have the benefit of a window, and his cheery face was enough to lift the spirits, unlike the skeleton chart on the wall behind him. There was barely space for his small desk, two chairs and bookshelf in what must have been the smallest room in his house.

'Monsieur Given, how are you today?'

'I'm afraid I'm not ill, Doctor.'

He chuckled. 'Well, that's not something to apologise about, is it? Makes a welcome change for me. What is it, then?'

'It's a little delicate. You attended at the death of Madame Lisette Perron, I assume?'

'I did. Sad case. Did you know her?'

I explained that I'd met her and some issues had been brought to my attention which made me wonder if her death had really been an accident, not least being Jennifer's assertion she saw the librarian on the bridge.

'I'm no pathologist, monsieur, so it may be possible to interpret her injuries in a different way. From what I saw, they confirmed the police view that she'd skidded from the road into the river.'

'You were happy to concur that she'd hit the back of her head when she crashed?'

'There was no reason not to. If, as was suggested, she'd ridden out of control over the grass and the bicycle slid sideways, she could easily have slipped backwards. There was no blood at the scene but, again, that wouldn't be unusual with the river high and fast-flowing. I didn't see blood anywhere else, and neither did Pascal.'

I'd found none myself on the road, the bridge or the grass and presumed, if there had been any, it would have washed away in the heavy rain.

'So nothing to make you think it wasn't accidental?'

'Sorry, nothing. She'd a fractured arm and some surface scrapes, both consistent with the police version of events, as I said.'

'Any idea of a time of death?'

'Not more than three hours. She was found around half past six, and you've told me Mademoiselle Parmentier saw her at just after four. Even if I didn't know this, I'd still have said she hadn't been dead for very long when I arrived. Rigor mortis hadn't set in, which usually happens after three to four hours. It might have taken a bit longer in the cold water but not too much.'

'No bruising round the throat, or other injuries?'

'None, other than the ones I've mentioned.' Doctor Hodin glanced towards his door. 'I'm sorry, Monsieur Given, I had no alternative when I made out the death certificate but to confirm Pascal's conclusion. Believe me, if I'd had any doubt I wouldn't have done so.'

'I'm certain you would, Doctor. Don't worry, I'm just trying to build the best picture I can of Madame Perron's last hours. All the facts don't seem to fit together neatly at present, but they will. In time. Thank you for seeing me, and if any tiny thing comes to mind perhaps you'll let me know.'

He agreed he would, and I left him to deal with the queue of patients now formed outside his door.

Pascal Jaubert was waiting when Jennifer, Marie-Clair and I arrived at the agreed time. There was a marked contrast in his appearance to the previous day with his hair combed and brilliantined and his uniform neatly pressed, and the man was clean-shaven other than his newly trimmed moustache. For a second I wondered if this was for my benefit until I saw the way he blushed when Jennifer shook his hand. He barely gave me or Marie-Clair a second glance when he offered her a seat. The effect her friend had on Jaubert couldn't have escaped Marie-Clair's notice, but she forged on regardless.

'You already know Jennifer, Pascal. I believe my friend, Monsieur Given, told you yesterday that she has some information for you. Are you willing to listen?'

The policeman dragged his eyes away from Jennifer long enough to answer. 'Of course. I'd love to hear what she has to say. Monsieur already gave me the bare bones, but it will be better coming from Jennifer's lips.'

He almost choked at the last two words, and Marie-Clair turned to me and rolled her eyes, then returned to Jaubert.

'Good. I hope you've some good questions for her too.'

Marie-Clair nodded for her friend to start, and she told him the same story she'd told me. He took great pains to write down every word, pausing occasionally to seek clarification on matters of detail.

'For the record, could you describe how the person you saw was dressed?'

'I've always thought Madame Perron very chic, even in the library. We've talked about it, haven't we, Marie-Clair?'

'We have.'

Jennifer turned back to Jaubert. 'She had a deep blue coat with matching hat and gloves. The scarlet scarf she wore was a really stylish addition. I'm not sure how suitable the outfit would have been for riding a bicycle, but standing there on the bridge she looked wonderful.'

The policeman consulted a file on his desk, looked at me and nodded, then returned his attention to Marie-Clair's friend. 'Well, the clothes seem to be correct. Did you see her face?'

'Only briefly, but enough to know it was her.'

'And you're certain?'

'As certain as I can be, Pascal. Why do you think I'd tell such a story if I didn't believe it to be true?'

'I'm only checking.' He glanced at me again. 'It's important I examine every avenue. Now please carry on.'

Afterwards, he carefully read the statement back to Jennifer.

'Is that correct?'

Jennifer nodded.

'Then I'll ask you to sign it.'

Marie-Clair interrupted. 'Haven't you any more questions?'

'Actually, Marie-Clair —' Jaubert drooled in the direction of his witness — 'Jennifer has been very thorough in her statement. I don't believe I do have any questions.'

Jennifer returned his smile and delivered our pre-agreed line. 'So are you going to investigate further, Pascal? I really think you should. After all, if Madame Perron was waiting on the bridge for someone at the time you thought she'd had her accident, then something doesn't add up, does it?'

The poor, smitten policeman ran a finger beneath his collar. 'Well, I suppose if you put it like that … I mean, it's most unusual…' He read her statement a second time, pausing and shaking his head every few lines, then slipped it into the case folder. 'I'll tell you what we'll do. Monsieur Given may continue with his enquiries, bringing anything he finds to me. I, for my part, will keep my eyes and ears open and ask one or two questions around the town. It is most important, though —' he glanced through his window to the mayor's office across the hall — 'none of this gets back to Monsieur Sitell. He's approved my initial conclusion and will not be a happy man if he hears he shouldn't have done so.'

I stood and shook his hand, Marie-Clair kissed him like a cousin and Jennifer flung her arms round his neck with a little more enthusiasm. I could almost feel the heat from his cheeks as we walked to the door.

THIRTEEN

As I'd decided I must take a serious look at Lisette Perron's death, because no-one else would, it seemed obvious to re-examine the only person who might have had a serious enough reason to want her dead. Although the thread from Ménière looking for army bases to killing the librarian to keep her quiet was tenuous at best, it was all I had other than a jealous husband.

For the ten minutes it had taken for us to walk from the square to David Ménière's house, Marie-Clair had questioned me on our next move. She'd kicked off with "what do we do now?" as soon as Jennifer left us and wouldn't accept my argument that Pascal Jaubert hadn't included her in his permission for me to continue. To be honest, I had no real reason to exclude her other than her lack of experience and a vague wish to keep her safe. I liked the girl. She was keen, intelligent and good company except when her nagging got the better of her. On top of this, I had no more *right* to investigate than she had, even if I had permission, so, equally, I had no right to tell her she couldn't do so. Though I pretty much like to plough my own furrow, I've always found a partner useful to bounce ideas off and to give a different slant on evidence uncovered so, in the end, I capitulated. I had one provision.

'You're not to go off on your own, it's too dangerous.' Advice I wish I'd always followed myself. A shiver ran through me when I remembered the last time I didn't and lost a good friend. 'You're to watch and listen. If there's some digging you can handle without me, I'll let you do it. Agreed?'

Marie-Clair's face split into a grin. 'Agreed.' Her tone and eyes told me this was only up to a point.

By the time we arrived, I'd reminded her of all the information we had on Ménière, including Mitchell's request that I keep him under observation. I didn't go so far as telling her my contact was military intelligence, only that our man was of interest to the "British authorities".

'So what's he done?'

'We're not sure yet if he's done anything at all. He's just a person of interest, someone who's been asking some odd questions and who might have a wireless transmitter hidden in his house. Until we have more information, there's no more than that.'

'Then what's the plan?'

I tapped my pocket. 'I promised I'd let him have a list of army bases, so I've put one together.'

'But if he's a spy —' her eyes widened — 'isn't that playing into his hands?'

'Not with this list it isn't. Two of them are easily found, visible from the main roads into Vieux-Croix, the others I made up. They're as far off the beaten track as I could make them and will keep him busy going round in circles for ages. If he comes back and complains, I'll think of some excuse.'

We agreed that I'd do the talking and if Ménière asked, she was a niece of Rachel's. He'd not know my wife's nationality so Marie-Clair being French shouldn't matter, though I'd lie if he questioned it. With luck, Ménière would invite us in and we'd get a better picture of the life he was living.

'If he does, I want to get into his kitchen to nose around for that transmitter — if there is one. Should the chance come up, you keep him talking. You'd better cough loudly if he comes looking for me.'

On the doorstep I rattled the knocker. It echoed in the way they do when a house is empty. I looked at Marie-Clair.

'Sounds like he's not at home.'

Her face dropped. 'Try again.'

I did — three times and still no answer. I peered through the front window, covering my eyes to shade the reflection. There was no fire in the grate, not even any ashes I could see. There were no papers, no cups, no mess of any kind to suggest the house was still occupied.

'Looks like he's gone. Let's take a look around the back.'

We ducked under the windows of the first two houses, particularly avoiding the scrutiny of the elderly woman on the end. The view through the rear window mirrored the empty rooms I'd seen in the front, with a spotless kitchen and no food in sight. I tried the door, but it was locked. Marie-Clair tugged the elbow of my coat.

'The aerial has been taken down.'

She pointed to the rings where the wires would have been fastened, and a hole through the wall where they would have fed into the house. We took a quick look round the garden, though it added nothing to what we'd already gathered. Ménière had lived here for a short time, set up and run a transmitter of some kind, and now cleared off, probably to repeat the process in another town. We returned to the front and knocked on the door of the helpful neighbour I'd spoken to previously.

'We're still looking for Monsieur Ménière, your neighbour. Thought we might catch him in if we came a different day. Have you seen him?'

'He left yesterday. Asked me to give the keys back to the landlord. Said he'd paid in advance, and now his work locally had finished he was moving onto the next job.'

'Mention where he was going?'

'Not that I remember.'

'Did he have anything with him?'

'Only two suitcases. Must say one of them looked heavy — fair puffing he was when he put it down.'

'That was all?'

'Don't expect he had much else. The house was furnished, and he wasn't here very long. Glad he's gone, though. Noisy devil, that generator going at all hours.'

'Generator?'

'Borrowed it from a farmer down the road. Asked when he arrived if I knew where he might get one, said he needed it for his work. I saw the generator's owner, René Dulap, call in the van last night to collect it from behind the house.'

I asked if he might lend us the keys for a few minutes to have a look round. The man looked like he was about to refuse, so I explained we had the blessing of Pascal Jaubert and he handed them over.

Inside, there was no more to be found. Two rooms downstairs with the most basic of furniture and only a single bed in each of the two upstairs rooms. The whole house was as clean as if no-one had lived in it for years, and I was sure that even if I'd had the equipment we'd be hard pressed to find a fingerprint of any use. Marie-Clair looked under chairs and beds, in kitchen cupboards, and in every nook and cranny but found no trace of Ménière's having been there. I locked the door when we left and asked Marie-Clair to pop the keys back.

When she re-joined me, the girl looked as miserable as I'd seen anyone in a long time. 'Is that it then? He's got away?'

'Only for now. Don't worry, Marie-Clair, we'll pass on what we've found to your cousin, and if he wants to take it from there, he can. Even if he just circulates a description of

Ménière to other areas, something might turn up. Then Pascal can question him and decide if there's a case to answer.'

'But what about poor Madame Perron in the meantime? She's lying in the ground and her killer's escaped.'

'Not necessarily. You really must learn a little patience, Marie-Clair. We're far from certain that David Ménière was actually involved; he was just an easy first line of enquiry. We need to continue to keep our ears to the ground for other possibilities. It's a small town, and the librarian must have known her killer.' I explained, by way of example, about Louis Décast and the row with his wife.

'So you think he did it?'

'Well, he has a motive, the inheritance, and they obviously didn't get on. But is he a murderer? I don't know yet. I'm only mentioning him to show how there may be others who would be happy to see Lisette Perron disposed of. We'll just keep asking questions and see what turns up. Someone will know something important, even if they don't know they know it.'

It was Thursday again, and Eric and I were scrapping with Phillipe and Daniel over tricks. They were two points up after an hour, and I fancied a break.

'Any of you want a cigarette? I could do with five minutes while I'll get the drinks in.'

Phillipe and Eric were both heavy smokers but didn't bother at the table because neither Daniel nor I did, so they jumped at the chance to go outside to feed their habit. I ordered three beers and a Diabolo then brought them back. Daniel emptied his earlier glass and pushed it to one side.

'Did you hear the news, James?'

'About what?'

'A bloke who'd been living here in Vieux-Croix has been found with his throat cut.'

Had someone discovered Ménière's little secret? It hadn't taken them long, unless he'd been followed from here or somewhere he'd been earlier.

'Who? Where?'

'Don't remember his name. David something. Not a local family. He turned up at the roadside near an airfield outside Dinard. Throat cut.'

'Do they know why?'

'I was told he'd been found with binoculars, and the police unearthed a wireless transmitter at his rented house. Neighbours reported he'd been asking questions about military camps nearby. Looks like he may have been a spy, and a local patriot or two didn't like it. From what I heard the police aren't looking for anyone, except perhaps some of his accomplices.'

'I met him.'

'You did?'

'Peston, at the post office, put me onto a man asking the same questions, so I made contact. I wondered if he'd had anything to do with the death of Lisette Perron. He only left a couple of days ago.'

The notion of the execution of a spy who'd been in our midst inevitably steered our conversation to the war for a few minutes before the others came back in. I played for another hour without enthusiasm because my mind wouldn't settle, and I left earlier than normal.

Back home, I penned another letter to Mitchell to give him the news that Ménière had left and was now probably dead.

The next day, I was leaving to post it when a letter arrived from the Paris hotel Ménière said he'd stayed at. The owner apologised that the friend I'd enquired about had been and gone. He'd stayed with them only two nights, on the dates he'd told me.

So, he couldn't have killed Lisette Perron.

On my way to the post office I called in to speak to Pascal Jaubert to find out if he'd heard anything of the man who'd been killed. He said he'd been contacted by the Dinard police, and the dead man was indeed David Ménière.

'I'm in big trouble because I didn't spot him down here, but what can I do? There's only me and a big area to cover. I can't see everything. I'm surprised Monsieur Sitell didn't suspect anything when he interviewed this Ménière.'

I told him what I'd told Daniel.

'You're saying you knew we had a spy in the town and didn't tell me?'

'I didn't know for certain; I went to talk to him on Wednesday and he'd moved out. All I had was gossip about him asking curious questions and a report of wires at the back of his house, which could have been anything. I thought I'd find out more before bothering you with it.'

Jaubert screwed up his face and patted his cheeks. 'I understand, but I wish you had said something. At least I could have claimed I was waiting for further information. Still, it shows you're a good detective.'

Praise I wouldn't have expected to hear from the policeman. Perhaps he might be thawing a little. An even bigger thaw came a few minutes later. We were still chatting about the dead spy and Jaubert asked me to use his first name.

'Please do, monsieur. I was born in this town, so everybody knows me, and they all call me Pascal.' He smiled, 'sometimes I wish they might be a little more formal, but what can you do?'

'Then please call me James. It might be helpful if we're to work together.'

I told him I'd be more forthcoming if I heard anything else which might interest him, then I used his windowsill to change my letter now Ménière's killing had been confirmed. Mitchell would be grinning at his desk in London when he heard of another leak sealed.

FOURTEEN

There'd been so much to do on the farm when I arrived home I'd not had time to think about the latest development. Most non-farmers would think it's an easy life: sow a few seeds in the spring then just feed the animals a couple of times a day until the harvest. Even I'd thought this was how it was before I took the job with Malo. The reality is different. Long days of heavy labour and the constant worry of bad weather and crop failure mean it's not a career for the faint-hearted. We were in a quiet period, but I still had plenty to do and my boss was being more than generous in being flexible with my time. The interruptions of the past few days meant I'd had some catching up to do.

I'd just slumped in my chair after our evening meal when the door knocker rattled, and I answered to find the policeman on the step. I invited him in.

'Pascal? Nothing wrong, I hope.'

'No, nothing. Well, not much anyway. Ever since you brought Jennifer Parmentier to see me, I've spent a lot of time thinking about what a fool I've been. I've only been in the job a couple of years and should be listening to a man with your experience. It was only my pride that stopped me accepting your help.'

'There's no need to apologise, Pascal. I might have done the same in your shoes.'

'That's very kind, James. However, I've been mulling over what you found about Lisette Perron, and I've come to the conclusion that her death as an accident doesn't add up after all.'

Not everyone can move at the same speed. Some of us make connections more quickly; others need to chew the cud thoroughly before they can swallow it. At least Jaubert had arrived at the same place as me in good time. I asked if he had thoughts on any suspects.

'This chap Ménière. What do you think?'

'It wasn't him; he was out of town at the time the librarian died.'

'Other than him, I've not thought of anyone. I know most people within ten kilometres and can't imagine any of them committing murder.'

'From what I've learnt, killers don't have big signs round their necks telling the world to keep clear. If they did, there'd be no murders, would there? Most of them don't even think they're capable of such an act until it's done. Anything on Louis Décast, the husband?'

'Louis? Might overcharge for a repair now and again, but he's no criminal. Why?'

'I was told he'd had an argument with Lisette, so I drove out to talk to him. He said he hadn't seen her for months before her death, even though he had. Clearly still bitter about how she'd treated him when they were together.'

Jaubert was quiet for a moment, and I could almost hear the wheels whirring until he grinned and pulled open the front door. 'Let's go and ask him some questions.'

Décast had been living on his own for a few months and it showed. His two-storey stone house, a couple of doors from the boulangerie in a short street off the square, looked well-kept from the outside. When he let Jaubert and I in, however, we had to step over vehicle parts and tools in his front room. The place smelt almost as much of grease and petrol as his garage had. His kitchen wasn't much tidier, with unwashed pans and dishes in the sink, and, on the side, a tablecloth which looked like it had been gathering stains since his wife left. He lifted a cup from the table, looked inside, screwed up his nose and offered us coffee. We both declined politely. He was still in his overalls.

Pascal explained I was giving him a hand. Décast leant back and peered through his bottle-thick glasses at me for a minute.

'You're the one came to the garage last week with Malo Legrand's car. You never said you were a policeman.'

'I'm not. I used to be, in England. As Monsieur Jaubert says, I'm just giving him the benefit of my knowledge. On murder cases.'

Now Décast looked at the policeman. 'Murder? What's this about, Pascal?'

'New evidence has come to light since your wife's death. I'm sorry, but it points to her having been murdered.'

The mechanic slumped in a chair, his lips moving but no sound coming out. He slid both hands over his bald patch and clasped them behind his trembling head. 'I knew something like this would happen.'

'Why?' I asked.

'My Lisette was a passionate woman. Fond of fun but a terrible tease. She'd lead a man on, then when she'd had her fill she'd throw him over for another without a second thought. This suits some men who don't want a long-term involvement.' He spat in the fire. 'I expect others might take it hard and want revenge.'

'Is that you, Louis? Jealous? Your wife had one affair too many and you decided to punish her?'

He sat bolt upright. 'Me? You think I'd harm Lisette?'

'It's well known you two didn't get on, fought all the time.'

'No, no, no, that's just being married, isn't it? You show me a man and wife who don't have rows at one time or another. I'd never hurt her. Wouldn't hurt anyone.'

Pascal interrupted. 'You were seen arguing shortly before she died, Louis. What was that about?'

He shook his head. 'Nothing. Just personal stuff.'

'If it was nothing, why did you tell Monsieur Given you hadn't seen your wife for ages?'

Décast glared at me. 'Because it was none of his business. None of yours either.'

'Was it about her will, Louis? That must have made you angry.'

He stood, shaking, fists clenched. 'I was annoyed, but that was all. Not angry enough to kill my wife.'

The policeman stepped forward, pushing his face nose to nose with Décast's. 'Sit down, Louis. You don't want any trouble now, do you?'

He did as he was told. Pascal may have been carrying a little weight, but he was younger and taller than the mechanic, and carried the authority of his office on his shoulders. He returned to his questioning.

'You were about to tell me about the will, Louis. Cutting you out is what I was told.'

'Huh. The will wasn't worth a bean. Not really. An old house in need of repair and a few francs to bury Lisette. I could sell a couple of cars and make more.'

I took over again. 'So what were you arguing about? You might not want to say, but it will be worse for you if you don't. Monsieur Jaubert will have to take you into the police station and all your neighbours will know about it.'

'If you must know, she wasn't happy about the boot being on the other foot.'

'Sorry?'

'I've struck up a friendship with a woman. Someone in the village near my garage. Lisette heard of it and came at me in the street. Said I'd no right, that we were still married. Didn't like it when I laughed in her face and told her she should mend her ways before having the nerve to tell me who I can and can't see. It all got a bit heated, as it always did, and I thought she would hit me. Then Daniel Bisset came round the corner and she scurried off. Lisette wouldn't want anyone seeing what she was really like.' Décast stood and looked out of the window. 'That was the last time I saw her.'

'Are you saying you didn't meet her again by the river on the day she died?'

'Definitely not. I was working on a car all afternoon for a customer then delivered it to his home in Évran.'

'What time was this?'

'Suppose I got to him about four o'clock. We took a little spin to make sure he was happy, he paid me and we called in for a beer or two. Then I caught the bus back here. When I arrived, I was told a woman's body had been found. It was only later when he —' Décast jerked a thumb at Pascal — 'came round I heard it was Lisette.'

'I hope this is all true, Louis. You'll need to give us the names of both your lady friend and this customer of yours so we can check them.'

He gave me their details. 'You can talk to them if you want, but I'm telling you I had nothing to do with Lisette's death. If you think someone killed her, then you need to speak to Francine Charbonne.'

'Francine?' said Pascal. 'From the boulangerie?'

'Of course. How many Francine Charbonnes do you know?'

I asked Décast why we should talk to her.

'Her husband just finished an affair with Lisette, and Francine is bound to have heard about it.'

On Saturday morning the market was quiet. I spent my time in the early spring sunshine reading a three-day old English newspaper, though the news was depressing. The front page carried stories of the successful evacuation of a naval base at Scapa Flow off the north coast of Scotland. The story next to this discussed the imminent invasion of Denmark and Norway by Germany. Events on France's Eastern border were relegated to an inside page, even further back than coverage of a minor riot at Dartmoor prison, but the commentator speculated it would only be a matter of time before Nazi pressure would threaten French defences.

As it approached twelve o'clock and it had been twenty minutes without a customer, I was wondering if it might be worth packing up for the day, so I started to tidy the front of my stall. I'd been at the job less than a couple of minutes when someone coughed at my shoulder.

'Not closing already, Monsieur Given?'

I turned to see Doctor Hodin. 'Not if there are customers waiting. What can I get for you?'

He asked for several items, which I weighed and put into his bag, but he then hovered for a few moments after I took his payment. I thought he'd forgotten something.

'Was there anything else, Doctor?'

'After we spoke, Monsieur Given, I got to thinking about your questions and I couldn't rest without checking. My notes are very thorough, as they have to be in the circumstances, and I rang a colleague in Paris who would be much more familiar than I with violent deaths. He'd see serious accidents and even killings on a regular basis, so I went through my findings with him.'

'And did he see anything?'

'Nothing conclusive, but the bottom line is he threw enough doubt on my conclusions for me to think Madame Perron's death may not have been accidental after all. His main concern was the position of the head wound. He thought it more consistent with a blow from behind than a fall.'

'Are there more tests you could do?'

'Not without disinterring her body, and I'd not get permission for something so drastic without stronger evidence. All I can do is apologise for perhaps being a little too casual in my original conclusion. I'm happy to pass this information on to the police if you think it would be helpful.'

'It would be more than helpful, Doctor. Anything which throws more light on Lisette Perron's death could be useful in convincing Pascal Jaubert to reopen the case. It's good of you to have taken another look.'

He promised to call straight away to see the policeman when he'd finished his shopping. 'You seem to be fairly certain someone murdered Madame Perron. Do you have a suspect?'

'I can't say I'm certain, but the evidence is pointing that way. As for who did it, I haven't a clue. I had a man in mind, but it seems it couldn't have been him. I hope we can convince the police to become properly involved and ask questions.'

'Well I'll do all I can to help.'

Doctor Hodin said goodbye and then continued on his way. When he'd gone, I wrote a note to Marie-Clair telling her what he'd said and the outcome of my talk with Louis Décast. I'd hardly finished writing when trade picked up and I was rushed off my feet for an hour or more, so I was glad to hear the church bell strike twelve. I joined the other stallholders in the task of clearing up the market-place. Everything from Normandy, cheese to spanners, was packed into boxes and piled in vans, cars and carts until the next market, be it in another town or the following week. Women chatted whilst they worked and the men eyed the clock, hoping for a beer before going home with what was left of the takings. I exchanged a few pleasantries, refused the beer, made sure everything on my cart was secure then delivered my note through Marie-Clair's letterbox without knocking.

Rachel had cooked a good old-fashioned vegetable soup for lunch and dished out a substantial bowl once I'd unloaded and washed. She placed a basket of bread in front of me on the table. I lifted a piece, ripped it open and sniffed.

'That's good. Did you buy it in the town, at Francine Charbonne's?'

'As usual. Why?'

'Just wondered. You teach her son violin, don't you?'

'On Mondays after school. You're usually still out. He's not very good, though.'

'Better or worse than Marie-Clair?'

She crossed her arms and knitted her brow for a moment. 'Different.'

We both laughed.

'What do you make of his mother?'

'Good baker, but otherwise I don't know her so well. Once or twice she's walked down with Raymond but leaves him at the door. Mostly he comes on his own. We'll exchange the odd word in the shop if she's not too busy. What's this about?'

'Someone said her husband had a fling with Lisette Perron.'

'Really? Men, I ask you.'

'What's that supposed to mean?'

'Well, have you seen Francine? She's attractive, not much older than me, and very good-humoured. Why can't men just be happy with what they've got instead of looking for greener pastures all the time?'

I grabbed Rachel's hand and pulled her over onto my lap. 'Is that what I should be doing, looking for pastures new?'

She play-slapped me behind the ear. 'Not if you know what's good for you, James Given.'

'Now, that's what I'm interested in.'

'What?'

'If I was to go with another woman, would you take your revenge on me or on her?'

'This is theoretical, yes?'

'Yes, of course.'

She thought for a moment, then went back to her seat. 'I don't really know. I'd probably blame you. After all, this theoretical woman, whoever she is, isn't married to me, is she? She's not betraying any trust, but you would be. Is this about Francine?'

'It could be, though I just need your thoughts generally on the subject. If jealousy could be relevant to the librarian's death, I need to consider how a woman would view betrayal. Would you do me a favour?'

'Only if you stop talking and eat your soup. It will get cold.'

'Would you ask Francine Charbonne to call round for her son's next lesson? You can tell her you'd like to discuss how he's getting on with the instrument. I'd like a chance to chat to her. I can do it while she's waiting.'

'How very devious you are,' Rachel smiled, 'though I'm not really happy doing it.'

'Why not?'

'Well, it's a lie, for one thing, and I can't see how Francine could be involved. She seems so nice.'

'It's only a tiny white lie, isn't it? And I'm not saying she is involved; I'm just following what Louis Décast told me. But if you don't want to do it, then I'll find another way of talking to her.'

'No, no, it's fine. I'll take a walk and catch her in the shop this afternoon. If I see her there, then she'll be too busy to talk so won't ask why she needs to wait until Monday.'

Rachel was right, I did need to be devious. It occurred to me how much easier this would have been if I still had the authority of being a policeman. No subterfuge, no excuses, just pick them up and pull them in for questioning. So, at last, I'd remembered one advantage of the job.

FIFTEEN

Sunday, as had become the pattern, passed with Rachel and I going to church, a good lunch and snooze afterwards, a quick check on Malo's animals, then a decent walk in the late afternoon if the weather was fit. In the evening we'd settle to listen to the wireless or read, and I'd think about the jobs that needed to be done in the coming week.

Monday was my day for odd jobs around the farm. I'd always start with tidying the barn and cleaning the crates we'd used for the market. This done, I checked with Malo if he had any specific projects in mind, and as he hadn't, I worked my way down the list I'd compiled the previous evening. A couple of weeks earlier the wind had brought down part of a hedge in the field farthest from the house and I'd been putting off fixing it, but the weather had stayed fine and there was now no excuse not to get on with it. Once I'd completed the smaller jobs I collected a bill-hook, a saw and roll of wire, then tramped a quarter of a mile and set to work, with my thoughts split between the task in hand and what I'd discovered regarding Lisette Perron's death.

There wasn't much. There was a good chance she'd been murdered; of that I was now fairly sure based on the testimony I'd heard. The unexplained tracks on the riverbank, Jennifer Parmentier's report of seeing Lisette waiting for someone, and the doctor's revised view pointed in that direction. What I didn't have was a reason for her to be killed. She'd possibly uncovered David Ménière's activities but he probably didn't kill her, at least not if his alibi was genuine. There was also her infidelity, but from what I'd heard this might put any number of suspects in the frame. I needed to find out more about Lisette and who she knew. I also needed to find out from Mitchell if she was reporting on anyone other than Ménière.

The day grew colder in the afternoon and clouds on the horizon suggested snow might be on the way again, so I put away my thoughts to speed the job in hand. Half an hour later, I was disturbed by Marie-Clair's voice on the path beside the hedge.

'Monsieur Given? You are there?'

I stood and peered over. 'What are you doing down here, Marie-Clair?'

'You sent me a note. I haven't been able to come until now. My father wants me to keep studying and not to run about solving murders.'

I grinned. 'And have you?'

'What?'

'Solved a murder?'

'No, not yet, but I will — or at least *we* will.'

She babbled on for a full minute about how happy she was that Doctor Hodin had confirmed the librarian had been killed, and how excited she was that there were now real suspects to investigate. I told her that the doctor's verdict was far from certain. Her jaw dropped.

'You're not saying you won't investigate now?'

'No, that's not what I said. Only that we need to be cautious. We can't go accusing anyone of a crime which may not even have been committed. We'll take it slowly, one step at a time. If you ask your parents to tell you everything they know about the librarian, no matter how irrelevant it might seem, that would be a good start.' I consulted my watch. 'I have to go back home; there's someone I need to talk to. This repair will wait until tomorrow to be finished.'

We walked back in the direction of the house, Marie-Clair shivering on one side of the hedge and me on the other, and I talked her through all I'd found so far. I left her with a warning.

'Don't share any of this with anyone. If there is a murderer out there, we don't have a clue who it is, and I don't want you in danger. Understood?'

'Understood.'

With this she turned off the track and hurried off home. I smiled as I pictured her later, pencil and notebook in hand, interrogating her mother and father.

Kicking off my boots at the back door, I heard Rachel speaking to someone at the front. She introduced me when she invited them in.

'James, this is Madame Charbonne and her son Raymond. You've met before?'

I nodded to Francine Charbonne. 'Only Madame, in her shop. I've not had the pleasure of meeting this young man.'

The boy, about ten years old, tall and skinny, was pushed forward by his mother to shake my hand. His cheeky smile broadened as he did so.

'Very pleased to meet you, monsieur. My friends say you were a detective. Did you catch lots of murderers?'

No secrets in a small town.

Raymond's mother told him not to be so rude, but the grin only widened. Rachel invited him through for his lesson and told Francine they would talk about his progress afterwards.

I offered her a seat and a coffee or tea. She accepted a chair and refused a drink. The woman was, as Rachel had mentioned, attractive though a little overweight, an occupational hazard I assumed if one is surrounded by cakes all day. She had long blond hair, sparkling teeth and a wide smile like her son, and I agreed with my wife's analysis that any man might be content to have her by his side. I asked how long the boy had been playing the violin.

'For about two years. His school began lessons, but then the teacher moved away. I was very pleased when Madame Given arrived and Raymond could continue.'

'Do you play yourself?'

She laughed. 'Sadly no. I wish I could. But I'm happy that my son can learn.'

We chatted for a while about how he was getting on. Unfortunately, the noises I heard escaping through the door didn't quite live up to the glowing account Raymond's mother gave. I asked if she'd always lived in Vieux-Croix.

'Not always. I came from Paris when I married Gerard — he is from here — and we took over the bakery from his father. It is a nice town. Quiet but nice.'

'It is nice. Though not without excitement.'

'How so? Ah, you mean the death of poor Lisette?'

'That's right. Did you know her well?'

She shook her head slowly. 'We were good friends for a time.'

'You fell out?'

'No. We just drifted apart a little. I became busier in the shop and she had friends she'd known before I arrived. It was such a shock when she died. I still can't believe it.' Francine reached into her handbag for a handkerchief and dabbed the corners of her eyes. 'I am sorry, monsieur. Lisette was a lovely woman, always so full of life.'

Raymond's fiddling stopped in the other room, and Rachel opened the door to invite his mother through. I was left wondering if Francine was unaware of her husband's reported affair with her friend. If she was, she hid it well and must have been a competent liar.

When Francine and Raymond Charbonne left, I walked with them into the market square then wandered round to Pascal Jaubert's office. I asked if I could use his telephone in connection with Lisette's death.

'It is there, on the desk. Help yourself, monsieur.'

'I'm afraid it's a little private — but I'll tell you anything I find.'

He tutted and went into the street for a cigarette. I didn't tell him I was ringing London.

A woman answered the number Mitchell had provided and told me to wait when I asked her the pre-arranged question. Mitchell was on the line within a couple of minutes.

'This had better be important, James. This is a secure line, not for social calls.'

I explained it wasn't a social call and that I was still following the David Ménière connection.

'But he's dead, isn't he?'

'He is, but he didn't kill Lisette Perron. I have an alibi for him being in Paris. Can I ask you something?'

'Go ahead.'

'Did she mention Ménière by name when she contacted your department?'

He asked for a minute so he could grab the file. I heard him rattle open a filing cabinet then leaf through papers before he picked up the handset again.

'She doesn't name him, or anybody for that matter. She only says that she's found something which might interest us.'

'So she might not have been referring to him at all. It could be someone entirely different.'

'It's possible, I suppose. But two spies in that little corner of France? Hardly likely. We're waiting for a fuller report from the French authorities, though they have their hands full at the minute so it might take a week or two. If anything turns up, I'll let you know.'

I thanked him and hung up.

Not likely, Mitchell had said. But possible.

I joined Pascal outside his door. He was talking to the mayor and grimaced when I walked out. Sitell tipped his hat, then glanced at the policeman.

'Good evening, Monsieur Given. What are you doing here?'

'I came to have a form signed by Monsieur Jaubert. British paperwork, I'm sure you understand.' I tapped my breast pocket. 'He did so then very kindly let me use his desk to complete the rest so I can pop it in the post on my way home.'

There seemed to be little point in getting Pascal in trouble by telling the truth, and I was pleased I'd thought of a story so easily on the spot. Sitell nodded.

'We try to be helpful, monsieur. Perhaps you might like to walk with me part of the way? I believe you'll be going in my direction.'

I had to agree and needed an excuse to leave him before we reached the post-box.

'You and your wife are settling into our little town, I assume?'

'We are, very well thank you. People are very kind to us as strangers.'

'I hear you've taken up my suggestion to attend Mass.'

'Indeed, I've found Father Guen to be a good man and we've met several new friends. Though I don't think I've seen you there often, monsieur.'

147

'I'm afraid I'm not a regular attender. I'm so busy, even on Sundays. I go whenever I can,' he laughed, 'more often in an election year. That's why I went to the christening — a grandchild of a good supporter.'

The callousness of his remark made me dislike him as much as most of the other politicians I'd known. Behind his friendly face lay an operator, a man wanting to hold on to the power he'd managed to attain, like his kind the world over. I hadn't known him long enough to know if he had principles or if he was just in the job for the pay and the control it gave him over people's lives. I hoped it was the former. It annoyed me he'd had the gall to ask about my politics, yet he immersed himself in it virtually every day to achieve his ends.

As we approached the Bar du Marché I spotted my cards partner, Daniel, and waved. He gestured for me to join him. Normally I'd shake my head and walk on. Instead, I stopped and turned to the mayor.

'I'll let you go on, Monsieur Sitell. I need to speak to my friend inside for a few minutes. It has been good talking to you.'

Without giving him time to reply, I shook his hand and dashed away to swing open the door into the warm sanctuary. Inside, despite the smoky fug, I breathed a deep sigh of relief.

Without waiting to ask, Daniel made a beeline for the bar, refilled his own glass and ordered a Diabolo Menthe for me. Only a quarter of the tables were occupied, all by men with cigarettes trailing smoke which hung like clouds below the ceiling. The wallpaper pattern was drawn in dark relief where fumes had condensed in brown tar.

Daniel brought the drinks over to the corner and we chatted for fifteen minutes, long enough for Sitell to be well out of sight. I thanked my friend for the Diabolo and said I'd see him on Thursday for our game, then was heading for the door when Louis Décast came in.

'Afternoon, Louis. Glad I've bumped into you. Could I have a word?'

I sat him at a table and bought him a beer. He downed half on his first gulp and wiped the froth from his lips with the back of his hand.

'I was ready for that, Monsieur Given. How can I help?'

'I've spoken to Francine Charbonne.'

'And?'

'She seemed to have no hard feelings towards Lisette.'

'You asked her directly?'

'Well, no. I mentioned your wife and she had nothing but good to say about her. If she doesn't know about the affair, what's the point in stirring it up? If she had known, I'd have expected her to tell me to mind my own business. The only regret she appeared to have was that they were not as friendly as they once were.'

'She told you that?'

'Yes.'

Décast laughed out loud. 'They were never friends, not really. Lisette would be nice to everyone and some people would misunderstand. That's what happened with Francine. When she first arrived, they met at a couple of functions and next thing you know Francine is inviting Lisette round for tea, or out for a walk. Lisette went once or twice but quickly pulled away. She said there was something about Francine she didn't like.'

I asked what it was, but he said he didn't know, just that his wife told him Francine gave her the shivers.

'Are you sure she knew about your wife and her husband?'

'I can't be one hundred percent certain, but Lisette hardly kept her activities secret. Not even from me. One thing I'm certain of is you can't believe everything Francine tells you. I've known her for years. She's a liar and a good one. Butter wouldn't melt in her mouth.' He swigged the remains of his drink and I bought him another.

'Tell me about your wife, Louis. Anything at all that might explain her murder.'

'I don't think I can tell you any more than I told Pascal, but ask your questions and I'll give you everything I know if it helps find who killed her.'

By this time the bar had filled up and before I could ask even one question, two of Décast's friends joined us, taking the other seats at our table. There was now no chance of a private conversation. I'd told Rachel I'd only be half an hour and it was close on an hour already, so I left, with a promise I'd be in touch in a day or two, then headed home.

SIXTEEN

A few days later, I'd just left through the back door when I heard a knock at the front. Rather than walk back through the house wearing my boots, I shouted for the caller to wait, then nipped round the outside to find Marie-Clair on the doorstep. She waved a notebook above her head.

'My parents have known Madame Perron for ages, since she came here.' She tapped the notebook. 'I've written it all down.'

'Then you'd better read it to me while we walk. I've work to be done.'

She looked down at her recently polished shoes, then pulled a face. 'Back to the far field?'

'I'll do that later. Come through to the barn. I need to repair some boxes and resharpen my hedge-cutting tools first.'

Marie-Clair followed me the forty feet across the yard, making me grin each time she tip-toed around animal droppings. Inside I dusted down an old apple crate and bowed. 'Please take a seat, milady.'

'Hmm. There's no need to be nasty just because I didn't want my shoes dirtied. I had a real telling off yesterday from my mother after I'd been down that muddy track. Do you want me to tell you what my parents said about the librarian or not?'

I apologised, still smirking, and asked her to go ahead. I started to sort damaged boxes from a pile stacked in a corner and laid them to one side as she flipped open her notes.

'Madame Perron was born in Vieux-Croix, though her parents only moved here two years before she came along. She had two older brothers, but they were killed in 1916, within a month of each other, her father also killed a year later. She was serving in London in the army at the time. When she came back, her mother never got over their deaths and committed suicide about ten years ago. So tragic.'

A story I'd heard many times. The French suffered terrible casualties in the last war, military and civilian, and there'd be few villages or towns where they'd not lost a number of young men and women. Even across the road from my house a small stone tablet listed the names of five men, two of them brothers, who'd perished in the first skirmishes.

'So she was left on her own? When did she marry Louis?'

'They married nine years ago. They were quite old, don't you think?'

'Not really.' I wasn't about to concede that one. Rachel and I were older than Lisette Perron when she and Louis Décast tied the knot, and we'd been married less than a year.

'According to my father, she'd lived alone until she met her husband, though she had a succession of boyfriends. Dad said he thought she was quite attractive but then Mum frowned, so he added "for a librarian".' Marie-Clair flipped through her notebook. 'She had a couple of jobs as a typist when she came back from the war then took over the library after the last person retired.'

'Did your parents know if she had any enemies?'

'Well, not enemies as such, but plenty of people who might hold a grudge.'

'Like who?'

'Men she'd dumped, women whose boyfriends she'd stolen.' The girl screwed up her face. 'There were quite a few of those.'

I finished with the boxes, noting what repairs were needed, and moved to the bench to lift my billhook. Malo had shown me how to sharpen it, pushing a cigar-shaped stone along the blade edge time after time, on one side, then the other until it was honed to perfection. At least that was the theory. Only time would tell if I could reach the level he had over sixty years. I fixed the implement in a vice and started the job then turned my attention back to Marie-Clair.

'Anyone with something more than a broken heart or hurt feelings?'

'Not that they could think of. My father said the same as Pascal: she was a librarian, how many enemies could she have?'

'Well, she had at least one, didn't she? Someone who wanted her dead.'

'I still think it was her husband.'

'And his alibi?'

'Easy. We only have his word he left when he did. He could have fixed the car earlier, driven to the bridge to meet and kill Madame Perron, then gone straight to his customer. My father said it would only have taken him fifteen to twenty minutes to get to Évran from there. I bet if you asked the car owner he'd not be able to tell you exactly what time Monsieur Décast arrived. It would have to be before quarter past four for the husband's alibi to stand up. Have you spoken to his customer?'

'Not yet. It's quite unusual, and exceedingly dim, for someone to provide an alibi which they know can be checked. Most criminals are stupid but rarely that stupid, and Louis didn't strike me as unintelligent. He'd need some brains to figure out his timing and to leave the car out of sight. Jennifer saw none near the bridge. Still, you have a point, and I'll explore it when I've an hour to spare. For my money I still believe Louis. From what everyone says, including your parents, our Lisette Perron liked to run around, and Louis knew this when he married her. Why should he snap over yet another fling?'

'What about the will?'

'Nothing worthwhile in it. He already has his own house and a decent, steady business. He'd hardly kill her for such a small amount. I've known men kill for less but none with a few shillings already in the bank. I think we're looking at someone with a stronger motive than money. We just need to find that motive and we'll have a clearer view.'

I pushed the sharpening stone one last time along the blade, wiped the edge with a damp rag and moved to the door to inspect the tool in daylight. Satisfied, I turned to Marie-Clair.

'I'm sorry, but I really do need to get on with this hedge now. Do you have any more to tell me?'

'That was about it. My parents couldn't think of anything remarkable about Madame Perron, even though they'd known her a long time. But what about the other suspect?'

'Who?'

'The lady from the boulangerie, Madame Charbonne. You mentioned in your note that Louis Décast pointed the finger at her.'

'He did, and I spoke to her. She seemed blissfully unaware of her husband's dalliance, though Louis has thrown some doubt on her truthfulness since then. I'll need to think more about her. For now, we'll have to look more widely.'

'Well, my parents gave me a list of the people they thought were Madame Perron's friends, so I'll see if they have anything to add. If I'm not sure about any of them, we can arrange for you to talk to them too.'

'That's a good idea. If you hear anything to give us a lead, dig a little if you can. I'll call to see you late tomorrow and you can tell me what you've found.'

It took me the rest of Tuesday afternoon to finish the gap in Malo's hedge, and he'd found another on the other side of the farm which also needed fixing. I started work on it but hadn't finished before dark and had to return again next morning. I asked Rachel to let Francis know I'd miss our get together for coffee and to tell him I'd be in touch to rearrange.

After lunch, Malo and I spent the remainder of the day sowing cabbages in one of the fields and potatoes in another. Heavy work, and I felt like collapsing in front of the fire when I'd finished but knew Marie-Clair would be rapping on my door if I didn't keep my promise to call to see her. I washed, changed and trudged into town hoping my exhaustion would lift enough to make the effort worthwhile.

Marie-Clair's mother smiled when she opened her front door, then invited me in and took my topcoat, pointing to the dining room I'd been in last time.

'My daughter is waiting in there, monsieur.'

I turned go through, but she touched me on the forearm. 'May I ask you something?'

'Of course.'

'This policing, is it a suitable career for a young woman?' She glanced towards the door of their sitting room. 'I ask because my husband does not approve; he says he does, but I know that deep down he wants more for her. Yet Marie-Clair is so determined it is what she wants. They argue about it all the time.'

I shrugged. I wasn't sure what she meant by "more". Why should being a police officer be seen as more or less worthy a career than teaching, commerce or the legal profession? 'All I can say, Madame Levaux, is that your daughter seems an intelligent girl with an enquiring mind, both good qualities for an aspiring detective. If she joins the police, she'll see a side of humanity which most people are shielded from and, yes, from time to time she'll face danger. On the other hand, if your husband stops her following her dream you may lose her.'

I thought back to my own youth, when I was even younger than Marie-Clair. The arguments with my father about his vision of my future and how it differed from mine. The slipping away in the night, leaving a note and hard feelings, to sail from port to port for a decade. We'd made up later, but the resentment on both sides still bubbled up from time to time.

The mother put her hand to her mouth. 'I tell my husband this, but he does not want to listen. He says she must become a teacher or a wife.'

'Then you must try to convince him. Your daughter won't be satisfied by living her life through a home, a husband and a string of children. She may make a very good teacher, but she'll also make a good detective if she puts her mind to it.'

Madame Levaux nodded and opened her mouth to reply when Marie-Clair popped out her head.

'Oh, it's you, Monsieur Given. I thought I could hear voices. Do come in.'

I followed her into the dining room, glancing back to catch a worried smile from her mother before I closed the door.

The table in the middle would have seated a dozen in comfort, half as many again at a push. Marie-Clair offered me an ornate chair with a maroon velvet seat, took one opposite and flicked through her notebook. She was halfway through before she stopped.

'I've spoken to a dozen people supposedly friendly with Madame Perron. Most of them knew no more than my parents. Some less. One or two told me to clear off, that I shouldn't be asking questions about the dead. Not a single one of them likely to be a suspect.'

'And how could you tell?'

'They … they all seemed so nice and helpful. Even the ones who wouldn't say anything weren't nasty about it.'

'Have you checked what they told is true?'

The girl hung her head. 'No.'

'Then we can't be sure, can we? I've known killers you wouldn't suspect in a million years. Decent and honest on the outside but deep down simmering with hatred. Remember what was said of Francine Charbonne, "butter wouldn't melt in her mouth".'

'Sorry.'

'No harm done. But if you become a detective, you'll need to look beyond how people appear and what they say. Never take anyone at face value. Now, did you find anything new at all?'

'Only in relation to Madame Charbonne. One of my mother's friends knows her quite well. She said Madame Charbonne told her she thought her husband was being unfaithful but didn't know who he was seeing.'

'So she knew he was having an affair?'

'Seems like it, and it wouldn't have been hard for her to guess who with. Madame Perron has quite a reputation.'

'And we can believe the person who told you? She couldn't have been trying to put us off the scent?'

'I don't think so. I've known her all my life, and my mother is very fond of her. Despite what you've said about ignoring appearances, I can't see her as a killer.'

'All right, we'll accept, for now, that she's telling the truth. If you write down in detail everything you've learnt, we'll pass it to Pascal.'

'Like an official report?' Marie-Clair beamed, and I laughed.

'Just like an official report. Do it now and I'll take it to him on my way home.'

For the next ten minutes I sat thinking whilst she wrote. We had another suspect, but the motivation was flimsy if everyone knew what Lisette was like. It might have made sense for Francine Charbonne to take revenge against her husband, but why should she do so against a serial man-hunter? If the wives of all Lisette's conquests wanted to do the same, she'd have to stand in a very long queue indeed. No, what was behind this was a much stronger reason. Self-preservation? Money? Jealousy? What if the killer wasn't local? It appeared Lisette had lived in Vieux-Croix most of her life, but was there anything in the woman's past, something from her time in London perhaps, that might have prompted her murder?

Marie-Clair held up a sheet of paper. 'I've finished.' She laid it on the table again, signed it with a flourish, pressed blotting paper on it a final time, then handed it over. I skimmed through and nodded when I reached the end.

'Well done, Marie-Clair, it's very thorough. Put it in an envelope and I'll drop it into the police station.'

Pascal Jaubert had just locked his office when I arrived. He looked at his watch.

'Good evening, Monsieur Given. You are looking for me?'

'I am.'

'Is it urgent?'

'Not particularly. I can come back tomorrow if you've finished for the day.'

He consulted the watch again. 'No, you are fine as long as it won't take too long. I am visiting my mother for supper, and she doesn't like to be kept waiting.'

'It should only take a moment. I thought I should tell you what I've been doing in relation to Madame Perron's death.'

He turned the key in the lock and swung open his door. 'You'd better come inside and take a seat. I have a feeling this may take more than a minute or two.' He took his seat beneath the tricolour, waved me to the other chair and folded his arms. 'Please go ahead, monsieur.'

I talked him through my discussion with Doctor Hodin, and Pascal confirmed the doctor had passed the new information to him. I also explained I'd spoken to Louis Décast again and whilst there was some doubt about him, I was sure he was unlikely to have murdered his wife. Taking out Marie-Clair's report, I went through it with Pascal, point by point, whilst he made his own notes. He looked up when I'd finished.

'Not really much to go on, is there, monsieur?'

I had to agree. 'Other than Francine Charbonne's knowledge of an affair between her husband and Lisette, I'm afraid you are right.'

'But she didn't exactly lie, did she?'

'Not exactly. My concern would be that she didn't react at all negatively when we talked of Lisette. When she seemed to be regretting a lost friendship, I assumed she just didn't know about them. Now we know that she did. Will you interview her?'

The policeman leant back in his chair and thought for a few seconds. 'I won't interview her, as such, but I will have a word. I've known Francine a long time. Well enough, I hope, to be able to tell if she has anything to hide.' He checked his watch again. 'Now, is there anything more?'

'No, that's it, but may I ask you a question?'

'Of course.'

'Do you mind me investigating this?'

He rubbed the back of his neck with the tips of his fingers. 'Not at all, monsieur. We have agreed. You are an experienced detective, and I am just a lowly village policeman. In time, I suspect you will cause trouble for me with Monsieur Sitell, but you're not, for now at least, charging round like a bull in a china shop, and any waves you and Marie-Clair are creating are only little ones. As long as you keep me informed, all will be well. Now, I really must be going or else my mother will have fed my supper to her dog.'

SEVENTEEN

The evening had turned wet and windy, with hailstones rattling down in frequent showers. I had my collar turned up and hat brim turned down as I hurried through the square towards my weekly card game. As I passed the boulangerie, a voice shouted from above.

'Monsieur Given, is that you?'

I peered through the rain to see Francine Charbonne leaning from an upstairs window. I raised a hand. 'It is, madame.'

'Could I speak to you for a minute? I'll be down in two ticks.'

True to her word, the bell on the shop door tinkled in less time than I'd have thought it possible for her to get downstairs. She waved me in.

'Come inside, monsieur, it is a terrible night.'

I didn't hesitate.

The shop smelled of flour and sugar and lavender. I guessed the lavender was Francine. It felt eerie to be in the shop with empty shelves and racks, and only a half light filtering down from the stairs leading to their living quarters. The air was thick and warm, heat left from earlier baking retained when the doors were closed and windows shuttered for the night. I'd only been in once or twice but then it had been bright, with baguettes stacked on shelves and beautifully crafted delicacies displayed on trays.

'How can I help you, madame?'

'I had a visit today from Pascal Jaubert.'

'Oh?'

'He said you believe I had something to do with Lisette's death.'

'Did you?'

Francine frowned and then went behind the counter. She scrabbled in a drawer, pulled out matches and lit a lamp on the wall. The yellow glow cast deep shadows, making the room even ghostlier than before. She said nothing until I repeated the question.

She shook her head. 'No.'

'Then why did you pretend you were friendly with Lisette?'

'Because I was friends with her once.'

'But not since you discovered your husband was having an affair with her.'

'What?'

'Your husband was seeing Lisette Perron; you found out and decided to get rid of her. Is that how it was?'

She grabbed the edge of the counter and squeezed until the white showed through on her knuckles. I may have assumed too much after all.

'No. I didn't. I wouldn't. Lisette? You're telling me Lisette was the woman he was seeing? I knew he had some floozy but didn't know it was her.' She let go of the counter, relaxed and looked me directly in the eye. 'That explains it all.'

'Explains what?'

'After Lisette was found dead, Gerard stopped going out in the evenings. He'd usually take the dog out for an hour, or at least that's what I thought. Instead, he began coming home after ten minutes then sitting in his chair staring at the fire. He even started bringing me little presents. Flowers, chocolates, even a scarf one time. Must have realised I was all he had left.'

I asked where she'd been at the time Lisette died.

'I usually close the shop at three o'clock on Saturday. It takes me half an hour to tidy and clean, then it depends what I feel like. That day I'd had a stinking cold, so I took to my bed for a couple of hours. I took some linctus and slept until Gerard woke me with a coffee at around five o'clock.'

'He was with you?'

'No, no. I'd popped into the back to tell him I was going to bed, then he came up to check on me later.'

'So he can't verify you were there, and you can't verify he was there?'

'I suppose not, but why would I need an alibi? There's no reason for me to want Lisette dead, I've already told you.'

Did I believe her? I wasn't sure. I asked to speak to her husband.

'Gerard would usually be in the bakery at the back at this time —' she pointed to a door behind the counter — 'but he is out this evening. He has gone to a restaurant in Tréfumel to discuss a large order they have for a wedding. I don't know when he will be home. It would be better if you come back in the morning. Say, six o'clock?'

My knees wilted at the suggestion of such an early hour, but I said I would.

'And Monsieur Given…'

'Yes?'

'I'll be having a word with him before then.'

The bakery was stifling, as might be expected, when I walked through the side entrance, even though the world outside was still dark. Gerard Charbonne, shirtless, stood between a long table and two ovens, using a large wooden paddle to unload baguettes through the open door of the smaller one. He looked round when I greeted him.

'I'm afraid we're not open yet, monsieur, not for another couple of hours.'

'Yes, I know. I don't need the shop, it's you I want to see. Didn't your wife mention I was coming?'

'Haven't seen her. I only arrived home an hour ago,' he laughed. 'I was with a customer last night, and he has an excellent wine cellar. We finished our business over dinner, and it was a bottle or two lighter by midnight, so he put me in a spare room to sleep it off.'

'So she hasn't spoken to you?'

'No, I expect she's still asleep. I came straight in here.' The baker lifted a tray of bread from one oven shelf and moved it to a lower one. 'Please forgive me if I don't stop; these will burn if I leave them.'

I told him to carry on. 'I'm working alongside Pascal Jaubert, looking into Lisette Perron's death, and need to ask you a few questions.'

He lay down his paddle. 'I'm not sure what I can tell you. It was very sad, but I didn't know her well.'

I laughed. 'I hope that's the story you'll stick to when you speak to Madame Charbonne later.'

'What do you mean?'

'You should know by now there are no secrets in this village. You were having an affair with Lisette. So why are you lying?'

Gerard stuck his hands in his pockets and looked at the floor. 'Why do you think? I wasn't about to shout it from the rooftops, was I? Not if I wanted to keep it from Francine.'

'Well, I'm afraid it's a bit late for that now, Gerard. If Lisette hadn't been murdered, then your wife may never have found out. As it is, she has, and you're in big trouble.'

'Murdered? Lisette?'

His surprise seemed genuine, but then feigning it wouldn't have been difficult.

'So, let's go back to the beginning. How long were you seeing Lisette?'

'About a year. We'd had a couple of dances at a Christmas function, then hooked up a few weeks later. The middle of February, I'd say. I finished with her a month before she died.'

'Are you sure? Your wife said you kept going out at night right up until Lisette was killed.'

'I'd just got into the habit. I used to take the dog for a walk every evening. If I was calling on her then he'd get tied up in her garden, if not then we'd wander round for an hour. Got me out in the fresh air away from this place. After Lisette went, it knocked the stuffing out of me. We'd finished, but I was still fond of her.'

Gerard started taking bread from the oven again, shaking his head when he saw how brown the baguettes had become. When he'd finished he lifted the whole batch into a wicker basket and carried it through to the shop. On his return, he opened the second oven, peered inside, closed it again then sat on the edge of the table.

'They'll be fine for a while. You know, Monsieur Given, I've had a lot of time to think about Lisette since she died. I love my wife. I really do, but there was something about Lisette, something that made me feel young and alive. You're married?'

'I am. Less than a year.'

'Then perhaps you won't understand. When a couple have been together for a while, they fall into a pattern. Monday is chicken, Friday fish, Saturday the market, that kind of thing. The unexpected goes out of their relationship. Lisette was different every time I saw her. You'd never know what she would say or do. So full of life. And she read all the time in her job, so her head was full of new ideas, day after day.'

'You do know you weren't the only one?'

'Of course, but it didn't matter. It wasn't love; it was friendship. I knew we weren't going to be together for ever. I didn't want it and neither did she. It was good while it lasted.'

I asked Gerard where he was when Lisette was killed. He rubbed his chin, then repeated the same story as his wife. Gerard said even though the shop was only open for three hours on Sunday morning, there was still almost as much work to do as other days, with patisserie expected for lunch and brioche needing to prove overnight. He'd watched his wife go upstairs then carried on working until he took her a drink at about five.

'When we were sitting down to dinner, a neighbour knocked on the door and told us the news. I felt physically sick, and it took a massive effort not to give my feelings away to Francine. It was then I decided to try to treat my wife better, perhaps bring a bit more fun back into our marriage.'

In a way I felt sorry for the man. I couldn't justify his affair, but I could see he loved his wife and may not have strayed if he'd been able to keep the same kind of excitement going with her as he'd felt with his lover. Or maybe this was just an excuse from an unfaithful man who thought he saw the greener grass.

With both the Charbonnes now as possible suspects, and each providing the alibi for the other, there was no more I could do until I'd gathered something concrete on one of them.

EIGHTEEN

I was thinking of Gerard Charbonne's words about the routine of his marriage when Rachel and I walked down to the village on Friday night. We'd married on a Friday and every month since had gone out for the evening to celebrate. Nothing too elaborate, just an hour in the bar of the Hotel la Conche, a bit longer if we bumped into friends. She'd take a glass or two of wine, I'd stick with my soft drink, and we'd chat, happy to be out of the house for a while in each other's company. It struck me that although this *had* become a routine, like the baker had described, it was one I enjoyed. It cemented our friendship, not weighed it down. A night we both looked forward to.

We walked through the small foyer and nodded to the owner's wife at the reception desk.

'Good evening, Madame and Monsieur Given, lovely to see you again. We are quiet this evening; you'll have no trouble finding a table.'

The family-run hotel only had around a dozen rooms, but the bar had an opulence suggesting the builder had dreamt of a grander future. Its windows, wallpaper and tiled floor sang of the age when it was designed fifty years earlier, and successive occupants had maintained the quality of furnishings in keeping with his vision.

I left Rachel in one of our usual plush chairs near the fireplace and went to the bar. There were only two other couples, at tables as far apart as it was possible to be, and a man slumped at the bar. He'd a half empty glass of what looked like cognac in front of him, and from time to time he'd laugh then cry into his palms. In another time and place, he could have been me. Gaston Nouel, the present owner, gave me my drinks, shook his head in reference to the drunk, then tugged him by the sleeve.

'Robert! Time to go home, don't you think?'

The man lifted his head and squinted at Gaston. He mumbled something I couldn't quite catch, then lay down his head again. The barman tugged his sleeve once more. This time there was no response, so he came round the front and lifted Robert to his feet, supporting him with an arm round his back.

'Come on now, off we go. These nice people don't want you spoiling their evening, do they?'

I sat down with Rachel as the two wandered, crab-like, through the double doors and into the night, leaving us giggling at the sight.

Ten minutes later, Gaston returned, held up his hands and apologised for his absence. 'Sorry, folks. Our friend Robert Renan enjoyed himself a little too much this evening. He's safely home now, though I wouldn't want his head in the morning.'

We finished our drinks and I went to the bar to order more. Gaston poured them and pushed them across.

'I can only apologise about Robert again, James. He's had his troubles lately. Been hitting the bottle a bit.'

'Poor man. What sort of trouble?'

Gaston grunted. 'What do you expect? A woman.'

What he'd mumbled before Gaston took him home then made sense.

'Was it Lisette Perron?'

'It was. Mad about her, he was, but she couldn't be bothered. He'd come in here night after night talking about her, how he'd been to the library and asked her out again and she'd refused. Then she died, and he's been a mess ever since.'

'In what way?'

'He comes in after work, drinks without eating, then rages about how she'd go out with any number of other men but not him.'

'Does he know why?'

'Not that he's said. But you can see why, can't you? His obsession is creepy. I wouldn't have gone out with him either if I was her.'

I asked if Renan was ever violent. 'Got into fights? That kind of thing.'

'Not in here, I wouldn't allow it. He's a decent man when he's sober, but I heard he had a girlfriend when he was younger, and he'd be rough with her when he'd taken a drink. I think she moved away because of it.'

Another customer came to the bar, so I went back to Rachel and told her what Gaston had said. She asked the obvious question.

'Could he have attacked the librarian, do you think?'

'I don't know. I'll need to have a word with him, I suppose. It seems unlikely if he's only violent when he's drunk, but they could have met, and she could have said something to tip him over the edge. Perhaps Lisette told Robert why she didn't want to go out with him and he didn't like it.' I lifted my glass. 'Anyway, don't let this spoil our evening, plenty of time for me to follow it up tomorrow.'

Marie-Clair hovered round my market stall on Saturday morning until there was a quiet moment between customers. She'd squeezed the fruit, sniffed the potatoes and weighed vegetables in her hands for half an hour, with the air of a young woman seeking the best quality and value for her weekend purchases. Each time I served someone Marie-Clair had waved the next customer through, waiting for a gap so we could talk privately. She asked if I'd found anything new, so I told her about Robert Renan.

'I agree with what you were told; he does seem creepy.' She glanced towards her house. 'Give me five minutes. I'll ask Mum if she knows anything.'

Marie-Clair hurried across the square and round the corner. When she came back, she had to go through the same performance as earlier until I was clear of customers again.

'You'll be getting a reputation as fussy if you keep this up. Did your mother have any information?'

'She confirmed what Gaston Nouel said. There was a young woman he went out with a few years ago, and it was rumoured Renan gave her a black eye one night when he got drunk. Her father went round and gave him a good thumping afterwards, but she went to live with an aunt in St Malo. Mum also said she seemed to remember him being locked up overnight for fighting more than once when he was in his twenties.'

'That shouldn't be too hard to check. I'll ask Pascal to look at his records.'

'Do you want me to do it? I don't mind.'

'No, I'll nip round when I've finished here. He may come by anyway; he sometimes does, to show his face to the stallholders. Are you free later?'

'I have to do some shopping for my mother, then homework, but I'll be at home in half an hour.'

We agreed I'd call at her house when I'd talked to Pascal. I spent the rest of the morning, when I'd time between customers, making notes on what we had so far.

After lunch, Rachel was none too pleased when she heard of my plans for the afternoon.

'But you've been out all morning, James, from first light. Do you have to go?'

'I was hoping to see Pascal Jaubert at the market, but he didn't show, so I need to go to see him. Then I'll need half an hour with Marie-Clair, that's all. I'll be back before you know it.'

Rachel scowled. 'You're spending more time with that young woman than you are with me these days. Not that I blame you.'

I knew better than to laugh. 'What's that supposed to mean?'

'She's young, pretty and intelligent. What more could a man want?'

Now I did laugh, then reached across the table and took her hands. 'A man, as you put it, has all that he wants in you. More than pretty, more than intelligent. Perhaps not so young…'

A smile flashed and Rachel slapped my hand.

'Just as long as you're not thinking of running off with her. I don't want all these stories of extra-marital affairs putting ideas in your head.'

'I'm not thinking any such thing. You're the one who asked if I'd help her, and I promise that's all I'm doing. The girl is keen to learn, and it now seems we have some kind of case for her to practise on. I'm happy to stop if that's what you want.'

'No. I know you have to find who killed the librarian if you can; you'll not find any rest until you do. Though I do wish you could leave it to the police so I could have you back again. It's just me feeling neglected.'

'Well, I'll be as quick as I can, then we'll take a walk when I get back. Happy?'

'Hmm. Ecstatic.'

'Robert Renan? I know him a little. A decent man. Why do you ask?'

'He was in the hotel bar last night, Pascal, so drunk he had to be helped home by Gaston. It seems he's hit the bottle hard since Lisette Perron's death.'

'Guilt?'

'I don't know, perhaps. I heard he can be violent.'

Pascal went to a filing cabinet in the corner, searched through the second drawer and extracted a folder. He skimmed the two or three sheets in it as he sat at his desk again. 'What you have heard is true: he got into trouble when he was younger. He spent a couple of nights in the cells for fighting, but he's no criminal record. There was also a complaint from a girlfriend, but she withdrew it when she moved away. He's never been in trouble whilst I've been in the job. I suspect, like many of us, he grew up.'

'Well, it sounds like he had a serious fixation on the librarian. Crying into his glass because she wouldn't go out with him.'

'Do you want me to have a word?'

'Not yet. I'll ask around. See if there's any more to it than a sad man who's lost the girl of his dreams.'

Fifteen minutes later, I was in Marie-Clair's dining room with our notes spread across the table. In one column we had all we knew about the victim, then one for each of our possible suspects. I told Marie-Clair we needed to add another to this group.

'My contact in London said Lisette hadn't named David Ménière in her report. We know he'd met her, and asked some suspicious questions, but he also had an alibi for the time she died. We'll call the new person Mister X for now.'

'And now Ménière's dead so not really a suspect.'

'That's not strictly true. I agree we can put him to one side, but alibis are broken all the time. He's the only one we've found with a motive not related to her love life, he had much more to lose than the others, and was probably committed and desperate enough to kill someone for what he believed in. Suppose he had someone pose as him at the Paris hotel, leaving him free to dispose of his accuser over here? If he was part of a network of spies, it would be in all their interests to assist him in avoiding detection. For my money, without the alibi, he'd be top of the list.'

'It's interesting when you look at it that way, isn't it? It's so easy to follow the obvious and ignore other possibilities. See, for me, I'd have gone for each of the suspects as they arose, the evidence looked so compelling at the time. With your experience you see other things.'

Marie-Clair walked round the table, rearranging the slips of paper in Lisette's column. She looked up.

'You know this will become more difficult? It's a small place, and everyone knows by now that you're looking into her death as murder.'

'It is a problem. Some people will clam up to protect themselves or their neighbours, some will invent stories just for the attention. Either way, we'll have our work cut out. How much time can you spare from your studies? More importantly, how much time will your father let you have?'

She told me she was on top of her studies and not to worry about her father. 'He might rant and rave, but it's only for my own good he does it. As long as he can see I'm working, he'll let me do what I want with my free time. So what shall I do?'

'First we'll try to make sense of all these notes, then decide who we need to look at further. After that, I'll have a clearer idea of the next steps. We'll start with the victim: what do we know about her?'

Marie-Clair scanned our papers then stood, straight-backed, hands clasped behind her like she was reciting for her teacher or the court. 'Lisette Perron. Aged 44. Librarian. Reconsideration of evidence by doctor suggests she was hit on the head then dumped in the river to make it look like an accident. Last seen about quarter past four and found dead about six o'clock. She was in contact with the British authorities. Known to have had a string of lovers, some of whom were married.'

'Good, well done. So far we've four men, one woman and a possible sixth person of unknown sex on our list. Correct?'

Marie-Clair double-checked the material on the table, counting the names on her fingers. 'Agreed. David Ménière, Robert Renan, both Charbonnes, the husband, and Monsieur or Madame X.'

'We also have to keep in the back of our minds the possibility it was someone from outside the area who we've no information on yet. Let's put that to one side for now until evidence turns up to point in that direction. How many of them have alibis?'

'Two if we discount the Charbonnes. David Ménière and her husband, Louis Décast.'

'Then the first thing to do is check those. I'll contact Louis Décast's customer. Will your parents allow you to use their telephone?'

'Of course.'

'Then you call the hotel in Paris. Give them a description of Ménière and ask them to confirm. Tall, blond, well-built. Say you're my secretary and we're just checking because it would be unlike my friend to have been there and not made contact.

If they're reluctant to give information, tell them I'm worried about him because he hasn't appeared at his next destination, but I don't want to contact the police until I'm sure. That should loosen them up. A tip for you there: any mention of the police usually oils the wheels. As for the other suspects, do we need to look more at Robert Renan?'

'I thought Pascal said he'd not been in trouble for years.'

'That doesn't mean he couldn't have snapped if Lisette gave him the brush-off again. He was in a pretty bad way about her when I saw him. I'll call on him and ask a few questions. Next?'

'Francine Charbonne. Says she was in bed when Lisette was killed, but no-one to confirm it. Claimed not to have known her husband was seeing the librarian. She did know he was seeing someone and appeared surprised when you spilled the beans. Could she just be a good actress?'

'Good point, but that applies to all of them, doesn't it? No-one has put up a hand and admitted to being a murderer. She'll stay on the list. You ask around about her. Did anyone see her on the street between the time Lisette was last seen and when her body was discovered? Has she spoken to anybody about Gerard's affair? Try not to make it too obvious; we don't want her neighbours becoming alarmed about her. At least not without good cause.'

Marie-Clair asked me to wait a minute whilst she scribbled in her notebook. When she finished she removed her glasses, cleaned them with the edge of the tablecloth, then put them back adjusting the arms so they sat squarely on her face. She shook her head almost imperceptibly.

'It's all so thorough, Monsieur Given, yet I can't help thinking it's a waste of time. I believe Gerard Charbonne is our man.'

'On what basis?'

'Just a feeling. He was the last to have an affair with Lisette Perron and may have been concerned his wife suspected.'

'But how would killing her have helped?'

'Perhaps if he finished with her, as he said, she threatened to tell his wife.'

'We can't rely on "perhaps" or hunches. These guesses only work in the end if they're backed up by evidence. Especially if it goes to court.'

'He has no alibi.'

'No, he doesn't, so we'll keep him on the list too until he can be excluded. We'll both keep asking questions to see if anything else turns up.' I ran my finger along the shortest column. 'And that leaves us with our mystery man.'

'Or woman.'

'Right, or woman.'

NINETEEN

As promised, after I returned home, Rachel and I rambled through Malo's orchard then across the fields down to the river. The apple trees were heavy with pink, sweet-scented blossom and we watched stock-still whilst two hares boxed in their spring courtship ritual. I avoided the temptation to walk all the way to the bridge, knowing Rachel would accuse me of using our walk as an excuse to do more investigating. I risked this again on our way home when I called into the Hotel la Conche for Renan's address, but she just gave me a look and a shake of her head.

Gaston didn't want to give it to me at first, saying the man would be in the bar by five o'clock and I could catch him there. I explained I'd prefer to talk to Renan in private and before he'd had a drink. I also said I'd make the request through Pascal Jaubert if it made it any easier. He gave me the address.

I couldn't leave Rachel again on Saturday, nor next morning, so it was early Sunday afternoon before I could look for Renan. His house was about ten minutes' walk from the market square, on a lane behind the church. Stone built and tidier than I'd expected, it stood slightly back from the road with a well-tended front garden boasting lavender and tightly pruned roses. There was no answer to my knock at the front door. I cast an eye up and down the road to check for curious neighbours and, seeing none, I nipped through a side gate and round the back. The rear garden was as cared for as the first but laid out with apple trees, fruit bushes and a recently weeded vegetable plot. Renan wasn't there, nor did he appear at the back door after I knocked.

Although I'd wanted to catch him when he was sober, I had no alternative but to return the way I'd come and ask in the watering holes for him. There were only three and I tried the hotel first. Gaston hadn't seen him.

'He's not been in since Friday. Maybe his head was so sore he's learnt his lesson. I thought he'd have shown up after you came yesterday but he didn't. Have you been to his house?'

I told him I'd just been and there was no sign of him. Gaston promised to contact me if Renan showed up. The second bar was one I didn't use — not for any reason other than a slight preference for the others. The owner, Marcus Viellard, hadn't seen Robert Renan either.

'Not been in for weeks. Wouldn't have him in anyway, he was in such a state when he drank. Used to come in often, have one glass of wine and a chat then go home. Fine, decent man. Hardworking and good company but hopeless with drink in him.'

'He started drinking heavily?'

'About three weeks ago. Switched from the wine to cognac, and not just one glass but as many as he could pour down his throat before he passed out. Once the alcohol kicked in he'd start raving about that woman.'

'Lisette Perron?'

'That's her, the one who died. They're saying you think she was murdered, is that right?'

I nodded. 'Possibly.'

'Either way, Robert was hit hard by it. He'd been chasing her for years, but she wasn't interested. Don't know why, he's a good man, most of the time, and well-set-up. He got drunk a couple of times and I took him home. The third time he did it

I went round and told him not to come back until he sorted himself out. I heard he'd started going into Gaston Nouel's place. You tried there?'

I said that I had, thanked him for his help, with a promise to call in again, then made my way to where I played cards on Thursday night. So we had a mild-mannered man, who two bar owners said was decent and hard-working but had started drinking when the librarian was killed. Did the fact he became so agitated when he was drunk show he had sufficient passion to lash out when angered and kill someone? Was his drinking just remorse at Lisette's death? Or guilt, as Pascal suggested?

Martin Absil, the owner of the Bar du Marché, had nothing further to offer. Renan rarely used his place, but Martin knew him well enough and confirmed the man's usual nature. I asked him, the same as the others, to let me know if he saw Renan.

'Will do, James. Did Louis Décast find you?'

'No. Was he looking for me?'

'Popped in last night. Asked if you'd been in. I told him you're only usually here for your cards on Thursdays. Said he'd something to tell you but he'd catch you at some point.'

I left the bar and wandered home to a relaxing lunch and a quiet afternoon by the fireside.

Rachel had been gifted a chicken by Malo and cooked it in the Breton style with cider, leeks and mustard. Later we settled by the hearth, each with a book. Every month, Sarah, my sister, sent a parcel of second-hand novels she'd found in junk shops and rummage sales, and this potluck approach had expanded my reading habits. Our brother, Eli, had started the treats and she'd continued when he joined the army. Two things I missed from England, without doubt, were my daily newspaper and my wireless. I'd buy *Le Figaro* once a week, but it wasn't the same. My French was much improved, but the constant effort of translating less common words made it more of a chore to read than a pleasure. My current book was *The Lost World*, a tale of fearless exploration by Professor Challenger and his followers into the unknown regions of South America. I had just approached the high point in the action when there was a tap at the door. Louis Décast stood outside. I invited him in.

'No thanks, monsieur, I just called round to pass on something I heard. I thought you might find it useful.' He looked sheepish. 'I also hoped it might get me off the hook.'

'In that case, I think it might be better if you *do* come in.'

I swung the door open and gestured to a seat. Rachel gave me one of her looks, slowly closed her book and went through to her music room. Before I'd even poured coffee for Louis and me, the strains of a Mendelssohn violin concerto were wafting over us. We listened for a few moments to her soulful playing until Louis broke the spell.

'I told you Francine Charbonne's husband was having a fling with Lisette?'

'You did, and I've spoken to them both. He seems to have no motive to do her harm, and Francine didn't know about the affair with your wife.'

'Is that what she says?'

'Yes.'

'And you believe her?'

'I have no reason not to. She seemed upset to hear about it.'

Louis snorted. 'Well, she's lying. I told you not to believe anything she said.'

'How do you know?'

'Because a friend overheard them arguing about it.'

Twenty minutes later, we were on the doorstep of a terraced cottage in the oldest part of the town. The woodwork looked recently painted, and the row of pots filled with sprouting geraniums suggested it would be pretty in a month. I recognised Clementine Theroux from the market, but we'd never spoken other than the minimum needed for her to buy her vegetables. I'd noticed she sorted through every box before she chose, whether looking for size or freshness I didn't know. She also always paid the exact sum, often made up of a large number of single centimes, as if she saved them just to pass on to me at the weekend.

In her mid-fifties, thin to the point of under-nourished and wearing clothes of decent quality, though I'd have guessed not new, she had the look of a woman who lived on her own or with a man who didn't take much notice of her appearance. Clementine scowled down her pinched nose and asked Louis what he wanted.

'Tell him what you told me, Clem, about Lisette and Francine.'

She popped her head out into the street and glanced in both directions, then spoke so quietly I had to lean forward to catch her words. 'They were fighting. Just outside the library.'

'Fighting?'

'Well, not throwing punches, just insults.'

I asked her when it was.

'It would be about a week before Lisette Perron died. The registration of my husband's business was due for renewal, and I'd been into the Mairie with some papers. They stamped them in the office, so I could check the date if you like.'

'Not just now, maybe later. Did you hear what the row was about?'

'I didn't hear how it started, only how it ended.'

'And how was that?'

'I came round the corner and Francine was very red in the face, waving a fist at Lisette. She warned her to stay away from the husband, Gerard, or else she'd do her some harm.'

'Those were her exact words?'

'Well, perhaps not exact, but close enough. Lisette looked frightened and dashed back into the library. Francine gave me a filthy look when I walked past then went off in the direction of the bakery. Disgraceful, if you ask me, two grown women acting that way in the street.'

'Have you mentioned this to the police?'

The woman wrapped her arms tight around her and shook her head. 'I didn't think anything of it until Louis said you were asking questions. I'm a woman who keeps herself to herself and doesn't go stirring up trouble where it's not wanted. Now, is there anything else?'

I clarified the time and place she'd seen the argument and tried to drag from her more details of what was said, but she came up with nothing clearer. We said our goodbyes and she stayed at her door whilst Louis and I walked to the corner. When we turned and were out of his friend's sight, he stopped.

'Does this take my name off your list, monsieur?'

'In what way?'

'Am I still a suspect?'

'How do you know Madame Theroux?'

'I can't remember how we met, but she's been a friend for many years. A widow, her husband died of influenza just after the war. He'd been gassed in the trenches, weakened his lungs. Why?'

'Because we don't trust alibis from long-time friends. How do I know the two of you didn't concoct this tale between you?'

'I wouldn't. I've already told you where I was. I only took you to see Clem because I thought it might help.'

'You can say that, and I might believe you, but you see the problem I have, don't you? Until I can confirm your earlier story with your customer, you'll stay under suspicion. Even if that lady is telling the truth, it doesn't mean Francine Charbonne took it any further, only that she was lying to me.'

Louis crossed his arms and sighed. 'In that case, I don't know what I can say to you, Monsieur Given. I didn't, and wouldn't, hurt Lisette.' He spit on the ground. 'Stupid as I am, I still loved the woman. She treated me so badly, but I was mad about her from the minute we met, and never got past that even though I knew she was cheating on me all the time.'

I'd see this often in cases. Someone discovers they're a prime suspect and finds it hard to accept the police don't simply accept their story at face value. They fully understand that not everyone tells the truth but are shocked when they're not believed.

'Don't worry, Louis. I'll be making a call to your customer in Évran soon, and if you did deliver that car when you said then you'll be in the clear. If you didn't, you, me and Pascal Jaubert will need to talk again.'

I left him worrying on the street corner and made my way home.

Thunder and gales rattled our bedroom windows for half the night, and it was near dawn before the worst of the storm blew through. I dragged myself downstairs and made a pot of tea, taking a cup up to Rachel before venturing out to the yard. It was still pouring, and everything which hadn't been tied down was scattered to the four corners or clattered back and forth on the concrete. On the horizon lightning sparked, and outside the thick walls of the house I could hear rumbles in the distance. With every one, the cattle in the shed by Malo's home moaned and bellowed. I went back inside to drink my cup and throw on a layer of heavy waterproofs.

Rachel got up and prepared breakfast while I checked the cows. It was just a case of ensuring they'd done no damage to their stalls or themselves during the night, then clearing their straw. After a quick hose down of the floor and the bedding being replaced they were ready for Malo's sister to come down to milk them.

After I'd eaten my breakfast of bread and blackcurrant jam, I walked the boundary of the farm, making sure the hedging had survived the night and noting where repairs might be needed before the next storm arrived. I was pleased to see the section I'd fixed had stood up to the night's battering. Malo farmed fifty acres split into a number of fields, so my walk around all the hedges took over an hour. Though not as big as some farms I'd seen in England, it was a decent enterprise built up over the years, with the two houses, two barns, the cowshed, an orchard and duck pond. As well as the arable crops and cattle, he kept pigs, chickens and a couple of goats. The place was never quiet, smelled like you'd imagine a farm to smell, and I loved it.

The rain had eased by the time I got back towards the house, and the job had been unpleasant, with deep mud in places, so treacherous I almost went down on my seat more than once. Before going home, I knocked at Malo's back door. He poked out his nose.

'Filthy out there, James.'

'It is. Are we still sorting out those two fields?'

'Not today,' Malo grunted and looked skyward, 'nor for a few days to come, I'd say.'

I told him I'd been round the boundary and it was all still in decent condition.

'Then there's not much else we can do today. Just keep on top of the usual jobs, and we'll get to those fields as soon as we can.'

Lightning flashed again, with a clap of thunder barely seconds after. The farmer pushed his door to close the gap.

'Seems like it's back, James. You get home before you're drenched again.'

As was the way at this time of year, the rain gushed for another hour then rainbows appeared with the sun breaking through retreating clouds. The afternoon was glorious and fresh. Rachel had two students planned, an older couple who'd played the violin as children and wanted to take it up again. I wasn't in the mood for their racket or conversation so made my excuses when they arrived and went for a walk.

I slipped and slid down the field opposite my house until I reached the road at the bottom, where I turned to follow it to the river. The spot where Lisette had been discovered was now even more churned than when I'd examined it, the result of curious villagers wanting a peek now the word was out her death might be more than an accident. I leant on the bridge wall for a few minutes, listening to the water gurgling beneath, and wondering why such a public spot could be a scene for a murder without anyone noticing. Perhaps its visibility was why the librarian had chosen the place, then she'd been unlucky that no-one was about when her assailant struck. If she had wanted the protection of being in view, why hadn't she simply arranged to meet in the market square or the café? Maybe she thought the bridge was far enough out of the village for it to look like a chance meeting to a passer-by. Or maybe she wasn't expecting to meet anyone on the road after all. If that was the case, how did the encounter result in her murder?

Beyond the bridge the other bank was as chewed as the one opposite, and there'd be nothing new to be found there, even if the swollen river hadn't scoured everything three feet above its usual waterline. I crossed the road and followed a path into woodland, where the afternoon rays shone through rows of poplars and birds trilled above my head in blatant courtship. A hundred yards in it was darker, and I had the same feeling of being watched I'd had when Marie-Clair and I were examining the riverbank. I stopped on the track and listened, but there was nothing to confirm my suspicion so I walked on, faster than I had before. I almost jumped out of my skin when a man stepped out from behind a tree, blocking my path. At least six inches taller than me, with tanned, grimy skin, long greying hair and an even longer beard, he'd have been threatening even in the centre of a town. He wielded a three-foot-long branch in his right hand.

'What you doing here?'

I swallowed hard. 'Just taking a walk, monsieur. Do you mind?'

'Don't want no-one wandering round my woods.'

'Your woods? You're the owner?' I thought this unlikely.

'I live here.'

'I'm sorry, I didn't know. I had no intention to disturb you, monsieur.' I nodded towards his club. 'So could you put that down?'

The man looked at the branch as though it was the first time he'd seen it, then dropped it to his side. 'Can't be too careful. Don't like people sneaking around.' A wide grin split the tramp's face. He dropped his weapon and stuck out a filthy hand. 'I'm Bertrand, Bertrand Fasquelle. I live here. Where do you live?'

'In the village. My name is James. How long have you had a home in the woods?'

Cracked, dirty, nails scratched his cheek. 'Ages. Two summers, maybe three. Do you want to see my place?'

'It would be a pleasure.'

The big man loped away down the track. For a moment I considered turning and running back in the direction I'd come, but then good sense overwhelmed the fear and I followed. If he'd wanted to hurt me, he'd have done it already. After a couple of minutes, the path veered sharply right, close to the road, then swung back into a small clearing with a ramshackle timber structure hard against the trees on one side. A fire burned quietly in a circle of stones in the centre with an iron pot suspended above it.

Bertrand dragged a log end from the edge of the clearing and placed it opposite one by the fire. 'Sit. Please.'

I did as he asked and looked around. He'd chosen his space well, amongst one of the clumps of firs which had sprung up unplanned within the plantation. The evergreen canopy offered shelter from the worst of the elements, and the needles underfoot kept ground cover at a minimum. Just beyond the clearing the firs gave way to the planted woodland, with good lines of sight in all directions. Bertrand constantly scanned the whole area whilst we sat. His shelter wasn't large. Big enough to lie down in with a small space to store a few bits and pieces, but if he wanted to live in the open air it was as much as he needed. He poked the fire with a stick, scattering sparks high in the air, then stood and peered in the pot. A loud crack rang in the forest behind Bertrand and he rushed to look out between the trees, then returned to the fire.

'You seem nervous, monsieur.'

'Can't be too careful, never know who's out there.' He poked at the fire again. 'Bad men, sometimes.'

'Bad in what way?'

'Over there —' he pointed towards the kink in the path — 'I saw one. Looking out. Then he went and hit the lady and put her in the water.' Bertrand shook, his eyes darting in all directions. 'Don't want him coming after me.'

'It's alright, Bertrand, he won't come now. There are two of us.'

The man seemed to take some comfort from this and began collecting sticks to build up the flames under his pot. 'You'd like a drink?'

I thanked him but said I wouldn't bother. 'Tell me about the man, Bertrand. Can you say what he was like?'

'Bad is all I know.'

'What did he look like?'

'Couldn't tell. His back to me then too far away. Lady had a bicycle, but he threw it over the bridge.'

'Was he tall, like you? Or smaller, like me?'

He stared at me for a moment then jumped up and backed away. 'He was like you. Same hat, same coat. You're the bad man, come to kill me.'

'No, no, Bertrand, I'm not him, believe me.' I stood. 'Look, I'll go away if you want me to. I'll do you no harm. I just want to know more about that man.'

The childlike smile appeared again. 'You're not him. You'll not hurt Bertrand.'

'I won't. Did you see where he went?'

'Watched him looking into the river, then he walked back up the road on the other side. Bertrand went down to the water when he was gone, but lady wasn't moving. Came back here and hid for a long time. Heard car and voices. When went out again, lady and bicycle there no more. Will Bertrand be in trouble?'

'I don't think so. You did nothing wrong. The woman was found by the police, so no harm done.'

We talked for another half an hour about his life on the road. In his simple way he told me he'd lived with his elderly grandparents in a cottage in the countryside until they died. He'd never managed to keep a job, and when they'd gone he'd had nowhere to live so set off rambling. The poor man survived on what he could gather in the woods and the charity of shopkeepers.

I left him with a few francs of small change and a pledge to visit him again. As I made my way up the hill to the village, I wondered who it was he'd seen. One thing was now certain beyond any doubt. Lisette Perron had been murdered.

TWENTY

Though Bertrand Fasquelle had described Lisette's killer as a man, he'd been too far away for it to be taken at face value, and, at the edge of the woods, the person had their back to him. Could it be a woman in disguise? I'm not tall, and the clothes I wear are nothing out of the ordinary, so it wouldn't be difficult to look like a man of my build. With this in mind, I thought it still relevant to keep Francine Charbonne on my list.

Before calling in to see her, I caught Pascal at the police station and told him what Bertrand said he'd witnessed.

He scratched his head. 'It doesn't really take us any farther forward, does it? You were already convinced Perron had been killed, and the ravings of a man of the woods are hardly likely to make me change my opinion. What are you asking me to do?'

'You could go to talk to him yourself, then decide if what he's saying is worth consideration. Also...'

'What?'

'The poor man is scared he'll be in trouble because he didn't tell anyone what he saw. You can perhaps put his mind at rest. After that, you might keep an eye on him from time to time, make sure he's fed and healthy.'

'I'll take a trip when I've a minute tomorrow, but I'm not promising to become his nursemaid. I'll leave that to the likes of you.'

We spoke for another few minutes of how life on the road would be difficult for the likes of Bertrand, and when I left Pascal he wore a smile which told me he might go a little further than his bluster suggested. It took me only a couple of minutes to walk round to the boulangerie, where the bell jangled on the door, bringing Gerard Charbonne from the back to the shop counter. He stopped when he saw it was me.

'I hope you've come to buy bread, monsieur, not to cause more trouble between man and wife.'

'Trouble in what way?'

'Don't pretend you don't know. You told my Francine that I'd been seeing the librarian. Who gave you the right to put a wedge between us?'

I snorted. 'I think you'll find it was you who put the wedge there, Gerard, when you couldn't keep your trousers on. As for having a right, I'm looking into the murder of your lover, and neither you nor your wife have a plausible alibi. I may not be a policeman any longer, but I have Pascal Jaubert's blessing to ask questions.'

'Well, she's not talking to me anymore and has kicked me into the spare bedroom. She's even taken herself off to Dinan today, shopping, and left me to look after the baking and the shop. Says she'll make me pay for what I did.'

'She's not here, then? It was Francine I wanted to talk to.'

'No, I told you, and I don't expect her back until evening, if at all. She's a sister up there and may stay if her temper doesn't calm down.'

I couldn't fathom why his wife had suddenly decided to take it out on Gerard. If Clementine Theroux's evidence was correct, then Francine had known weeks before I spoke to her. Was it part of a sham to make me believe she hadn't known about the affair? Or could she only be concerned that it was becoming public knowledge he'd cheated on her?

'There's no point talking to her, you know, Monsieur Given. Francine wouldn't have anything to do with killing Lisette. She wouldn't hurt a fly.'

'You've already told me she's in a temper, Gerard.'

'That's with me, and she's done nothing physical. Just decided to hit my pocket, that's all. Francine was here all day. In the shop in the morning and in bed all afternoon.'

'But you didn't see her. No-one did.'

'No, but I'd have heard if she went out. There are only two ways. Out through the bakery, and I was in there, or out through the front, and I'd have heard the bell. Like I did when you came in just now.'

He was right, I'd heard it myself when I opened the door. I turned and looked up. The mechanism was straightforward, a bell hanging from a large, coiled spring fixed to the top of the door. I pulled the door open once or twice and it rang each time, exaggerated by the swollen old wood catching on the frame. It might just be possible for someone to reach with a stick to prevent it ringing, but they'd not be able to guarantee success. If Francine couldn't get out that way, and would have been seen taking the other exit, then I'd perhaps accept her alibi. For now. But why did she lie?

'Even so, Monsieur Given, she'd have no reason to take revenge on Lisette.'

'Why not?'

Gerard stared at the floor. 'I didn't give you the entire truth before. I didn't finish with Lisette, she finished with me. She tried more than once, and I wouldn't let her. We'd leave it a day or so, but I'd go and knock on her door and she'd have me back. Then one evening she didn't; she left me standing in the street. I caught her at the library, and she said we couldn't carry on. She was seeing someone else, and it would be difficult if he found out she was seeing me as well.'

'Difficult in what way?'

'Lisette didn't explain. I assumed it might be someone she thought would be jealous.'

'And she didn't tell you who it was?'

'She didn't. Lisette was no angel, been with a good many men in the village — and beyond. It could have been anyone.'

So there was another man to find. Another to add to the growing list of Lisette Perron's conquests who might not take her promiscuity lightly. If it was true, it took the spotlight off Robert Renan because he, at least, wasn't having an affair with her.

'Well, you put your thinking cap on, and if you come up with a name let me know. In the meantime, tell your wife to meet me at the police station on Wednesday at two.'

Marie-Clair sat opposite me at my kitchen table. There was a small, red, leather-bound diary between us, with the year 1940 embossed in gold on its cover. She'd arrived at my house with it in a brown paper bag shortly after I'd returned from talking to Gerard.

'And you found this in Lisette Perron's belongings? You broke in?'

'I couldn't help myself, monsieur. I'd been thinking of all the affairs she'd had, and the idea came to me she must have written something down. I'm sure I would if it were me.'

'I sincerely hope you're not considering such a course of action, young lady.'

Marie-Clair blushed. 'No, monsieur, certainly not. I was just trying to put myself into this woman's head, that's all.'

The thought of this young woman exposing herself to danger in this way caused me to speak more sharply than I should have. 'A good idea, but it doesn't warrant burglary, does it? I asked you not to put yourself in danger. God knows what harm you might do, to yourself or to others who don't deserve it.'

'It wasn't really burglary. The kitchen window wasn't shuttered, and it was ever so easy to lift the latch then climb in. Anyone could have done it.'

'Well, let's hope your cousin, Pascal, takes the same view if he hears about it. So what did you find inside?'

'The house wasn't at all what I'd expected. Old, needed quite a good coat of paint and tidy up outside. Bit of a dump, really. I've only ever really seen her at work, so I thought there might be lots of books, but there weren't, only a few, and they were all borrowed from the library. I also thought her bedroom might be full of colourful drapes and cushions, like you'd imagine a loose woman's to be. It was a bit like my own, very boring.'

'What does that tell you?'

Marie-Clair groaned. 'Not to pre-judge people?'

'Correct. That's the way to wrong conclusions. Get an idea in your head then make the facts fit. Bad police officers do it all the time. Good ones try not to. Anything else?'

'Not that I could see. If we knew nothing about her, I'd have thought the house was lived in by an elderly spinster with a boring life. I half expected to find two or three stinky cats wandering about the place. The only thing of interest was this diary.'

'You've looked through it?'

Marie-Clair smiled sheepishly. 'Of course. I had to decide if it was worth bringing to you, didn't I? There are entries on most pages, but mostly they're as dull as everything else in her house. It's only the one on the day she died that might be relevant.'

I picked up the journal and flicked through to the date three weeks earlier when Lisette's body was found. Marie-Clair was right. In normal circumstances the three entries probably wouldn't have prompted a second glance. The first was a list of groceries to be collected, the second a reminder of a delivery of books. It was only the third, an appointment, which was of any interest. In the librarian's neat hand was written: *Afternoon. Meet for explanation.* No specific time and no name.

'What do you think, monsieur? Is it important?'

'I don't know. It takes us no further forward, though, except to confirm she was meeting someone, and it was planned. She didn't just bump into a random passer-by who killed her for no good reason. It was someone she knew, and she knew them well enough to remember without naming them in her diary.'

'So what will we do now?'

I wrote the contents of the page on a fresh sheet of paper, checked it through, then pushed the diary back to Marie-Clair. 'You'll take this to Pascal, explain what you've done, and hope he lets you off because he thinks the information is worth the crime. As soon as I've time, I'll go to the mayor and ask if he has any idea who his librarian might have been meeting that afternoon.'

It wasn't a task I was relishing. He'd politely told me to keep my nose out, and now I'd have to admit I'd continued to poke around. There'd also be the problem of keeping Marie-Clair out of trouble. All I could hope was the politician in him would keep a lid on his displeasure.

I pushed open the door to the police station and found Francine Charbonne frowning on a chair. Pascal waved through the window of his office, then popped out his head.

'I'll be five minutes, then you can come through.'

The boulangerie owner tutted. 'As if I've nothing better to do.'

The policeman went back inside, and Francine turned to me.

'What have you brought me here for? I've a shop that won't run itself.'

'You managed on Monday, though, didn't you? Went shopping, I hear.'

'Can't do it twice in one week, though. Anyway, you've not answered my question.'

'And I'm not going to, not yet, though I think you can guess. We're waiting for someone else, then we can talk when we join Pascal.'

On cue, Marie-Clair breezed in. 'Good afternoon, Monsieur Given —' a nod to Francine — 'Madame Charbonne.'

'What's this child doing here?'

'This child, as you put it, has been assisting me and Pascal to investigate our librarian's murder, and she's been making a decent job of it too. Very decent for one who is only learning the ropes.'

Marie-Clair beamed and took a seat as far away from the other woman as she could. We waited in silence broken only by Francine's fidgeting feet until Pascal called us into his office, asking me if I'd drag another couple of seats through. When we were settled, he addressed Francine.

'Thank you for coming in, madame. Doubtless you're aware Monsieur Given and Mademoiselle Levaux have been making enquiries around the death of Lisette Perron?'

'I am aware, yes, and this man has caused serious distress in my house as a result.'

'For that I may owe you an apology. But we'll see. Firstly, my friend here needs to ask you something.' He swung an open palm in my direction by way of invitation.

'You say, Francine, that I have caused a problem for you and your husband. However, this wouldn't have happened if you'd bothered to tell me the truth.'

'What? Where have I lied?'

'You told me you weren't aware of your husband's affair with Lisette Perron.'

'I wasn't. I didn't know it was Lisette he was seeing, only that he was up to something. I was shocked when you gave me her name.'

'That is what you said, and your very fine acting made me believe you. Now I know you were seen warning her to keep away from your husband.'

'Now, wait a minute. I didn't kill the woman. I threatened her, but I'd never have followed it through.'

'So why did you lie?'

Francine glanced at Marie-Clair, then Pascal, whose raised brow said he wanted an answer, then back to me. 'Because I was scared this would happen. I discovered Lisette was the one and I went after her. We argued, then she was dead a few days later. How would that look? I even had to pretend to Gerard that I still didn't know. It was a blessing really when you let slip her name, thinking I already knew. At least then I could get back at him.'

I nodded for Pascal to take over.

'You're sticking to your story you were in bed when Lisette died?'

'Of course. I can't prove it, but I was.'

'Then I think you can go for now, madame, but if we find you've not been truthful again, it will be the worse for you.'

The policeman scribbled a few notes, closed his pad and stood. We also got up, but he asked me and Marie-Clair to wait, then led Francine to the door. He said a few words before she left through the outer door, head bowed.

Pascal didn't bother to take a seat when he came back in. 'I went to see your man in the woods, Monsieur Given, and I'm afraid he's gone. Traces of his fire were there, still smouldering, so I'd not missed him by much. I looked around, but there was no sign. He could have been anywhere.'

Another piece of bad news. I'd liked Bertrand, even beyond feeling sorry for him, and now we'd chased him from his home. I thanked Pascal for trying. I had my appointment with the mayor, so he let us out to the hall. Marie-Clair didn't turn to go home.

'Did you believe Madame Charbonne, monsieur?'

'Well, it wouldn't be the first time I've heard her reason offered for lying to the police. People are funny, and some of them even think we're stupid. They imagine they can tell a story and not be found out. If Louis Décast hadn't been so keen to get himself off the hook, she might have got away with it. I'm still inclined to believe her story, though, so unless we can find some stronger evidence Francine was involved, we'll take her word. You keep your ear to the ground, though I doubt anything will turn up. She's just been silly, that's all.'

I've always found self-important men to be more difficult to access than really important ones, and so it was with Alain Sitell. I couldn't imagine what would keep the mayor of a small commune so busy, but it had been day and a half before he could "squeeze me in" as his clerk had said.

The mayor sat, as he had last time I was there, behind his desk, which was now covered with files. He rose briefly, nodded when I was shown in and waved the back of his hand across the stacks. 'Paperwork, Monsieur Given, the bane of my life. Hmm. The cross I have to bear, I suppose.'

I wasn't sure if he was saying this just for effect, perhaps as an excuse for why he'd made me wait so long. Another boost to his ego, or was this the life of a minor cog in the vast French machinery of government?

'I remember it well, monsieur; police work has much the same problem.'

'I imagine it does. Still, all that is behind you now, isn't it? So, what can I do for you today?'

'The diary of Madame Perron has come into my possession.'

The mayor raised an eyebrow.

'It would be better, for now, for me not to say how I received it. However, it contains little of interest other than one entry which you may be able to help me with.'

'Me? What would I know of her diary?'

'Only as her employer, monsieur. The item appears to be an appointment, and I wondered if she might have discussed it with you.'

'Well, she would occasionally, but I can't see what this has to do with anything. I thought we'd agreed Madame Perron's death was an accident and you were to leave it to the police to deal with.'

I leant back and rested my chin on my knuckles. 'By chance, some small issues have arisen which suggest it might not have been accidental. Each, in themselves, not conclusive, but taken together they add up to something more sinister. I've presented what I've found to Monsieur Jaubert, and he's agreed I should ask some questions and keep him informed every step of the way.'

'Pascal has allowed this?'

'I have to say he has not encouraged it, but he has seen, as I'm sure you do yourself, monsieur, that it would be wrong to stick with one conclusion if new facts suggest an alternative. Please do not blame your police officer. I can be a little stubborn when I take a scent. Old habits die hard, as my wife likes to tell me.'

'Then I suppose you'd better show me what you have. I wouldn't want to stand in the way of an experienced detective like yourself.'

I took the sheet of paper from my inside pocket, unfolded it, and passed it across the desk, pointing to the relevant entry. 'It is this one which is puzzling me. You'll see it is quite vague, but it is the afternoon she died. Madame Perron was clearly supposed to meet someone. Would you know who?'

Sitell ran his finger across each line of the page until he'd read it all. 'This final entry refers to a meeting she had with me.'

'With you, monsieur?'

'Yes. Lisette ... Madame Perron ... had some changes planned for the library, and we'd agreed to talk about them.'

I asked him about the plans.

'This building was erected over a hundred years ago and lacks some modern amenities, so the council has agreed to carry out improvements and to add a small extension for a larger reference section. The library also houses the history of our commune in its documents, and their safety needs to be considered if the war escalates. We met at two o'clock to discuss these things and finished about three. As far as I'm aware, she went back to the library afterwards.'

'Did you tell this to Monsieur Jaubert?'

'I may have mentioned it as the last occasion on which I saw her, but nothing more formal. As you know, he'd decided she'd simply skidded from the road so wasn't asking any questions. Is it important?'

'It's hard to say. When it comes to murder any detail can be important, no matter how insignificant. Was there anything she said or did to suggest she was meeting anyone else that afternoon? An indication that something was bothering her?'

The mayor stood and walked over to the window, gazing towards the church across the square. 'She said nothing. We talked about the plans over a cup of coffee. I said I was happy with her suggestions and she left. You need to understand, Monsieur Given, I liked Madame Perron, but we weren't friends, just colleagues. I wasn't her confidant, nor she mine.' He spun back and faced me. 'Are you certain she was murdered?'

'As sure as I can be.'

'Great God. This is a small town, and we all try to get along. How can such a thing have happened?'

'Believe me, Monsieur Sitell, murders happen everywhere, not only in big cities. All it needs is a spark to light the embers of hatred, and a life can be taken without a second thought. What we need to find is what that spark was and where the embers were lying.'

'Well, you'll have my full support if you're convinced a crime has been committed. I'll speak to Pascal and tell him you have my backing.'

I thanked him and stood to leave.

'Before you go, Monsieur Given, there's one more thing. Please understand that if you are proved wrong and have stirred up a hornet's nest for no good purpose, you will be looking for a new home. I do not like to be made to look a fool and will do everything in my power to make your life here very unpleasant.'

I nodded and left without comment. I wasn't sure Rachel would appreciate hearing this ultimatum.

TWENTY-ONE

After I'd tended to my morning jobs, Malo asked me to deliver a bag of vegetables to his sick aunt on the far side of town. The April sun warmed my neck as I ambled through the back roads to her house, and I was glad of the walk. He'd told me she'd be resting in bed, so I tapped at the back door, dropped the bag inside where she'd find it, then wandered back to the post office to buy some stamps. When I reached the counter, Monsieur Peston turned and lifted an envelope from the shelf behind him.

'Ah, Monsieur Given, I have a letter for you. It will save Henri's legs if you take it with you.' He handed it over after reading the front and back, showing, once again, how there can be no secrets in a village. 'It is from England. Your father, perhaps?'

I checked the handwritten address and told him he was right.

He smiled. 'I would make a good detective. Yes? Like you were before you came here.'

This gave him a springboard for his favourite topic, and he regaled me for ten minutes, as he did every time the subject came up, with his love of crime novels. Had I read this one, or that one? Each time, I told him I hadn't, feigning interest but having none. I couldn't grasp the fascination with his choice of reading matter. To my mind, those I'd attempted were so full of basic errors, lucky breaks or American tough-guy bravado as to bear no resemblance to the reality of detective work. When he finally paused for breath, I thanked him and made my escape with the letter and stamps in my pocket.

I waited until I'd arrived home to open the envelope, taking a kitchen chair outside to take further advantage of the sunny day. My father's letter had been posted a week before. He'd heard from his brother that I'd visited, and it seemed Anna had convinced him they should go to England. Papa had spoken to people at the synagogue and discovered what needed to be done to allow my uncle and his family over. There were forms to be filled in and undertakings to be made. He'd written back to his brother to explain and to say he would find friends to register as their sponsors. My father even offered to provide the required financial guarantee if Uncle Gideon couldn't manage it himself.

He used the rest of the letter for family news. Meat rationing had been introduced, and they were all finding it a little difficult. Mama was fine. She had a few more aches and pains and she'd had a bad cold but was over it now. Sarah, my sister, continued to do well at school. They'd taken in a Kindertransport girl before I left, and Meena was becoming a great asset in his workshop. My father had heard from my brother, Eli, now posted to Portsmouth and awaiting onward transit to northern France when more troops were needed. I knew this wouldn't be long now that the Germans had finally invaded Norway. Papa said he prayed every day for Eli to be safe and hoped I'd do the same.

Rachel came outside, her hands covered with flour. Every week I asked her to go easy on the cake baking, telling her I'd prefer to keep my newly slimmer self, and every week she'd ignore me with a peck on the cheek and an "even more of you to love". She asked me about the news from home.

'All's well in the main. It looks like my uncle is going to England after all.'

'You don't sound too happy about it.'

'No, of course I'm happy for him. It's just…'

'What?'

'It's just it's made me wonder if we should go as well. By all accounts Germany's army is massive, and they'll overrun France with no problem. They could be all the way over here in a month.'

'You don't think the British can help hold them back?'

'I don't see it. It's a long border to defend, and there's only so many troops they can send. The best bet would be if the Americans joined in, but there's not much chance of that.'

She crouched down beside me, laying her head on my shoulder. 'But I like our life here so much. I'd feel awful if we had to give it up.'

We sat in silence for a few minutes, then I kissed the top of Rachel's head.

'Let's not worry about it for now.' I stood and helped her to her feet. 'We may not have much choice anyway.'

My wife pulled away. 'Why's that?'

'Because the mayor gave me an ultimatum. Solve this crime or get out of town.'

'You're joking, James. What have you done?'

'Me? What have *I* done? I've had nothing but pressure from all sides to dig around in this little town's dirt.'

'Don't give me that. You were happy to go along when it suited you. And now we're in real trouble. I hope you're satisfied.'

She dusted her hands on her apron and stormed away, leaving me open-mouthed.

A few minutes later I followed my wife indoors, then went to check our fake papers were still safe where we could find them.

On Saturday morning my mind was still on how upset Rachel had been. She'd simmered all day and come round a little when we went for our usual jaunt to the Hotel du Conche, but her annoyance resurfaced as the evening wore on. When I began to tell her the latest I'd heard on the wireless about the war, she said she didn't want to talk about it, that she found it too upsetting. With this topic out of bounds and knowing that sharing my thoughts on Lisette Perron's murder would be inflammatory, we sat in silence for much of the evening, then continued in silence on our walk home. By bedtime we were talking again, though not warmly. She'd still been asleep when I loaded the cart to take to the market.

Early April had brought a wider range of fruit and vegetables, and my neighbour's counter glowed with bright red Gariguette strawberries, the first of the season. Their sweet scent was irresistible, so I grabbed some for Sunday. A peace offering. The over-wintered and stored produce was now complemented with fresh harvests from the south and would expand wildly over the coming weeks as new food came into season. Malo's first crops were in the ground and growing well, but we still only had cabbages, cauliflower, carrots, potatoes and apples grown or picked the previous year, plus eggs and milk, to fill our stall. Even so, it was a good display and I had a steady flow of sales all morning.

It slowed down at about eleven o'clock, and I was able to sit back and take a look around. I was tempted to tuck into the strawberries I'd bought but thought better of it. Everyone else seemed to share my idea of taking a break when the customers thinned, and small groups began to appear, some smoking, all chatting and joking. I'd have guessed there were two topics of conversation: the war and how business had been that morning. Eric, Phillipe and Daniel were in one of the gatherings and waved for me to join them. Before I could, I spotted a figure I recognised leaning against the wall on the far side of the square. The man was by the café, arms folded like he'd not a care in the world. It was Robert Renan.

I asked the closest group of stallholders to keep an eye on mine for a few minutes and wandered over to speak to Renan. When he spotted me he walked away, turning right at the first corner. I followed. At the next corner he did the same, into a long narrow street behind the Mairie. Despite the bright morning, tall buildings kept it gloomy and I shivered in the shade. He was a good distance in front of me and I guessed he'd turn again at the end, hoping to return to the square then give me the slip. I went back the way I'd come, knowing I'd be able to cut him off if I increased my pace. Sure enough, he wasn't in sight when I reached the square and still didn't emerge for a few seconds after I reached the corner. When he did, he almost bumped into me and the look on his face was priceless.

'What you want, monsieur, chasing me round the streets?'

'I wouldn't have been chasing you if you hadn't run away.'

Renan looked both ways along the street. 'Wasn't running. I ain't done nothing.'

'Are you sure, Robert? A little bird told me you were very keen on Lisette Perron, and last time we met you were drunk to hell, cursing her name for all to hear.'

He leant back and cocked his head. 'When did we meet? I don't know you.'

'You'd remember nothing in the state you were in. I sat in the hotel next to you last week. You were slumped at the bar, rambling about how Lisette always rejected you. Did you drink too much one afternoon and decide you'd teach her a lesson? Only it was more than that, wasn't it? She ended up dead.' If

I'd thought he'd looked surprised when he walked into me, it was nothing to how he reacted now. It was as if I'd slapped him.

Renan dropped to the pavement and put his head in his hands. 'How could you say that? Lisette was everything to me. I'd never harm her. I loved her.'

'I've no doubt you did, Robert, but she didn't love you back, did she? I can imagine how much it hurt, how you'd want to punish her. Going off with other men like that and not giving you a chance.'

'Never gave me no chance. Uglier men and ones not so well-set-up, she'd go with. Years I'd asked her out and always, "No, Robert, you're not my type. Let's just be friends." I didn't want to be no friend. Worth more than that.'

'As I said, I understand. So where were you when she died?'

'Away.'

I asked him where.

'I was in Vannes, picking up some tools. Man, there is only one this side of Paris that makes them. Left home after lunch, got back about eight.' He began to shake. 'If I'd been here, I might have stopped it.'

'Anyone to confirm what you're saying?'

'Gave my mate, Jacques Falon, a lift to his mother's in Gaël, picked him up again on my way back. Can give you the address of the bloke in Vannes if you like.'

I told him to do it, though it was unlikely I'd bother following him up. It was a two-hour drive or more each way and, combined with the companion for the first part of his journey, his alibi seemed pretty watertight. Renan clicked his fingers and pointed at me.

'You check with them; you'll see I was nowhere near. Anyway, it's not me you should be asking questions of. Ask that mayor.'

'Alain Sitell? What are you talking about?'

'That's him. Her boss. She was going with him when she died, and he's married. I'll bet he had something to do with it.' He laughed hoarsely. 'Never trust no politicians.'

TWENTY-TWO

I found Marie-Clair waiting for me when I came out of church on Sunday morning. She asked if I could go round to her house with her so she could tell me what she'd found. I looked at Rachel for approval and she shrugged.

'If you must, you must, James, but try not to be too long. I'll have lunch on the table in a couple of hours.' She nodded a goodbye to Marie-Clair then turned back to me. 'Please don't spoil it.'

Her tone told me she wasn't only referring to our meal. As Rachel strode away, I almost apologised to Marie-Clair and chased after her but knew I'd not rest until I'd heard what the girl had to say. My wife and I would need to sort out what was bothering her later. As I walked from the church entrance, Francis Guen called after me.

'James, wait a moment.' He caught up and asked Marie-Clair to give us a couple of minutes. 'Are we still on for Wednesday? You've cried off the last two weeks, and I wondered if it was something I'd said.'

'Of course not, Francis. I've been busy, that's all. Usual place, usual time? I'd welcome the chat.'

The priest glanced at Marie-Clair, then looked across the square at Rachel disappearing into the distance. 'I'd imagine you would. Hope it's nothing better suited to the confessional?'

It took me a second to catch his drift then held up my hands. 'Certainly not. Just looking for a chance to talk to a friendly ear.'

'Well, I think I can manage that. I'll see you on Wednesday.'

Francis shook my hand, bowed towards Marie-Clair and made his way back to the stragglers outside the church, all of whom, I'd bet, were wondering what was going on.

Marie-Clair took me through into the dining room again, where she had more notes added to those we'd been through last time. She lifted a small pile and flicked through them. 'These are all to do with Madame Charbonne.'

'And?'

'No-one I've spoken to has anything bad to say about her, and none of them saw her on the streets the afternoon the librarian was killed. I even asked in two of the shops which would have been on her route to the river, in case either had spotted her walking past, but they hadn't. I suppose you're going to say it doesn't mean she didn't go, though. Just that she wasn't seen.'

I laughed. 'You're right, I would have said that. But this time I think we can safely say Francine Charbonne isn't our murderer. We're only a small place and little is missed. What you've found seems to support what she's said. Did you find anything else?'

'I rang the Hotel de la Paix in Paris, as you suggested. It was good fun pretending to be someone else. The manager spoke to two receptionists and they both agreed the man named Ménière who stayed with them fitted my description.'

'So we take him off the list. It was a long shot anyway, once I'd had their letter.' I told Marie-Clair about the shop-door bell and Gerard Charbonne's admission it was Lisette who'd packed him in, not the other way round.

'So he might still be a suspect?'

'It's a possibility, but I doubt it's him. He doesn't strike me as the type to knock his girlfriend on the head with a rock.'

Now Marie-Clair smirked. 'I thought you told me it wasn't possible to tell a killer from the way they look or act.'

'Cheeky pup. Caught me out, though, didn't you? Keep looking for inconsistencies like that and you'll make a good detective. I suppose what I'm really saying is Gerard will move down the list, without being taken off altogether. Likewise Francine, though she'd be even further down. If anything turns up on either of them we can take another look, but for now we put our energies in other directions.'

We both turned when there was a knock at the door. Marie-Clair's mother pushed through with a tray of coffee and cake.

'I thought you two might be a bit peckish.'

I tried to refuse, patting my waistcoat, but she'd have none of it.

'Nonsense, Monsieur Given, what would your wife think if I didn't offer you a little hospitality?' She shot a look at Marie-Clair and all the papers on the table. 'I'm surprised my daughter hasn't already done it. Now, you tuck in. It looks like you'll need something sweet to get through that lot.'

I thanked her and we chatted about how I was settling into the village. She told me how pleased she was with her daughter's progress on the violin with Rachel's help and, having heard some earlier attempts, I could see how the family would be grateful for any improvement. After ten minutes or so, Madame Levaux left us and we returned to sharing information. I filled her in on my conversations with Alain Sitell and Robert Renan.

'Wow! So our esteemed mayor was another of Madame Perron's conquests. Does that put him on our list?'

'I imagine it does, at least until I can talk to him about it. Renan seemed certain enough but, then again, he's been drunk for the last month. He was also so obsessed with that woman he could be imagining anything. I'll see Pascal in the morning, and we'll talk to Sitell. I doubt he'll see me this side of Christmas without official police backup.'

'What about the victim's husband? Any news there?'

'I begged Malo to let me use his telephone yesterday and called Louis' customer in Évran. He confirmed Louis arrived with him mid-afternoon and they went drinking for a few hours afterwards. There's no way her husband could have been back if we have the right timeframe. Your friend saw Lisette around four and she was discovered dead soon after six, so that's fairly clear-cut. You don't think Jennifer could be mistaken?'

'Well, I'd assume she'd know when she caught the bus; they're only every couple of hours so a bit difficult to mix up. She'd have known Madame Perron well enough from the library to recognise her, even from across the road. Didn't Jennifer also describe her clothes, and they matched the ones she was wearing when she was found?'

I scanned our notes, now loosely sorted into "possibles" and "rejections", and massaged my forehead. 'I'm just clutching at straws here, Marie-Clair. We know someone did this, but for the life of me I can't make the connections.'

The church bell chimed twice, and I grabbed my watch from my pocket.

'Oh God, Marie-Clair, I'll have to be going. Rachel will skin me alive. I'll let you know what I've found when I've spoken to the mayor. You have another word with Jennifer and go through her story again, to check those times. I can't see it will do much good, but you never know.'

I threw on my jacket and left. By the time I'd dashed home, I was drenched with sweat and Rachel's face was like thunder.

Suspects were disappearing fast. Although I'd told Marie-Clair I thought Gerard Charbonne wasn't in the frame, there was no justification for this when I thought about it again. He'd been having an affair with the victim, and she'd thrown him over for a new flame not long before she was killed. His wife was a jealous woman, and Gerard would be concerned about her finding out. On top of this, he'd no corroborated alibi. He'd provided a story based on preparing the next day's bread, but I'd not a clue how long that might take or if it was even necessary to do it the day before. If it was, then he might even have paid someone to do it for him and keep their mouth shut.

Gerard had proved he could lie to both his wife and to me. He'd kept his relationship with the librarian secret for months and he'd told me he'd ended it, when it was his lover who had. I wondered what else he might not be telling the truth about. From his bakery to the river bridge would be a ten to fifteen-minute walk, so half an hour maximum there and back, plus perhaps another quarter of an hour to meet Lisette, kill her, then dispose of her body and bicycle. Francine saw him at about half past three, and Jennifer saw Lisette waiting for someone at a few minutes after four. Gerard could easily have left soon after talking to his wife and been home, baking, for half past four at the latest, in plenty of time to make a drink and wake her at five o'clock, as she'd reported.

Marie-Clair had asked around the village about Francine, and I cursed that I hadn't told her to enquire about Gerard at the same time. I decided I'd need to ask Pascal Jaubert to talk to Gerard as well as to the mayor.

Pascal was at his desk when I went in to see him after my early morning jobs that Monday. I filled him in on the reasons I'd had a look at the Charbonnes, Robert Renan and Louis Décast, and what I'd found to reject some of them.

'You've made progress, monsieur. We now know who *couldn't* have done it. Are you any closer to proving who could?'

I bit my tongue and didn't respond to his jibe. Instead, I passed on my latest thoughts about Gerard Charbonne. After I'd finished, Pascal folded his arms and rocked his chair back on to two legs.

'Is that it?'

I took a deep breath. 'Not quite.'

'Go on then, spit it out.'

'There's a small matter of your boss and the victim.'

'Monsieur Sitell? Tell me more. This is one I've got to hear.'

I got up to leave. 'If that's your attitude, Pascal, there's no point in me talking to you. I'll figure a way out of talking to him myself. Or perhaps I'll just leave the whole thing to you, then you can sweep a murder under the carpet if that's what you want.'

'Wait, Monsieur Given. I apologise. The mayor is, as you say, my boss and it seems so unlikely he could be mixed up in this I may have reacted inappropriately. Please sit. Please.'

A minor battle won, but all of this treading carefully was getting on my nerves. It wasn't simply an idle threat when I said I'd walk away, something I'd considered more than once.

'I'm not suggesting Monsieur Sitell had anything to do with Lisette's death, only that I've been informed they were having an affair at the time she died. I think you should ask him about it.'

'Who told you this?'

'Robert Renan.'

'Huh. Do you think it's sensible to take the word of a drunk, monsieur? Someone who was crazy about Lisette? So crazy he is jealous of everyone?'

'You've echoed my thoughts exactly, Pascal. But still, it's worth checking, don't you think? If Robert is mistaken, what's lost?'

Pascal's jaw dropped. 'What's lost? Only my career down the pan, that is all. I'll not be staying in this job long accusing my boss of cheating on his wife now, will I?'

'Then don't. Just get me in to see him and stand by my side when I ask him about it. You only have to tell him I have some new evidence and I'll only share it with him. You can pretend to be shocked when you hear what I say. At least you'll get to see his reaction. What do you think?'

TWENTY-THREE

Alain Sitell's face was as dark as the weather and my raincoat dripped on his carpet whilst he left me standing next to Pascal later that day. No more of the bonhomie of my earlier visits. This time his desk was clear, with nothing to distract from the power vested in his office. Even President Lebrun now seemed to be frowning down on us.

'Pascal tells me you have something you wish to discuss with me, Monsieur Given. Something so sensitive you couldn't reveal it to him.'

I'd no idea what the policeman had told him. When I'd left in the morning, Pascal had simply agreed he'd ask the mayor to see me urgently, without making any promises. He'd sent one of the village lads to fetch me and I'd dashed through the grey drizzle straight away. Pascal met me on the step and said I had ten minutes, not a second more.

'I have to lay my cards on the table, monsieur. I have heard a rumour that you were having … how should I put this … a liaison with Madame Perron at the time she died.'

The explosion I expected didn't come; neither did the iciness of a wary and calculating man. Instead, he chuckled.

'Really, monsieur, I'd have thought you'd be more cautious about what you believe in a small village. You have told me you were a detective in England, and I have checked. My sources inform me that you were well respected, but I cannot see how that can be if you make such a simple error. Who told you this?'

'I don't think it's such a good idea to say at this stage, monsieur.'

Pascal began to speak and I shot him a glance to stop, but not before the mayor noticed.

'Ah, so you've told Pascal?' A crocodile smile went the policeman's way. 'Perhaps he may wish to share the name with me later?'

'Quite so. He's completely at liberty to do that, but I'd prefer it if, as you say, you wait until we've finished.'

'I have no problem at all with that suggestion, monsieur. I assume this won't take more than another minute or two if you have no other questions.'

'I'm afraid you didn't exactly answer my last one.'

'I wasn't aware you'd asked one. You merely said you'd heard some tittle-tattle from a —' another glance at Pascal — 'so far unnamed individual that I was seeing Lisette Perron.'

'So, let me try to put it more clearly. Were you having an affair with the dead woman?'

This time there was a cough and a slight flush to his cheeks. He turned to the policeman. 'Perhaps Pascal might leave us for a few moments?'

'I understand you'd like to keep this private, monsieur, but I think I'd prefer it if he stayed. I'm sure you can see that in the circumstances what you have to say may be of interest to the police.'

'Yes, I *can* see that. And I don't want to hinder your enquiries in any way.' He indicated the two chairs by his desk. 'Please take a seat. Both of you. I apologise for not offering sooner, but I have a meeting and thought we'd be finished quickly.'

I removed my wet coat and sat next to Pascal, whose knee shook twenty to the dozen.

The mayor swivelled his chair in my direction. 'Before I answer, could I ask you a question, Monsieur Given?'

'Certainly.'

'You have not been in our country long, but you know a little of our customs, do you not?'

'I like to think so.'

'Then you'll know it isn't unusual for men in my position — men of importance or wealth — to take a mistress.' He chuckled again. 'It is almost expected of them.'

'And, for you, the latest was Lisette Perron?'

Sitell shook his head. 'No. Lisette was not "the latest", she was the only one. Ever. Clara and I have been together for over twenty-five years. We were engaged before the last war came and married as soon as I left the army. There has never been anyone else until this year.'

'So why now?'

'If you've spoken to anyone in this place, any man at least, you'll have heard that Lisette was fun to be with. She flirted with me all the time, as she did with everyone. My wife and I went through a bad patch around Christmas, and Lisette was … available. It meant nothing to either of us. I was going to end it soon, and then the poor woman died.' He looked at Pascal then back to me. 'Listen, this doesn't have to get out now, does it? I wouldn't want Clara to know, and I have political rivals who'd take great pleasure in using it as a stick to beat me with.'

It never ceases to surprise me when, even in the midst of a murder investigation, people look first towards how it might inconvenience their life. It's no indicator of guilt, but it does show how selfish and self-centred we can be. I wasn't about to give the mayor any comfort.

'Pascal and I will be discreet, monsieur, but tongues have already wagged. I'm sorry, but I can't guarantee they won't wag more.'

Sitell looked at the clock and clapped his hands. 'Then I suspect I'll just have to live with the consequences, but now the time has come when I really must dash. As I've said, I have a meeting and I'm already quite late.' He opened a drawer and removed a black attaché case, then got to his feet. Pascal and I also stood.

'Before you go, monsieur, could you tell me your whereabouts between four and six on the day Lisette died?'

'I'm sorry, I can't. I'll need to check the diary with my secretary and get back to you.' He threw on his coat, lifted his case and, arms outspread, ushered us to the door. 'Now, I have to go. I'll let Pascal have the information tomorrow.'

I pointed Pascal to his office door when we stepped into the corridor after leaving Sitell.

'We need a word.'

He unlocked and waved me into a cool room with curtains drawn. Even when he pulled them apart, no more light seeped in from the murk outside, but he remained looking out of the window. 'What is it?'

'You knew about your boss and Lisette, didn't you?'

'What makes you think that?'

'Come on, Pascal, you'd not miss much in this commune, and it's obvious if Robert Renan knew then you'd have known. I've seen it in your face ever since I told you what he said.'

Now he turned to look at me, a mixture of anger and embarrassment in his eyes. 'I hear a lot, Monsieur Given; much of it I wouldn't share, not even with you. In my opinion there is not a chance in hell of the mayor having killed Lisette Perron. I know him and I respect him. For this reason, I kept his little secret. What would be served by me blabbing it around?'

'Well, I'm annoyed you chose not to tell me, Pascal. Surely you'd see such information might be relevant in a murder enquiry, even if we discounted it later.'

'As I've said, *I* didn't think it was relevant.'

Had I still been in the force and a junior officer had responded like this, I'd have torn him off a considerable strip. I didn't have that option any longer and diplomacy, not my strongest suit, was required. Mentally I drew a deep breath. 'I'm sorry, Pascal. You're the policeman here, and I'm only acting as an amateur. I didn't mean to criticise. Could we start again?'

He didn't move or speak for several moments, then he shrugged and offered me a seat. 'I'll have a word with the mayor's secretary later, and she'll give me his diary commitments on the day the murder happened. I'm sure we'll see nothing untoward.'

'Could I ask you how you knew about the affair?'

'I didn't, not conclusively. You'll remember the mayor mentioned his political rivals? One of them, a councillor, Michel Elphine, came to me the day after Lisette's body was found. He said he saw the two of them talking in the market in February but thought nothing of it until he saw her later the same evening behind Monsieur Sitell's house. He didn't see her go inside but knew the mayor's wife was away for the weekend.'

Behind my chair I clenched my fists. 'Have you spoken to the mayor about this?'

'No, I haven't. Elphine was just stirring up trouble. He wants to be mayor and I thought it was part of a plan to remove my boss. If I'd gone to him and he denied it, then I'd be in big trouble. If he'd admitted it, then he'd only have told me the same as he told you; there was nothing to be gained and only problems to be had.'

I'd had enough bosses to understand his dilemma. None had been a potential suspect in a murder investigation, but several didn't like to hear any views different to their own. In my early days, where it didn't seem too important, I'd been tempted to take the easier route, like Pascal. I don't believe I ever did, but sometimes the quiet life had looked attractive.

We agreed there would be no point in me interviewing Michel Elphine because he'd seen nothing other than Lisette in the vicinity of Sitell's house. I left Pascal to check the mayor's diary, though I suspected there'd be nothing incriminating there. Sitell had already told me he'd been with the librarian until an hour before she was seen on the bridge. I had no doubt there'd be a blank afterwards, proving nothing and offering no progress. Another dead end.

Rachel greeted me at the back door when I arrived home. The space between us hadn't warmed since our argument the previous week, but at least we were civil and amicably distant, even if she was spending more time practising than usual.

'You've a visitor. Your cousin Anna, she arrived about an hour ago.'

My Uncle Gideon's daughter turned in her seat by the fire. Though she smiled broadly, I detected concern in her eyes.

'Anna, is everything alright?'

She stood and hugged me. 'Everything? No. But most things.'

'Then why are you here?'

Rachel gasped, 'James, how rude.'

'I'm sorry, that came out wrongly. It's just we weren't expecting you and assumed you'd brought bad news.'

'Don't worry, James, I would have reacted the same way myself in the circumstances. I thought I should come and tell you that we are moving to England soon. The way things are, I didn't know if I'd get another chance.'

'You're taking up my father's offer?'

'When he wrote I wanted to go straight away, but father said we should wait, then when the Germans invaded Norway and Denmark last week he conceded it won't be too long before they come here. We've completed the necessary papers and will leave as soon as we are able.'

'That's excellent news.'

'But there is a problem. Father is unwell. He picked up influenza soon after you visited and hasn't been able to shake it off. It's now gone on to his chest and he's so weak he's taken to his bed.'

'Then he can stay with us until he's better.' I looked across to Rachel and she nodded. 'You and your mother must get away if you can. When Uncle Gideon improves, I'll make sure he joins you.'

'That's most kind of you, James, but I hope we won't need to take you up on it. They're saying we might be able to travel within a month, so he will be well again by the time everything is ready.'

Rachel moved away to prepare the evening meal, having invited my cousin to stay for the night. I didn't fancy sleeping a night on the settee so the women could share our only bed, but it was the least I could do. Anna filled me in with all the news from Dol-de-Bretagne until dinner was on the table, and the three of us chatted through the evening. The two women got on well, and it wasn't long before I was able to escape to the sink and let them get on with it. I'd lived long enough without a wife to know my way round a kitchen and dishes, so I spent the time washing up and turning round Lisette Perron's murder in my head. Usually by this point in a case I'd have a clear idea of one or two realistic suspects, but with this one there was nothing.

By the time I'd finished putting everything away, I'd only become frustrated with my lack of clarity and decided I definitely needed to talk to Francis Guen. I made a round of hot drinks then carried them across to re-join the conversation by the fireside until bedtime.

TWENTY-FOUR

The fog of cigarette smoke in the café stung my eyes for the first five minutes, then started again when Francis lit up. He laughed as I dabbed away tears with my handkerchief.

'You'll have to take it up, James, that's the only answer.'

I'd never smoked, not really. A few cigarettes out of bravado when I was first away at sea, but I'd not felt any effect, good or bad, and decided it wasn't worth the bother. So now I had to suffer every time I was in a café, bar or any public place. It still wasn't worth beginning to smoke just to avoid that. I added another sugar to my coffee.

'May I ask you a question, Francis?'

'If it's about that young Marie-Clair, then you'd better bring it to my office.'

'It's not. It's this case I'm working … helping … on.'

'Not my area of expertise, James, but I'm willing to listen.'

This was why I'd known it would be a good idea to become friends with Francis. From the moment we'd met, he'd struck me as a man who'd have a friendly and non-judging ear, and he'd shown this each time we'd spoken. Our weekly conversations in the café were laced with his good humour, but he'd also shown an ability to sense if something was troubling me and to offer a few supportive words without being too obvious.

'It's hard to know where to begin. I've been so mixed up since I was asked to take a look. My last couple of cases in England proved to me I didn't have the stomach for it any longer, that's why I left the police. I came here partly to get away. Then someone dies, recorded as an accident, and I find myself investigating the death. Not seriously, just a little exercise to show Marie-Clair how it's done.' I shook my head. 'I should never have agreed to do it.'

'Never regret helping someone, my friend. Kindness is usually repaid, if not by the recipient then by God in His own good time.'

I wanted to tell him I was none too sure about God, that I'd seen too many bad things in men to believe there to be an overarching plan. But Francis was a good man, with his strong belief, and I didn't want to erect a barrier between us.

'It's not repayment I'm looking for, though, it's peace. If I hadn't agreed to Marie-Clair's request, I'd not have discovered Lisette Perron was murdered. Once that was obvious, the seeds were sown. It's like I jumped on a runaway horse hurtling towards a precipice. I couldn't stop myself from raking and sifting to find an answer. Some stupid, uncontrollable, desire for justice. Now I've nothing but problems.'

'Like what?'

'First off, I can't see a way through the woods. There's no-one jumping out at me as an obvious candidate for having committed the murder.'

'I'd expect this isn't the first time that's happened, though, is it?'

'Not at all. A policeman thinks he's lucky if there's an obvious suspect right from the start, but one usually emerges fairly soon, or there are at least pointers to motive and opportunity. With this, there's nothing. I could cope with that because something eventually turns up, but I can't see where to go without having any authority.'

A smile flickered across Francis' lips. 'So you like to be the boss?'

'What? No.'

The smile widened. 'Really?'

'Well, I do admit it would be helpful to be able to tell Pascal Jaubert what to do without having to beg and cajole all the time. He's able to hold people in a cell until they give some answers and I'm not. That's frustrating. We have these novels, the ones our postmaster loves, about amateur detectives who manage to worm a confession out of a guilty party by guile, but I'm not built that way. I like a direct question and the authority to expect a reply, that's all.'

'You're not going to get that, though, are you James? Not unless you join the police here.'

'I know, I know. It's why I'm trying to use Marie-Clair. She's grown up here and knows the people. She seems to be able to ask questions without them clamming up. Maybe it's the language and she can be more subtle than me, or perhaps it's just her personality. People are willing to talk to her, like they are with you. I'm too used to the uniform and the warrant card.'

Francis drained his cup and gestured to the waiter to bring us two more. We sat in silence until they arrived. 'Is that it, James? Just the case? Is everything alright at home?'

'Everything is fine ... apart from Rachel being mad with me about the mayor.'

'What's Alain Sitell done to you?'

'Nothing. Yet. He's just promised to make our lives hell if I stir up trouble about the librarian and then nothing comes of it. Rachel's been angry with me for almost a week because of it. She's really happy here and doesn't want to have to move. Neither do I for that matter.'

'So if you sort out the other problem, this one goes away.'

'I imagine it would.'

'Then you know what you must do, don't you? Put on your friendliest face and convince everyone to open up.'

'Easier said than done. As I said, I'm not like you.'

'Come on, James, do you think I find this simple? I'm trained, the same as you. We both wear a costume to suit our role.' He fingered his dog-collar. 'I have this and my church, you've had your police station. Now, it's possibly true that our personalities led us down different paths, but you've honed yours and I've honed mine. You now just need to train yourself differently.'

Sometimes you can be told the glaringly obvious, a solution you knew to be there all along, and still you can't take it on board. There was no doubting that Francis was right, all I had to do was change a little, but the pedestal I was building for my difficulties was becoming too high. I thanked Francis for his advice, said I'd give it some thought, and changed the subject.

Most weeks my talks with Francis lifted my spirits, but today's hadn't helped. In some ways it had pulled into focus how serious this crime had become in my life. I was still miserable after my evening meal, and Rachel asked me what was wrong. As is the way of these things, I said it was nothing and she asked me again five minutes later, then five minutes after that. When she asked me the fifth time, I snapped.

'Nothing's wrong. Even if there was, what would it matter to you?'

'Oh, James, this mood is becoming silly. Stop being such a child.'

'If you think I'm being childish, then perhaps I'll just go and talk to someone who appreciates me.' I grabbed my coat and lifted the latch. 'I've some things to go through with Marie-Clair anyway. I'll see you later.'

I only heard her call the first part of my name before I slammed the door behind me. This stupid running away put me in even worse humour than I was in before. I hadn't really intended to go to Marie-Clair's, I'd only said it as the only route of escape, even knowing another discussion of the case wouldn't make me feel any better. On the other hand, I couldn't go back home without a decent interval and, in the humour I was in, a bar was not a good idea.

Marie-Clair opened the door. 'Oh, Monsieur Given, it is late, did we agree to meet this evening?'

'No, I'm afraid we didn't. I just ... I thought ... well I hoped you might be free to talk about Lisette's death. If it's inconvenient, we can do it another time.'

'Not at all,' she smiled, 'I was only reading. Come in and come through. It may not be too warm in there as we've let the fire die down after dinner, but it will be better than disturbing my parents.'

As if on cue, the lounge door opened and her mother looked into the hall, suspicion clouding her face. I explained and apologised a second time which seemed to satisfy her, and she closed the door, leaving Marie-Clair sniggering behind me. Inside the dining room I asked her what was so amusing.

'Adults can be so distrusting sometimes, don't you think? I'm sure she thought we were up to something. I mean, the very idea.'

Not the most flattering comment she could have made, and it did little to improve how I was feeling, but then she was half my age, and more likely to consider me as a father figure than a potential suitor. Madame Levaux clearly had more knowledge of the ways of the world than her daughter.

'So what do you want to talk about?'

'Could we go through all the facts one more time? I've spoken to Pascal and the mayor. Have you managed to talk to Jennifer again?'

'She stuck with her story, adamant she'd not mistaken her bus time and certain it was the librarian she'd seen. I pushed her to remember if there'd been anyone else and she was certain there wasn't. And she'd not seen a car parked. I think we have to accept her version of events. What did you glean from your conversations?'

I went through them both in detail and she added notes to her growing collection.

'So we're no further forward, monsieur?'

'It doesn't look like it. Every time we identify a possible suspect, an alibi appears or there's a barrier to asking further questions. Let's check and double check now we've confirmed the timetable, see what we've missed.'

The next hour was spent sorting pieces of paper into ever more complex combinations, even considering if two or more individuals could have been involved in the murder. The exercise was as unfruitful as it had been last time we'd done it. At the end, Marie-Clair asked the obvious question.

'Are you still convinced it was murder?'

'I am, but there's nothing concrete from the doctor, only a suggestion she might have been hit over the head. Other than that, we have your friend's sighting of Lisette, with her bicycle, waiting on the bridge, below where she was supposed to have run off the road, and the half-ravings of the tramp I met in the woods. If I had to take this to the coroner, I'm not sure he'd be convinced.'

'Then why don't we just leave it where it is? You've shown me how such a crime should be investigated, and that's all I

230

asked. If we're not absolutely certain a crime has been committed, why would we keep looking?'

'Because the evidence we've gathered makes me believe I should carry on. We have someone dead whose lifestyle created potential enemies at every turn, and I've seen plenty of cases where jealousy and betrayal turned into murderous revenge. If you're going to make a decent police detective, you can't give up just because you can't make the numbers work. You have to keep trying until you do.'

'So what are you planning to do now?'

'I'll keep sifting and thinking, and hoping Pascal puts his shoulder behind the investigation. So far, apart from accompanying me, he's done nothing. Anyway, for now there's not much more we can do, and I'd better go home. I'll be in touch if anything occurs to me.'

I stood and turned for the door.

'Monsieur?'

'Yes?'

'You seem annoyed tonight; have I done something wrong?'

'No, Marie-Clair, I'm sorry. It's me I'm angry with. I can't find a way through this riddle no matter which way I look at it. There's something there, something I can't quite see, and it's making me bad tempered with everyone around me. But don't you worry, we'll get there in the end.'

She let me out onto the dark street, and as soon as she closed the door I turned in the opposite direction to home. There was just too much going round in my head. The lanes were deserted and the houses shuttered for the night as I wandered, trying to put my thoughts in order. Alain Sitell and Gerard Charbonne were the only ones left in the frame and only on the flimsiest of evidence. What about the man in the woods? Could he have described not what he'd seen but what he'd done, in some odd delusion? Or was there a 'Mister X' after all, someone we hadn't encountered, from outside the village?

After aimless and unproductive wandering for half an hour, I found myself outside the entrance to the library and wondered if it all hinged on this place. I even chuckled for a second when it occurred to me that her death could have resulted from an unpaid fine or an overdue book. Was the killer someone she knew from here and nothing to do with her love life? My first suspect had been David Ménière, a man who'd been asking Lisette for local maps. Was there someone else she'd upset through the library?

I left my thoughts hanging and trudged round the corner, into the square. I stood across from the Bar du Marché, empty now of customers and closed for the night, and turned over the gossip passed on by my card-playing companions, all of which had come to nothing. Behind me the church bell struck, and I waited until the eleventh chime died away before heading home, even less sure of sleep than when I'd left Marie-Clair's house.

A light still burned behind the curtains, so I guessed Rachel would be waiting when I went in. She sat by the fire, a shawl around her shoulders, and woke, startled, when the latch clicked shut. She glanced at the mantel clock.

'What time do you call this to be coming home, James? Where have you been?'

'Nowhere.'

'What do you mean "nowhere"? You've been out for hours. Have you been drinking?'

'No.'

'Then where?'

'I was with Marie-Clair. I told you.'

Rachel stood, a fierce light in her eyes. 'Until this time? What the hell's going on, James? Are you having an affair with that girl? You see more of her than you do of me.'

'Don't be stupid. You're the one who told me to help her. Now I see her I'm accused of this nonsense.'

'I don't think it is nonsense. When you're not working these days, perhaps even when you are working for all I know, your head is somewhere else. I've seen the way she looks at you. You'd not be the first man to fall for a younger woman.'

I laughed sourly. 'It's not her I'm thinking about, it's this damned murder. If you'd not nagged me to get involved I would be sleeping easy in my bed now, not walking the streets looking for answers.'

'So it's my fault, is it? I'm not the one spending all my time away from the house. I'm not the one rubbing the mayor up the wrong way and putting our lives here in jeopardy. And I'm not the one spending nights with a woman half my age.'

I walked over to Rachel and put my arms round her, but she pushed me away.

'You were almost killed last time you wouldn't let an investigation go, James, and I can't see you do it again. Anyway, I'm going to bed. You can get a blanket and sleep in here.'

Next morning, Rachel was as cold as ever over breakfast, and we hardly spoke before I went out to continue the final ploughing with Malo. There's something spiritual about walking a field behind a heavy horse, the ground behind you in great lumps of freshly turned soil, or finely broken and sown with the new season's crop. With his bad shoulder and my weak leg, we laboured all morning and finished two fields, then sat in a corner surveying what we'd done. The farmer lit his pipe and puffed great plumes of smoke into the still air. He lifted his cap and squinted at the sun.

'Doesn't get much better than this, James, does it?'

'No, I don't think it does.'

'It's why I keep on farming. Sometimes I think I'm growing too old, then we get a morning like this one. Four generations of the family on this place and me with no children to hand it on to.'

'That's sad. I expect you'd know everyone in the commune.'

'Mostly. A few, like yourselves, moved in from other places, so I'd not be so familiar with them. In the main, though, they've been here since they were born.'

'What do you make of the Charbonnes?'

'Gerard and Francine? Nice enough couple, run a good bakery and shop. My parents were great friends with his, but we're not so close. She moved in when they married. We get on fine, just don't see each other too often. Enora would know her better. Why?'

I said it was just idle curiosity, that I'd met them both and found them pleasant and it was just a stranger's desire to get to know the locals. I'd learnt a long time ago not to show too much interest in a potential suspect. 'What about the mayor? How well do you know him?'

'Alain Sitell? Not had much to do with him. He arrived here in his early twenties to help out Maurice Dauphin in his timber yard. Said he'd not been able to find much work at home when he left the army after the war, so he was glad of the opportunity to get back on his feet. Old Maurice died a few years later, and Sitell bought the business from his widow. The man had settled in and got to know the locals. He worked hard, did his bit in the community and found himself elected to the commune council. Not a job many wanted at the time, so there was no opposition. Got a decent head on him and moved up to mayor a few years back.'

'So he's not from the village?'

'No, somewhere in the east I'd guess. Never heard really. His accent would be over that way.'

Malo and I chatted for a while longer, then I left him to go for my lunch, hoping Rachel was in a better frame of mind. She wasn't in when I arrived, but on the table was a sandwich, a note and a letter.

I turned up the corner of the sandwich: cheese, made not too long before I got in, judging by the freshness of the bread. The note, in Rachel's handwriting, told me she'd gone for a walk and might be a couple of hours. The envelope bore a Paris postmark and the return address of my stamp dealer there. I could see no evidence of tampering. Inside, there was a recent catalogue with Mitchell's letter tucked between the last page and the back cover. In it he thanked me for the news about *our mutual friend*, meaning David Ménière, and confirming that he had *sadly died*.

He went on:

I've heard he had little in his possession when he went, poor fellow, other than the address book he kept with him always. It is interesting to see that one of his friends is continuing to pass on his messages even after he has left us. I have my own friends trying to identify who it is so we can send our good wishes.

I read this to mean the transmissions to Germany were continuing, David Ménière's contact list had been found, and Mitchell's codebreakers were working on it. The remainder was drivel, aimed at disguising the important section of his note.

He finished with a gentle warning to keep my eyes on the rising sun — a reference, I assumed, to the Germans on France's eastern border, and with a promise to let me know about *our friends* if he heard anything.

I screwed up the letter, threw it on the fire then broke up its ashes with the poker.

Did Mitchell's information point to a 'Mister X'? Could Lisette have discovered another person sending secrets to the Nazis and been unaware of Ménière's activities? It seemed unlikely two spies would've been sent to the same area, but I knew nothing of the world of espionage. Perhaps they were working together or, possibly, were working for different arms of the military and were each unaware, like their masters, of the presence of the other.

I re-read Rachel's note several times and picked at my lunch until it was time to go out to the fields again.

Rachel stayed within herself the whole of the evening. I was allowed to return to our bed, but there was an icy barrier between the two sides. It continued all the next day, and by seven o'clock I was ready to clear out to the bar with Daniel, Phillipe and Eric. Too ready.

When my wife left the room, I raided the cash we kept in a sideboard drawer and tucked it into my waistcoat pocket. I'd double it, courtesy of my friends, and perhaps take Rachel for a meal to thaw the Arctic conditions.

Phillipe was late and we were in to our second round of drinks before he arrived, with me on the Diabolo Menthe as usual. He joined us and won his first two hands, scooping our centimes into his pot with great show. Eric pointed to his empty glass and Phillipe stood to collect refills.

'I'll get these in and then take some more cash off you three mugs.' He laughed. 'You still on the children's stuff, James?'

He'd pushed the wrong button.

'It's easy to win when there's nothing to lose, Phillipe. If we were playing for real money, you'd not do so well.'

Daniel and Eric looked at each other, then at me.

'It's true, he'd lose his nerve and drop out if the stakes were too high. A serious gambler doesn't have that problem.'

Phillipe turned red and puffed out his chest. 'I'll show you, rosbif. Throw your francs on the table, and we will see who is the better man.'

I unfolded half my notes, three days' wages, and laid them down in front of me. 'There, that should give a good start. Now get those drinks in, and make mine rum this time. A double.'

For me, drinking and cards have never gone well together. I am a quiet, pleasant, drunk, becoming mellower, rather than sharper, with every glass, and I became very mellow as that night rolled on. Phillipe won the first hand, and the next two. I won a couple by virtue of being dealt unbeatable cards. It wasn't long before Daniel and Eric left the game, admitting they'd already lost more than they dared tell their wives. The slide began. Hand after hand went to Phillipe. He wanted us to stop when I ran out of money, but the alcohol in me begged him for the chance to win back what I'd lost.

Daniel and Eric shook their heads, told us we were idiots, and left. Others in the bar drew up their seats when I took the second wad of notes from my pocket. Drinks arrived out of nowhere and I lost more and more focus as my empty glasses filled the table.

Rachel found me on the pavement outside the library, shivering, vomiting and weeping. She put her arm around my shoulder and wiped my mouth with a handkerchief.

'Come on, James, what's this all about?'

The best I could do was garble about dead people, and bad people, and good friends, and her.

She told me not to worry, that we'd sort everything out, and she held me for a long time.

As I staggered home with her support, I had a vague memory of Phillipe trying to give me back my cash before the bar closed, and me telling him where he should put it. He gave an appropriate response and stormed off to let me find my own way to my bed. That would be one more apology I'd need to make when I sobered up.

The house was cold. Rachel sat me in a chair, threw a blanket over me and stoked the fire with logs from the basket on the hearth. Within minutes the flames licked the sides and I started to warm through, helped by the hot drink Rachel had wrapped my fingers round. She knelt on the rug beside me and lay her head on my lap.

'We shouldn't argue, James, it's not good for either of us.'

My head had cleared enough for me to understand, but my tongue wouldn't do what I wanted, so I grunted and stroked her hair. We sat until the fire died, with me ebbing in and out of sleep. Rachel got up, took me by both hands and pulled me to my feet.

'Let's get you to bed. We can talk in the morning.'

TWENTY-FIVE

My head thumped like a steam hammer. I wanted to be sick and felt guilty as hell. There'd be a lot of explaining to do. I refused breakfast other than a large mug of coffee. Rachel ate hers slowly and without speaking.

'I'm sorry. Last night was stupid. So, so, stupid.'

She leaned across the table and took my hand. 'Stupid is true, James, but we knew this may happen. You told me when we met that you were a drinker who fell off the waggon from time to time. We can only count our lucky stars you don't do it often.'

I swallowed. 'It wasn't just the booze.'

'No, I know. You didn't want to fight with me. But couples do sometimes. I saw my parents stop speaking to one another for days on end when I was young. It didn't mean they weren't in love.'

'It wasn't that… Well it was, but only partly.'

She let go of my hand, shuffled back on her chair and closed her eyes. 'What then? What else have you to tell me? Was I right about you and Marie-Clair?'

'Nothing like that.' I took a deep breath. 'I've spent all our money.'

'How… What…?'

'Last night. Took what we had in the house and blew it all in the card game.'

Rachel jumped to her feet and dashed to the sideboard, opened the drawer I'd emptied the evening before, then swept all the contents aside in a frantic hunt for the cash. She did the same with every other drawer before turning back to me, her voice shrill. 'James! How could you? The drinking is one thing — but this?'

I got to my feet and began to pace the floor, fingernails digging into the scalp above my ears. 'What can I say? I'm sorry. I've not done anything like it for years, not since I was at sea.'

'So why now? Surely not because I accused you of cheating on me?'

'That didn't help, but it was more, much more.'

'Like what?'

'Like the Perron woman's murder and me getting nowhere with it. Like Sitell threatening to have us chased out of town, and like…' My next words wouldn't come.

When Rachel spoke again it was softer, conciliatory. 'Go on, James, spit it out. It must be damned important for you to drink all night and gamble away all our hard-earned cash.'

'…and like what was happening to us. I thought I'd lost you and didn't know how to get you back. I was mad and scared at the same time.'

Then we were in each other's arms, clinging as if our lives depended on it. We stayed locked together for minutes until Rachel relaxed and pulled away.

'For an intelligent man you're such a fool sometimes, James. I was angry with you, but you should have more faith in our marriage than that. I love you too much to lose you easily.'

'You do understand there's nothing going on between Marie-Clare and me, don't you?'

'If you say so, I'll believe you.'

'Even if I wanted to, she'd not have me.' I told Rachel how Marie-Clare had unwittingly made it very clear I was a little too old for her.

She burst out laughing and took my hand again. 'Then I expect you're stuck with me.'

'I expect I am.'

'Losing the money's bad but we'll not starve, though I'll never understand why you did it. What will you do? Are you giving up the hunt for Lisette's killer?'

This is what I wanted to do but knew I couldn't. 'I can't, it's not in me. How could I live here knowing there's a murderer in the village and I walked away without trying to bring them to justice? You wouldn't want me to do that, would you?'

'I would if it means you're safe from harm.'

Two coffees later, my head still felt like prize-fighters were inside, knocking seven bells out of each other, and I told Rachel that Phillipe would probably give me our money back. The pounding got worse. I covered my ears until I realised it was on the door, not in my brain. I dragged myself over and swung it open. Malo was on the step.

'Come quick, James. A man is on my telephone. From England. Hurry.'

He scurried off with me limping in pursuit across the yard, despite the explosions behind my eyes, and into his house, where he pointed to the dresser.

'There, he is there.'

I lifted the handset. 'Hello?'

'Given? Mitchell here. Can you talk?'

'Give me a moment.'

I asked Malo if he'd let me take the call in private. His frown told me he'd rather stay to listen, but he shuffled through to his living room and closed the door behind him.

'I can now. What is it?'

'You had my letter?'

'A couple of days ago. Very inventive.'

'Good. Then you'll have worked out we found Ménière's contacts. My boys have been working on the code since we received it, and it's revealed the name of someone living in your neck of the woods. Chap called Sitell.'

'Alain Sitell?'

'That's the one. You know him?'

'There must be a mistake. He's our local mayor. I'm told he's been here for years.'

'Well, his name's in our friend's book. No doubt about it.'

I asked what he wanted me to do.

'Ask one or two questions if you can, without arousing his suspicions. I'll get one of my chaps over your way soon to take care of him. It may be a few days, though. Alright?'

Mitchell hung up after we'd agreed I'd do as he asked and that I'd be in touch if I discovered anything to show he was wrong and didn't need to send anyone to "take care" of Sitell.

I was shaking as I wandered back to my own house. I'd no doubt Mitchell was right in his assessment of Sitell being a spy; why else would he be in Ménière's coded list of contacts? So what might he have done to cover it up?

I grabbed my coat and hared along the lane to the Mairie, deciding I'd pull Pascal Jaubert in straight away before tackling Sitell. In the event, I could have saved myself the rush because the policeman's office was locked and shuttered. I asked the mayor's secretary where he was.

'A tree has fallen down on the road to Dinan, two kilometres outside the village. He's driven there to direct traffic around it. I expect he'll be back after lunch. Can I take a message?'

'Maybe later.' Now I had to confront Sitell on my own. 'Is there any chance the mayor is available?'

'I'm afraid he's not here either. He's going to a meeting in Saint Brieuc today with his wife. The mayors of all the communes in the department will be there.' She looked at the clock. 'If it is important, you might catch him at home before he goes.'

She explained where Sitell lived and the quickest way to walk there. I followed her instructions through the lanes out to the edge of the village. His house was smaller than I'd thought it might be. Somehow his title and the grand building he worked in suggested he'd be a wealthy man with an equally grand home. Instead, it was a modest single-storey place that had been built about fifty years ago, with a regimented front garden which looked like it was tended by council workers. There was no sign of a car.

I knocked at the front and waited. No reply, so I knocked again, waited with the same result, and so tried round the back. Here there was no garden, only a concrete yard with a large barn behind where logs were stacked on one side and sawn planks on the other under a canopy. I rapped on the back door and had no better luck, then tried the handle, but it was locked. Clearly I'd missed Sitell. There was nothing strange to be seen when I peered through the windows, so I turned my attention to the barn. To my surprise, it wasn't locked. Inside were several machine saws of different sizes and the sweet scent of sawdust. Papers littered a desk against one wall. I rifled through them, but they were only orders, receipts and supplier's catalogues.

A metal cabinet stood in one corner and I opened it to find trays of hand-tools. As I closed its door I noticed a cable running at the back and saw it exited through a hole in the back wall. At the other end of the cable, five or six feet away on the side wall, it did the same. Why would wiring be brought inside for so short a length then led out again? I knocked the side wall beside the cabinet and the cold, hard, rap confirmed it was solid brick. Doing the same on the back wall brought a hollow thud. I tried a door, which I'd assumed led to the outside of the barn. It was locked. A hammer and chisel from the tool cabinet soon fixed that. When the lock splintered, the door burst through to a windowless room, only four feet deep, easy to miss from the outside. It was bare except for a shelving rack, a chair and a table. The rack supported a transmitter of considerable power, judging by its dimensions. A Morse telegraph key, several notebooks and a cardboard box lay on the table. I flipped through the notebooks. Columns of numbers and letters, and instructions printed in German. My examination of the box revealed a stack of handbills similar to the one shown to me by Francis Guen, so now there was little doubt of the barn owner's affiliation.

It took only another minute to return outside and locate the cable. As expected, it trained up the wall to connect an aerial to the equipment inside.

TWENTY-SIX

I found the police station still locked when I arrived back, so I went home and tried to work. Each job I tackled ended with frustration as my impatient clumsiness caused problem after problem. I decided to check the hedge repairs, to turn my pacing of the barn into something productive, but my mind wandered as much as I did and I discovered I'd missed two holes when I walked back via the same route. I bothered Malo for the use of his telephone twice, with still no reply from Pascal.

He didn't return until late afternoon.

When I walked into the policeman's office, he waved me away.

'I'm sorry, monsieur, I have no time now for this case, unless you have something new. It has not been a good day.'

'As a matter of fact, I do have new information.'

'Enough to bother me with?'

'I think so, but what's the problem, Pascal?'

'I'm tired, hungry and annoyed, having spent the whole day arguing with people wanting to use the blocked road and blaming me for the inconvenience. The men sent to cut up and move the fallen tree arrived without adequate tools so had to go back to their depot to collect the right ones. They delayed the damned operation by several hours, leaving me stuck out there.'

I suggested we walk to the hotel to get something to eat before I brought him up to date. Regardless of my earlier restlessness, there was no rush to drag Pascal into action. He'd be reluctant until he had food inside him, and it was likely the mayor's meeting would be followed by a formal meal, so he'd not be home until late, if at all. It seemed a much better idea to butter up the policeman, pass on my new information and let him make up his own mind.

After a glass of wine, some cheese and a baguette, Pascal was more rested and relaxed. After a second glass he opened up and told me he'd grown up in Vieux-Croix. He'd never wanted to be a policeman, but his father had cajoled him into it, believing it to be a more stable career than that of a professional singer, which would have been his first choice.

'It wasn't what I wanted either, Pascal. I found myself in the job after a friend was murdered. Before that I was at sea, then fruit-picking. That's why we came over here when I left the force, to travel round the grape, apple and vegetable harvests, earning a living in the sunshine wherever we could.'

'So you, Monsieur Given, were unhappy, as I am?'

'Not all of the time. Until a couple of years ago, I'd found the challenge interesting and the arrests satisfying. I felt I was doing something, but I started to believe we'd never defeat all the evil in the world, so what was the point of me carrying on? My last two cases convinced me I should stop and follow my heart.'

Pascal nodded, said he understood this, and asked why I'd come to see him. There was no way to dress it up.

'I think Alain Sitell is our murderer.'

The wine slowed the disbelief on his face, but it arrived eventually. 'We've been through this before, monsieur, but go ahead and explain.'

'Your mayor saw Lisette on the afternoon of her death. Did you look in his diary for what he was doing afterwards?'

'There was nothing, but this doesn't mean he killed her, only that he can't account for his movements. If I didn't have an appointment but was out of my office, then I probably wouldn't be able to do so either.'

'And you remember Sitell denied, then admitted, being Lisette Perron's lover.'

'Accepted. I was with you when he explained his secrecy.'

I'd only been softening him up with these scraps of information; the next one was a knockout punch. 'Your mayor is a German spy. I uncovered his transmitter and codebooks.'

Pascal didn't respond for a full five seconds as the gears turned in his head. 'What?'

'A contact in London reported your mayor's name appearing on a coded list of contacts found in the belongings of David Ménière. So I went to talk to Sitell. He wasn't at his office or his home, so I had a look round behind his house. He has a room in his barn, fully equipped for passing secrets to the enemy.'

'This is a very serious allegation, Monsieur Given, and I'll need to report it to the relevant authorities, but it still doesn't explain why he'd kill the librarian.'

'I'm afraid you'll have to take me on trust for now, but I hope you'll agree we should talk to him. Even the spying is enough to have him locked up, maybe executed. The least you can do is bring him in for questioning.'

The policeman was between a rock and a hard place. Sitell was an important, powerful man, and if I'd got it wrong Pascal would lose his job and probably never work in the area again. If I was right, then he'd be in real trouble if he didn't act to apprehend a spy and a murderer. All of this played out on his face in the moment before he spoke.

'Because I trust your experience, I'll go along with you to talk to the mayor. Come to the office and give me a minute to make a telephone call. Then we'll decide what to do next.' He grinned. 'If you've got it all horribly wrong, I suppose I can still become a singer.'

We walked back and he asked me to wait in the outer office while he made the call.

When he came out, he shrugged. 'I rang a senior officer in Rennes, and he's instructed me to bring in Monsieur Sitell for questioning, keeping him in the cells overnight if necessary. They'll send an expert team over in the morning if we find more questioning is warranted. However, there is nothing to be done for a few hours until Monsieur Sitell returns. Go home and meet me back here at eight.'

I had three hours to kill before I needed to meet Pascal again and knew if I went home I'd not relax, so decided to take a look at Lisette Perron's house. Outside it was much as Marie-Clair had described it, quite run down, and I wondered if she'd inherited from an elderly relative then never bothered to carry out repairs. The window through which Marie-Clair had climbed looked too daunting for my bulk, so I smashed a small pane in the back door and released the catch. The librarian was in no position to complain.

Inside, the decor was drab, and I wandered from room to room, though I didn't bother with places Marie-Clair would already have searched. Instead, I concentrated on possible hiding spots. There were, as far as I could tell, no concealed cupboards in walls nor under floorboards. Nothing unexpected under the bed or behind the bath either. I looked out of the kitchen window for any outbuildings but there were none, though it was clear that gardening was not one of the librarian's strong points, with more dandelions than dahlias on display. She'd been dead a month, but this didn't excuse the sorry, unkempt state of the grass and borders.

I searched the entire house, with hardly a notion of what I was looking for. Before I left, I scanned the living room one last time. Marie-Clair had commented on the fewer than expected number of books, and as I examined them one stood out like a sore thumb: Alexandre Boreau's *Flore du Centre*, a substantial old tome on plants in central France and the Loire Valley. A book I thought decidedly out of place, having seen Lisette's garden.

As soon as I lifted it from the shelf, I could tell I'd found a secret. The book was much lighter than it should have been. I shook it and it rattled. Laying it on a table, I lifted the cover to reveal a hollow centre which held five carbon-copy typed sheets, a handwritten one and a small notebook containing a list of dates, telephone numbers and what appeared to be routing addresses, businesses similar to the stamp dealer provided to me by Mitchell. The last date listed was two weeks before Lisette was killed.

I skimmed through the typed documents, and it was clear they were reports she'd made on activity which could be of interest to military intelligence. The first three, on yellowed paper, were dated soon after the end of the last war, the next one two months before Germany invaded Poland, and the most recent date corresponded with the last entry in her notebook. The handwritten one appeared to be preparatory notes made before typing and sending. At the top, underlined, was the name *Alain Sitell*. Beneath this, she'd written *German?*, *Aerial* and *Meeting him to ask questions*.

I folded the papers and put them with the notebook already in my pocket, then left. I still had time to go home. I knew I wouldn't settle, but I needed to tell Rachel I'd be late. As I made my way through the market square, I saw Marie-Clair on the opposite corner. She waved and ran across.

'Any news, monsieur?'

'I think we may have our man. Alain Sitell. I'm going to his place tonight with Pascal to challenge him. With luck he'll be under arrest before long.'

'Wow. Can I come?'

I shook my head. 'Not a good idea; he may be dangerous when he's cornered. Leave it to me and your cousin.'

Marie-Clair bit her lip. 'But that's not fair. I've helped with this case, haven't I?'

'Of course you have.'

'And you'd not even have found anything wrong if I haven't pressed you to take a look, would you?'

'Listen, Marie-Clair, this is true, but the fact remains we should now leave it to the professionals. The only reason I'm going is because Pascal needs someone experienced with him. If I thought it would be safe, I'd ask him to let you join us.'

'Hmm. A typical man's response. You think a girl would get in the way.'

Nothing could be further from the truth. Even before she'd asked, I'd had a picture in my head of an earlier male partner being lowered into the ground. I knew I'd need to keep her away from any possible danger. I had to hope Pascal could look after himself.

I didn't bother to respond further to Marie-Clair's accusation. I simply told her to go home and I'd speak to her when all of this was done. I thought for a moment she'd continue the argument. Instead, she turned and I watched her walk away until she disappeared into the lane leading to her house.

We sat outside Sitell's house for an hour in the police car. Pascal had contacted his colleagues in Saint Brieuc and confirmed there was, in fact, a formal dinner planned. They'd agreed to keep an eye on his boss and to inform us when he left for home. Despite it being an hour and a half's journey for Sitell and his wife, Pascal had driven to collect me as soon as he'd received a message that the event was almost finished. When we arrived, I suggested he take a look inside the barn, but he refused.

'I'm not about to go poking around on the mayor's private property without him here. That may be the way you do things in England, but here we're respectful to our betters. We'll wait until he arrives then sort the whole thing out.'

In the dark we were able to see car headlights from a good distance, and Pascal tensed each time they came into view. At about half past nine, we watched one set meander down the lane until Sitell drew up outside his house and climbed out of the car. We got out of the police car so he would see us.

'Pascal? And you, Monsieur Given. What are you two doing here at this time of night?'

'I … I need to ask you some questions, monsieur.'

'What sort of questions? Can't this wait until the morning?'

'I'm afraid not. Can we go inside?'

Sitell asked us to wait, then strode back to speak to his wife. She got out, took his key from him, and scurried indoors. The mayor waited a minute then asked us to follow him. He led us to the kitchen. 'We'll be more private in here. My wife can sit in comfort in the other room and listen to the wireless. Now, what's this all about?'

Pascal drew a deep breath and straightened his back. When he spoke, the underling had gone and the policeman was in control. 'I have reason to believe you have been spying for Germany, Monsieur Sitell.'

'What? Don't be ridiculous.'

'So you deny it?'

'Of course, have you taken leave of your senses?'

'It's been brought to my attention you have a transmitter in your barn.'

For the first time, the confidence and bluster disappeared from Sitell's face. 'Who told you that lie?'

I stepped forward. 'Me, and it isn't a lie. As you know. Hidden at the back of your barn is a small room, and in there I found everything you need to contact Berlin.'

'It's merely a hobby, nothing to do with Berlin.'

I laughed. 'And the codebooks?'

Sitell glanced at a drawer in the white-painted dresser next to the back door. 'Whatever you've seen, Monsieur Given, it's clear you have no knowledge of amateur radio. What might look like codes to the untrained eye are simply call signs we use to identify each other. If you like, I'll fetch my books and explain them to you.'

'It sounds very plausible, but if that's the case, why did you murder Lisette Perron?'

He looked at the dresser again and moved over to rest against it, then addressed Pascal. 'Are you going to stand there and let him make these preposterous allegations, Jaubert?'

The young policeman, to his credit, shrugged and told Sitell to answer the question.

'Whatever makes you think I'd kill Lisette? That I'd kill anyone, for that matter?'

'I believe, in the course of your affair, she became aware you were up to something. Perhaps she spotted your aerial when she was sneaking round the back to meet you when your wife was away. Or perhaps David Ménière let it slip he knew you. Your librarian was on the payroll of British military intelligence so passed on her suspicions to them. Before she confirmed the truth, you found out you were rumbled and decided to take action. You agreed to meet her outside the village where the two of you would be less likely to be seen, then you clattered the poor woman with a rock when she told you of her suspicions and you couldn't convince her she was mistaken.'

Sitell tapped the top of the dresser with his fingernail. He appealed to Pascal again. 'I'm not sure what I can say to this. Surely you don't believe him?'

'The evidence is very compelling, monsieur, so I'm afraid I do.'

In a split second Sitell pulled open the drawer and he had a gun in his hand. Pascal leapt towards him. A bullet exploded. The policeman screamed and fell to the floor, clutching his knee. The mayor swung the gun on me.

'I really didn't want to hurt anyone.'

'And you think you can be a traitor and not hurt anyone?'

'Traitor? I'm no traitor, I'm a patriot.' He must have noticed my puzzlement. 'Ah, you didn't appreciate I'm actually German. I came here after the last war to help prepare for this one, picking up a French accent and past life along the way. Any number of us did the same. Fit into a community, build position and power, and pass sensitive information back to Berlin.'

'So this is what Lisette Perron discovered?'

'She and I were getting on so well. A handsome woman and very obliging. Lisette told me one night she was refreshing the German she'd learnt years ago, in case she needed it if there was an invasion. I said I spoke the language quite well and I'd help her practise. She realised I spoke it a little too well, then later, as you suggested, she saw the cables running outside the barn so put two and two together.'

As he spoke I caught a flash of a face at the window, gone as quickly as it appeared. Pascal groaned, clasping his leg.

'I should have taken the woman for a drive in the countryside and dealt with her where no-one would find her body for a long time.'

The kitchen door opened behind me, and Madame Sitell's pudgy face peeked through. She looked at the mayor, then me, then the policeman on the ground and back at her husband again.

'It's alright, my dear,' Sitell said. 'I'll be finished here in a few minutes. You go and pack a few things. We'll be going away.'

The woman smiled as if he had just said he'd poured them a nightcap. She turned and disappeared back to where she came from.

Sitell raised his aim slightly and peered down the barrel at my head. 'I'm sorry it has to end this way, but you can see I have no —'

The entire window behind him exploded. He ducked and I launched myself at him, knocking him against the dresser. The man's head cracked as it made contact with a shelf, sending the gun flying in Pascal's direction. The policeman grabbed the weapon and fired a single shot, missing Sitell, but he steadied his aim for another and held it there until I took it from him.

Marie-Clair appeared at the gap where the window used to be. 'Is it safe to come in now?'

TWENTY-SEVEN

By the time Doctor Hodin had arrived to look after Pascal, and police from the next town had turned up to escort Alain Sitell to the cells, it was well after midnight. It was another hour before I climbed into bed, and an early alarm meant I was almost dead on my feet when I set up our market stall. The constant drizzle did nothing to make me feel better. Fortunately, I only had to stay until mid-morning because the interrogation officers from Rennes had arrived and wanted to speak to me, so I sent word to Malo to come to take over. Just before he did, Phillipe ambled round to see me and I made a snivelling apology for my behaviour two nights earlier.

'It is not a problem, my friend. This happens to all of us from time to time. You haven't seen me angry and drunk but when you do, you will remember it.' He threw an arm around my shoulder and slipped an envelope into my hand. 'Here, take this back.'

'No, Phillipe, you won it.'

'Nonsense. You lost it, and that is not the same thing. Anyway, I've taken a few francs for a drink to compensate for your rudeness.'

I laughed, said he was welcome and shook his hand. The smile stayed with me until I left Malo in charge of his vegetables.

It was strange to think that the top man in the Mairie had now moved across the hall into the police cells. A uniformed officer stood behind the counter in the police station when I walked in. He took my name and I waited until a man in plain clothes called me to join him in Pascal's office. He and another quizzed me for an hour, then, seemingly happy I was no kind of threat, gave me the bare bones of Sitell's excuses for what he'd done. I called round to Pascal's afterwards to see how he was, and the policeman sat in an armchair, his mother fussing as if he waited at death's door.

When I got home, Rachel was busy in her garden and a telegram from my cousin, Anna, lay on the table, telling me that Uncle Gideon had taken a turn for the worse and had died peacefully the previous night. Despite my tiredness, I walked back into town to send three telegrams of my own: the first to Anna, passing on my condolences; one to my father, saying I'd attend Gideon's funeral; and a third to Mitchell, with the words *Another friend has come to light. I will contact my stamp dealer.* A quarter of an hour later, I collapsed into bed and slept the entire afternoon.

There was no cause for celebration in Sitell's arrest, only relief and the satisfaction of a case solved, but it was pay day, I'd had our cash back from my friend, and I thought Rachel deserved a treat. The restaurant carried the same grandeur as the rest of the Hotel du Conche. We'd not eaten there before, and Rachel spent the first ten minutes open-mouthed, pointing out the chandeliers, ornate mirrors, and gold-painted columns. With a grin I warned her not to crick her neck staring at the floral decorations on the high ceiling. She reserved her greatest praise for the tables.

'How can they make something so simple look so elegant, James? They're beautiful. We'll have to do ours like this from now on.'

'Well, perhaps not every night. I'm not sure my working clothes would do it justice. Not unless we're going to start dressing for dinner as well.'

A waiter brought the menus, bent towards me and whispered when he gave me mine.

Rachel raised an eyebrow when he walked away. 'What did he say?'

'He asked me who the gorgeous lady I'm having dinner with is. Wondered if she might be available later.'

She leant across the table and slapped my hand. 'He did not. Now, what did he really say?'

'It seems our hosts, Gaston and Madame Nouel, have heard of the arrest of Lisette's murderer and want us to have dinner on them.'

Over an excellent dinner of onion soup followed by local duckling, I told Rachel it looked like Pascal would make a full recovery, and though there'd been a lot of blood, there was no long-lasting damage. He'd be walking as well as ever before long.

'You know, he told me yesterday he'd grown up wanting to be a professional singer, but his father wouldn't let him. I think his mother might push for a different future now. Pascal could become one of your students if she gets her way.'

We discussed Marie-Clair for a few minutes and agreed we didn't know what she'd do, though she was even more determined to become a detective having had a taste of it. I said I thought a German invasion might put paid to her plans.

'What will happen to Alain Sitell, James?'

'He'd face the guillotine if just charged for the murder, but it will probably be a firing squad for sending information to Germany.' I shivered. 'I'm not sure which I'd prefer.'

'Did he give them anything important?'

'It's hard to say. He's only a minor official so wouldn't have known much. I expect he'd at least passed on the locality of all the military camps in Brittany and any troop movements he became aware of. That's enough, though. It shows he was willing to betray this country. One good thing is Mitchell's people will have intercepted messages, so with the benefit of Sitell's codebooks they'll discover any instructions he'd received about preparing for an invasion.'

'Why would he do such a thing? He made his life here. People trusted him.'

'That's the whole point, really. Part of his defence will be he wasn't a traitor. I had a long chat this morning with the men interrogating him, because they wanted to hear my side of the investigation. It seems he's being quite open about his reasons. He says he's German and his family suffered after the last war at the hands of the French. They took over all the businesses, including Sitell's family's engineering works, and his father took his own life when he couldn't provide for the family any longer.'

'How sad.'

'It is, but it doesn't excuse what he's done. When he arrived home from the Eastern Front, unemployed, he latched onto Hitler's message and was recruited to move to France and wait for the second coming. His mother had taught him French as a child, so he spent a few months travelling and improving his grasp of the language. By the time he arrived in Vieux-Croix, he'd honed his accent so well they assumed him to be an incomer from the east of the country. Sitell's mission was to settle, ingratiate himself into the commune and then take any position of power he could manage.'

'So he's been waiting all this time for a kind of revenge.'

'From what he's said, they're surmising he's not the only one. God knows how the police will root them out. There will be a very nervous collection of mayors and other officials around the country at the minute. Even if they're not spies, they'll face some pretty rigorous investigations.'

After a dessert to die for, Rachel sipped the last of her Bordeaux, leaned forward and asked the question we both knew we'd come to discuss. 'Now this is over, are we going to stay or move on, James?'

I swallowed hard. 'I'm not sure we can do either. The news isn't good, and I think the Germans will be here within a month.'

'But we have the false documents, don't we? Can't we just head south and adopt new identities?'

'Those papers will only hold up in an emergency. Mitchell warned me to avoid serious scrutiny and said they were to be used to escape if we needed to.'

I'd looked at them a few times and they'd have fooled me. They'd get us past a country copper or a soldier on a roadblock. Even in a cursory examination by our mayor one set had passed muster, but would they if the person looking was a German officer intent on finding Jews and subversives? I didn't think we should take that chance and I said so. Rachel closed her eyes and pinched her nose. The tears might come but not here, not in public.

'Then we'll have to go back to England, won't we?'

I nodded and took my wife's hand across the table. 'It will be safer there. We can come back when this has all blown over.'

Though I said this, I had no idea when it would be.

EPILOGUE

The Germans crashed through the Ardennes, on the French border, in the middle of May and we'd made it to England only days before. We were one couple amongst hundreds flooding over the Channel, with only the possessions we could carry. Calais had been chaotic and Dover little better, but we'd made it to Birmingham safely and reclaimed Rachel's house as our home. We knew the city was no longer for us and talked of plans to find somewhere near Kenilworth as soon as was practical. A cottage with an acre or two, space for a vegetable plot, an orchard and a few chickens was our dream.

In the meantime, I was fulfilling my father's dream, working alongside him in his tailoring workshop, the destiny he'd planned before I escaped to sea, then the police, twenty years earlier. I'd hardly lifted a needle and thread since I'd left at sixteen, so he kept me well away from the actual production of his wares, but I could help with the business side when I wasn't keeping myself fit carrying bolts of cloth up and down stairs.

My cousin, Anna, and her mother had arrived days before we did, and Papa had put them in the room vacated by my brother, saying they'd work something out if he needed to come home.

At the end of May, news came in a letter from Francis. Alain Sitell had been found guilty of treason and removed from the court to an army prison to await execution. He'd been found hanging in his cell only hours after he'd been put there, having asked his guards for a pen and paper to write some letters. One was to his wife, apologising for the trouble she was now in and two others were to Pascal Jaubert and Louis Décast, Lisette's husband, saying he was sorry. He used his final sheet for a note explaining he'd acted for the Fatherland and was taking his life to avoid another small and bitter victory for France.

Francis signed off his letter with his blessings for our future and a newspaper clipping reporting ten other sleeping agents had been uncovered since Alain Sitell, credit being attributed to Pascal for "his tireless work in uncovering the plot".

A NOTE TO THE READER

Dear Reader,

I hope you've enjoyed *Where Every Man*, or if you're only flicking through before you start, I hope you do enjoy it.

In the earlier Inspector James Given novels he was based in Warwickshire, but I wanted to give him some relief from his wanderlust and to get him out into the sunshine which he yearns for. Personally, I've had a love affair with France for many years and have always admired the wonderful range of fresh fruit and vegetables to be found on every market. This produce is grown from the far south of the country, to the far north, a distance of over six hundred miles, providing ample opportunity for James and his new wife, Rachel, to follow the harvest if they wished, and for me to place them somewhere new.

At the start of the novel, war between France and Germany has been declared but between the declaration in September 1939 and the invasion of France in May 1940, action was largely limited to the country's Eastern border, sometimes known as the 'phony war'. As result, James would have felt relatively safe in Brittany, though always mindful of serious jeopardy if the Germans broke through.

One issue which I wrestled with throughout writing *Where Every Man* was how to deal with the language. I could have peppered it with French words and phrases, providing translations, but this, to me, didn't make sense if the characters were speaking French most of the time. In the end, I decided to trust the reader to recognise this, so limited non-English words as much as possible. The use of such terms as 'monsieur' and 'madame' appeared relevant, so have remained.

The title is from William Shakespeare's *The Merchant of Venice* and makes reference to the nature of war and the myriad ways in which ordinary people contribute.

I love to hear from readers, so please contact me through my **Facebook page** or send me a message through **Twitter**. You can also see my latest news on **my website** and sign up for notifications.

Reviews are so important to authors, and if you enjoyed the novel I would be grateful if you could spare a few minutes to post a review on **Amazon** and/or **Goodreads**.

Thanks for reading!

Charlie Garratt

Sapere Books is an exciting new publisher of brilliant fiction and popular history.

To find out more about our latest releases and our monthly bargain books visit our website:
saperebooks.com

Printed in Great Britain
by Amazon